On a rare night out, single mum Lily stumbles into the arms of the dazzling Parker. They spend one passionate night together, but both know it will never be anything more. Lily has lost too much over the years to even want to try again.

A year later, devoted teacher, Parker, is excited to start the new year at her brand new school. Greeting the parents, she sees one familiar face in the crowd—the woman she met over a year ago. The woman she has been unable to forget.

Arriving at the classroom, Lily cannot believe her son, Bodhi, has Parker as his new teacher. This surprise was totally unexpected!

Their roles have changed now—as teacher and school parent—but the attraction toward each other has remained. And, as if the situation wasn't already complicated enough, there's Bodhi's dad: Who is he? And why on earth is he still hanging around?

As their worlds clash, Parker knows she needs to be super professional, even though her heart races when she sees Lily. With everything to lose, but their chemistry so strong, is it worth taking a gamble for love?

HER LITTLE SECRET

GEMMA JOHNS

A NineStar Press Publication

www.ninestarpress.com

Her Little Secret

First Edition, May 2024

ISBN: 978-1-64890-762-3

Also available in eBook, ISBN: 978-1-64890-761-6

CONTENT WARNING:

This book contains sexual content, which may only be suitable for mature readers. Depictions of grief and mention of life partner death due to cancer

Chapter One

LILY

"My feet are aching," Lily called out over the music. "I'm exhausted!"

Maree rolled her eyes at her friend. "Come on. Stop acting like an old lady. You're not even forty yet. We are partying til at least three." Maree was whining. "Just let down your hair."

Lily shook her head. Not for the first time that night, she vowed never to go out with Maree again. She pondered joking with Maree about the fact that her long hair was already down, but she figured she wouldn't be heard over the music. "I'll go sit down, then."

Maree grinned in response, but Lily knew there was no way she could get her to leave the dance floor. She had her eye on a petite blonde dancing off to the side. It was typical of Maree—as soon as her relationships finished, she'd be on the lookout for some new girl. "The best way to get over someone is to get under someone else" was Maree's motto, but it was definitely not Lily's way of thinking. Besides, meeting someone in a club wasn't exactly her cup of tea. The nightclub, the Palace, seemed like a meat market. That's what Maree enjoyed.

Spying a chair off in a quiet corner, Lily made a beeline for the bar, hoping the seat would still be empty once she got a drink.

She got herself a cola and dodged drunk people everywhere to sit down. As she approached the quiet chair in the corner, though, she noticed a woman sitting off to the side at the same table. She must have been there the whole time but had been blocked by the wall. "Do you mind if I sit? I wouldn't normally intrude, but my feet…" Lily couldn't believe she was asking—she usually wouldn't approach a stranger—but she was desperate. The woman was sitting quietly, so it shouldn't be a problem. Lily just hoped she didn't have a group of friends that would soon join her.

The woman shook her head. "Please, make yourself comfortable."

Lily smiled. "Thank you. What a terrible night," she muttered, more to herself than to the woman near her. But the woman responded anyway. "I'm Parker," she said. "So tell me why it's such an awful night, and why you don't go home?"

Lily rolled her eyes. She hadn't intended on chatting, but she had started it, clearly interrupting Parker's peace and quiet, so she figured she'd better explain. "My friend just broke up her latest U-Haul relationship. And she's clearly looking for another." Lily gave Parker a crooked grin. "Or something. That's her there, and she seems to have her eye on that blonde in the purple dress."

Parker craned her neck and glanced at Maree and the blonde in the purple dress. "Okay, and what are her chances?"

"I have no idea. I have seen them stealing glances at each other, but…" Lily shrugged. "Truthfully, I have enough trouble working out whether women are attracted to me, let alone whether Maree has a chance."

"Are you flirting with me?" Parker asked, smiling wryly.

Lily was confused. "Huh? Flirting?"

"Well, you said you can't work out if women are attracted to you. Was that a loaded comment? Like you're waiting for me to look in your eyes and say, 'I am,' or something. Because I'm not…"

"What? No!" Lily shook her head. She couldn't believe the woman was thinking that! She'd barely even looked at her. "No, I was just meaning… Never mind." Now she was annoyed. She couldn't even sit down without someone in the meat market thinking she was fair game.

"Sorry, I've made things awkward. It's just…that was a little forward of me, but I wondered if that's what you were getting at."

Lily blushed. "Sorry, I'm not here for that. Unlike Maree over there." She looked over and noticed Maree was now dancing closer to the blonde in the purple dress. Lily turned back to Parker and looked at her for the first time. She realised that if she was looking, Parker was exactly the type of woman who would turn her head. Short dark hair, broad shoulders, strong. Not her 'type' exactly, but sexy as hell. She had to look away.

"She's getting closer," Parker said, interrupting Lily's thoughts. She gestured toward Maree and the blonde. Lily followed her gaze. "I'd just noticed that too."

"What happens? She'll go home with her? If she's interested?" Parker was curious.

Lily shrugged. "Maree will do whatever the circumstances demand. She's a serial monogamist, and while she does go home with a girl on the first night, that's not usually her style. She'd prefer a phone number at the end of the night."

"A phone number." Parker smiled. "Cute. I didn't know people still did that. Not since 2005."

"You don't give out your number?"

"It's not that I don't give out my number, it's just…I hate the phone."

"I hate the phone too. Text me, email me, messenger me. Just don't call me."

Parker absentmindedly looked toward the dance floor. "My friend is in there somewhere too. I don't know where he went." It hadn't even occurred to Lily that Parker was there with someone. Actually, Lily hadn't really given any thought to why Parker was there.

"Do you have to stay til he comes back?"

Parker shook her head. "He does this. He might have already found some bloke. I don't know. He invites me out, and we usually just grab dinner, have a nice catch-up. But then some nights he pleads with me to come to a place like this, and bam, I don't see him again. I fall for it every time though. This is not really my scene." Parker gestured around the club. "I'm here for Nathan."

"That's…nice of you…I guess."

"Tonight we had incredible pizzas, so it's not a total waste of a night. I should probably head home soon, but I thought I'd sit for a bit, finish my beer, and then you came along." She gazed toward the dance floor, clearly scanning for her friend.

Lily frowned. "Does he usually return?"

"Generally, but it could be way past my bedtime." She yawned. "He doesn't seem to worry if I'm waiting, so I don't worry about him." She laughed dryly. "Hey, I don't even know your name."

"Lily," she said, smiling.

"That's a pretty name. It suits you." Lily blushed, but Parker kept talking. "Listen, there's a coffee shop around the corner. It makes the most incredible—"

"Lattes?" Lily asked, grinning. "I go there too. When Maree ditches me."

"Do you have caffeine this late at night?"

Lily shrugged. "I usually have no trouble sleeping, even when I do. Usually by the time I've danced the night away, I'm exhausted enough. Do you want to go?"

"I'd love a coffee, and I'm enjoying chatting with you."

Lily was pleased. It had been a long time since she'd enjoyed the company of a gorgeous woman, and though she wasn't planning to date any time soon, she was enjoying talking to Parker. As they sipped their coffee and shared a large chunk of caramel slice, they realised they both loved eighties music and reminisced about various music film clips.

"The *Thriller* one got my sister and I dancing every afternoon after school. We would try to moonwalk. Jacqui was really good at it. I was never as good as her."

"I used to moonwalk, and breakdance with my sister too."

"Oh yeah, breakdancing! That was fun!" Lily smiled, remembering how she and her cousins used to try to breakdance at parties.

"The children of today won't have anything like that in years to come," Parker said. "They'll remember just pouting into the camera, and planking, and all the ordinary stuff. The eighties were much better."

Lily agreed. She quietly pondered Bodhi's friends, and how much of their catch-ups were spent on game consoles, battling one another. She didn't bother mentioning Bodhi though. She wasn't trying to make a life-long friend, and she certainly wasn't going to date. She was, however, enjoying Parker's company and didn't want the evening to end. She couldn't help gazing at her when she wasn't looking and wondering what it would be like to kiss her. That unsettled her. It had been a long time since she'd even had thoughts like that, and she didn't need to start now. She shook her head and asked Parker what video games she'd played as a kid.

"My brother and I would play for hours."

Lily laughed. "I did, too, with my cousins. God, it was a long time ago."

"Well, we're not *that* old." Parker put her empty coffee cup down. "This is really great, getting to know you."

"Yeah, it's fun." Lily smiled. "I really should go soon though."

Parker glanced at her watch. "Did you drive or cab it?"

"I drove."

Parker asked her where she parked and whether she could walk her to her car. "That would be lovely," Lily said, and she was truly grateful. She never did love walking alone to her car in the city, and although she didn't know Parker, she felt comfortable and safe around her. As they strolled, they chatted about where they both lived—about ten minutes from each other—and how long their commutes to work were.

"The irony is I moved to Canberra and thought since everything is so close I'd have a short commute to work, but I'm going from Tuggeranong to Belconnen every day." Parker shrugged. "It's no drama, but it's about an hour out of each day, round trip. Still, it's hardly a Sydney or Melbourne commute."

"What do you do?"

"I'm a teacher. I've been at the school I'm at for nearly ten years now. I do love it. I sometimes wonder about moving closer to work though."

"I bet." Lily was disappointed to see they'd arrived at the car already.

"You don't have to drive your friend home, do you?" Parker asked as if it just occurred to her.

Lily shook her head. "No, I did text her earlier to let her know I was leaving. I didn't tell her I'd left with a woman. That would invite twenty questions."

"So your friend does that often, but you don't?"

Lily shook her head. "Never."

Parker looked disappointed. "So there's no chance of me getting your phone number, then?"

"I told you I don't do phone numbers. And neither do you, apparently."

Parker's eyes twinkled in response as she tried to hide a smile. "What about another coffee? At my house? Do you do that?"

Lily was silent. It sounded innocent enough, but even if Parker's invitation was genuine, she knew what would happen if she went home with her, and she couldn't say she wasn't tempted. It had been a long time since she'd enjoyed a 'coffee' at the house of a beautiful woman. She couldn't deny her attraction to Parker either. She could barely stop staring at her, but she had vowed not to have a relationship. It was incredibly tempting, even though it would have to be a one-night thing. Finally, she shrugged and asked, "Do you have instant coffee or *good* coffee?" She couldn't believe she was even considering it. There was something about Parker. She didn't want to end the evening yet, only enjoy being around Parker just a little longer.

"I have good coffee. Really good coffee." She smiled. "It's definitely worth the visit. I think you'll really like my coffee."

Parker's cheeky smile got her, and the inuendo excited her. More than she'd been excited in a long time. She glanced at Parker again and felt desire overtake her. In a very bold move, she stepped forward and kissed her lips. Gently at first, but as Parker responded, Lily responded also.

"Wow," Parker said when Lily broke away. "That was some kiss."

Lily nodded and smiled. She felt the same way. It had felt comfortable and passionate—just right. Exactly what she needed. "Do you have your car here?" Lily asked. Parker shook her head, so Lily opened the passenger door. "Then get in, before I change my mind." Lily had never seen someone jump in a car so quickly.

*

PARKER'S HOME WAS small and fairly minimalistic but very neat. Rows of shelving units lined her walls. Everything appeared so organised. She wasn't at all surprised to see the sleek, black couches had no cushions, and there was little decoration around the house.

They skipped the coffee entirely, and as they kissed, the intention between them for the rest of the evening became very clear—as if there was ever any doubt at the car park—but Lily had to be sure Parker understood. She broke away from a kiss and said, "Parker, there's one thing."

"Oh God," Parker said in mock concern. "Warts? Syphilis? Husband?"

Lily grinned in response. "No, none of the above. It's just…I'm not a relationship girl."

"You're not a relationship girl?" Parker seemed surprised.

Lily shook her head and said apologetically, "This is a one-off. I can't offer anything more than that."

Parker looked disappointed but made a joke about it. "So there is a husband?"

"No, I'm gay. Definitely no husband. I just don't need the complication. But I'm attracted to you, and you seem to be attracted to me, and…" she trailed off as Parker began kissing her again.

"I am very attracted to you, and I thank you for being honest. I do enjoy your company, and if you want to see if we could become friends…afterwards…I'd love that." Lily knew friendship would never work between them, but there was no way she could offer anything more than one night. Parker, though obviously disappointed, wasn't saying no. Lily was concerned her honesty might have ruined the moment, but she moved toward Parker again, and within moments, they were completely absorbed in their kissing. They made their way to the bedroom, where Lily was not surprised to find the bed perfectly made. She was already getting an insight into this tall, strong woman's character, but that wasn't what she was there for.

Parker moved her lips from Lily's and started kissing her neck. Lily moaned in response, and Parker began trying to find a zip to remove Lily's velvet dress. "Here," she said, laughing and pulling it up over her head. "It's a slip-on, slip-off dress. There's no zip."

Parker smiled. "Slip off—my kind of dress." Now Lily was lying in her underwear, but she felt more confident than usual. Parker looked impressed at what she saw and tugged on Lily's bra strap in a hint to remove it. In response, Lily unsnapped it and removed it for Parker, who buried her face in her breasts. She closed her eyes and enjoyed the sensation of Parker gently alternating rubbing her breasts and licking her nipples. She pulled Parker's shirt off and then smiled appreciatively. "Do you work out?" she asked.

Parker blushed and nodded. "Sometimes I go to the gym."

Lily traced her fingers over Parker's shoulders, mesmerized. She put her arms around Parker's back, and then traced down toward her jeans, tugging them just low enough to give Parker the idea. Parker took her jeans off, and within moments they were both fully naked and embracing each other. Parker really took the lead, and then, moving her way down Lily's body, she brought her to ecstasy a number of times before Lily took over, treating Parker to the same pleasure.

Afterwards, they lay in each other's arms, and Lily smiled at Parker. "That was incredible."

Parker nodded. "Pretty good together, aren't we?"

Lily agreed. "Yes, but it was definitely a one-off." Lily felt bad, but she had no other option.

"Why?" Parker asked. "Compatibility like that doesn't come along often." Parker sounded sad, and Lily felt awful, but she couldn't fix it for Parker. She just gave Parker a small smile, and said, "Sorry, but I really enjoyed this evening. Thanks for making it much better than I expected."

Parker shook her head. "No. Thank you! After Nathan left me, I figured I'd be home on the couch watching TV before ten! The night turned out much better than I ever expected."

"I'd better go now," Lily said, as she dressed.

A few minutes later, she stood at Parker's front door. "I might see you around."

Parker pecked her on the cheek and responded, "I certainly hope so!"

Chapter Two

PARKER

"And then she left," Parker said to Nathan.

"She just…walked out?" he asked, screwing up his face. "That's sooo not a lesbian move."

"She did. She'd warned me, but I'm not used to that. It was an incredible night. I'm not used to a woman running out on me."

Nathan shook his head, clearly bemused. "It's usually the other way around."

"To be fair, you know I'm not a player. But yes, if it happens, it's usually me who ends up running." Parker gave a small grin, pausing for a moment. "She's got me intrigued."

"You know the saying," Nathan said, "if someone tells you who they are, believe them. She's told you she's not a relationship girl, she didn't give you her number, just let it go." The waiter delivered them their brunch plates, interrupting their conversation.

Parker shrugged as she surveyed her breakfast, and then picked up her fork. "So, tell me about your night."

Nathan gave Parker a cheeky grin. "I went home with some incredible flight attendant. I ended up staying the night at his hotel."

Parker raised her eyebrows. "That's sooo not a Nathan move."

"I know! I woke up and thought 'Crap, what's my escape plan?' His flight out wasn't til six pm. And so when you texted and suggested brunch, it was the perfect getaway. I jumped at the chance."

"Here I was thinking you were jumping at the chance to see your best mate, given we didn't get much time to catch up last night."

"That too, darling. Of course." Nathan grinned at Parker, clearly realising he could have offended her.

Parker wasn't easily offended, though, especially when it came to Nathan. Besides, if he hadn't abandoned her, she might not have met Lily. Although Lily was determined it was a one-night fling, Parker hoped that maybe she'd come across her again. Canberra wasn't that big a city, so maybe they'd meet again through their networks or maybe they'd run into one another on another evening at the Palace. Parker half wondered if she should go there every weekend on the off chance of running into her but recognised that was an act of desperation.

She wished she'd asked Lily more questions. She didn't even know what she did for work. It really was a strange evening. They'd talked a lot and really connected on a deep level, but in hindsight, Parker knew nothing about her. She didn't even know why Lily didn't want a relationship. She did know that Lily loved *Friends* and *Seinfeld,* was a huge fan of KD Lang, and could do a mean moonwalk. She felt she knew who Lily was as a person, and she'd seen her vulnerable and open to her, but in terms of actual day-to-day life, or even how to track her down, she knew nothing.

"Penny for your thoughts, Parks," Nathan said. Parker simply shrugged in response.

"You have it bad, don't you?" he asked.

Parker didn't respond. She knew it was a one-night fling, and she wasn't going to let herself go crazy now, but she had to admit, Lily had been on her mind. Still, she would survive.

"Anyway, school holidays soon enough. That'll cheer you up!"

Parker smiled and nodded. "What are your plans?" She couldn't believe she hadn't already discussed this with Nathan. Normally they planned their holidays down to the day.

"I'm spending Easter visiting my cousins. I decided to drive to Melbourne, rather than fly this time."

"You should have flown," Parker quipped. "I hear the flight attendants are pretty cool."

"Touché." Nathan winked at her. "Melbourne should be fun. I'll spend five days there, maybe, and then come home. I'd like to relax a bit, but I'll be up for a night out on the second weekend."

That sounded good to Parker. She secretly hoped she might run into Lily, the first woman to capture her interest in a long time.

After she left Nathan, she decided to go straight home. She took a leaf out of Nathan's book and decided to make some holiday plans. She rang her parents and made plans to visit them in Sydney.

"That'll be lovely. Briony was planning to visit too. She might have told you. I'm sure Nick, Jenny, and the kids would love to come over for

Easter lunch unless they're doing something with Jenny's family. Maybe dinner then. Look, I'll speak to Jenny and make a plan," Parker's mum, Judy, said.

"Thanks, Mum. That sounds nice." Parker's sister, Briony, lived about an hour out of Sydney. Her brother, Nick, lived in Sydney, only about fifteen minutes from their parents. By that evening, Parker was pleased that the plan was locked in, and she would be sharing Easter Sunday lunch with her whole family. She couldn't wait even though it was still over a month away.

Chapter Three

LILY

Lily had just sat down to her cheese and mushroom omelette for dinner, when the doorbell rang. She frowned in confusion. She wasn't expecting anyone, and it was rare for people to drop in unexpectedly. She looked through the peephole and saw Maree, so opened the door.

"You don't usually pop in," Lily said, frowning, but then smiled. "Not that you're not welcome."

"I tried to not pop in. I've been texting you for about two hours," she said, shaking her phone. "But no response!"

Lily shook her head. It wasn't like her to not check her phone, but she'd had a lazy Sunday afternoon soak in the bath and had obviously forgotten to get the phone off charge.

"I'm sorry. It was on charge. What's up?"

"Where are Scott and Bodhi?" Maree asked, noticing how quiet the house was.

"Dinner at Scott's parents' house. I thought I'd take advantage of the empty house, so I had a spa bath and then made a very low key dinner. Do you want me to make you one?"

Maree looked at the omelette. "It looks good, and I'm starving. But you stay there. I'll make it while we talk."

Maree walked to the kitchen and grabbed the fry pan off the counter. She went to the fridge to get out eggs and cheese. "Have you got bacon on yours?"

Lily shook her head. "Not on mine, but there's bacon or ham in there if you want it. I just had cheese and mushroom."

"I need some meat," Maree said. "I might make mine ham and cheese." The two women cheerfully talked over Maree's cooking as Lily finishing up eating her omelette.

"How did you end up last night? The blonde in the purple dress?"

"I got her number, but no kiss or anything."

"That's just the way you like it," Lily said triumphantly. "You can go on a nice, romantic date."

"I'm sorry I didn't even see you leave. I got your message, so I knew you were heading home early. Was your night total crap?" Maree pouted in empathy for Lily. Lily shook her head.

"It was fine."

"Fine?" Maree's brow creased. "Netflix? Or curled up with a good book?"

"Actually, I went home with a woman," Lily responded. She hadn't planned on telling Maree—she didn't want to be questioned for hours—

but there was something about the way Maree just assumed she was home having a dull evening. Of course, the moment Lily mentioned how she'd actually spent her night, Maree's eyes lit up, and she asked a million questions. Growing tired of Maree's excitement and questioning, Lily sighed. She would have been better not telling her anything at all. Trouble was, she just couldn't get Parker out of her mind.

Chapter Four

PARKER
Ten months later

Parker was nervous as she got ready for her first day at work after summer holidays. She still had a week before the children would return to school, but the week was filled with preparation, meetings, and personal development training. For what felt like about the millionth time, Parker glanced down at her schedule for the week and sighed. Making the plunge to change schools after so long was always going to be stressful. She was so comfortable at the school she'd worked at for ten years, but she worried she'd got too comfortable. When Nathan had told her about the job vacancies at the school he worked at, she had jumped at the opportunity, although the change did concern her.

She relaxed as soon as she arrived at school and saw Nathan chatting to another teacher. He took her under his wing and began introducing her to all the people she hadn't yet met. She had met a few of them at her interview, and they'd all seemed lovely. She didn't want to rely too much on Nathan, but she certainly appreciated having him to introduce her. He spent the day making sure she knew her way around the school and met the people she needed to meet. At lunch time, she sat next to Nathan on one side of her and a vivacious blonde woman on the other side.

"I'm Kelly," the blonde said. "You must be the new grade three teacher?"

Parker nodded. "Nathan and I will be the grade three team."

Kelly shook her head. "There are three grade three classes."

"Oh, really? You didn't tell me," she said, accusing Nathan.

"I did so. I said the other grade three teacher was a little difficult. I don't really like her."

"Oh, I don't remember that," Parker confessed, then looked around the staff room. "Everyone seems nice though. So, which one is the difficult one?"

Nathan roared with laughter and looked at Kelly. Parker was confused and felt she was in the middle of some kind of joke, but it was going over her head.

"I'm the other grade three teacher," Kelly said, rolling her eyes. "Nathan thinks he's being funny, but he's not." Kelly was deadpan, but Parker could tell there was a lot of affection between them.

"So clearly the grade three teacher relationships are based on put-downs?" Parker asked.

Kelly shook her head and said, "No, that's just Nathan's style. I'm a very supportive colleague." She shrugged.

"I can deal with Nathan," Parker said, smiling. "We've been friends nearly twenty years."

"Wow, how did you meet? Did you go to high school together?"

"Oh, you flatter me, Kelly. No, we went to university together. We're oldies."

"Thirty-seven is hardly old. Gosh, even forty is young. Forty is the new twenty, darling," Nathan said, and Parker laughed in response.

"Yeah, if the new twenty is a ten pm bedtime, slipper socks, and wild nights at the movie cinemas instead of clubs." Parker joked.

Kelly was clearly amused. Parker liked her already. "So, tell me about yourself, since we're going to be teaching buddies."

Kelly shrugged. "Not much to tell. I'm a full-time teacher and dabbling writer. I am trying my hand at writing a new novel, actually," Kelly admitted in a shy, hushed tone. "I've always wanted to, but I got into teaching as a back-up plan, to ensure I actually got paid. A few years ago I just decided I'd better get started. I'm single, no kids. I like kids, but I'm not pining to have any. I wouldn't mind a guy though. But all the men I meet through work are married, awful, or gay!" She looked pointedly at Nathan, who shrugged in response.

"All the girls wish I played for their team," he said cheekily. "But they haven't got the goods I need."

Kelly swatted him away, clearly cringing at the visual image. "Anyway, I try to write five hundred words a day, but that gets challenging in report card time." Kelly shrugged. "No one else here knows I'm a writer because I'm using a pseudonym." Kelly was really speaking in hushed tones now.

"Oh, so you're actually published?"

Kelly shook her head. "About to be. My first book will be out early next year."

"Oh, wow, that's fantastic. What genre?"

Kelly shot a look around the room. "Romance. Well, romance probably sounds quite demure. My books are not demure." She blushed but smiled as she talked. "I'm just guessing it's probably not your type of book."

Parker tried to hide her smile. Clearly Kelly had read her as a gay woman, and obviously Kelly's books were of the fifty shades variety! Still, Parker didn't discriminate with her reading, and if she and Kelly became friendly, she would, of course, rush out to buy her debut novel.

"Maybe not, but I hope you'll keep us informed about the book," Parker enthused. "I'd love to read it."

Nathan stage whispered, "She held his quivering manhood in her hand and said, 'Fellipe, you are exquisite. Fill me now!'"

As Nathan pretended to quote from the book, Kelly shook her head at him and said, "How did you get a copy of my manuscript? You've quoted it word for word."

Parker liked Kelly already.

Chapter Five

LILY

Lily stretched out her legs and yawned, then lay back on her beach towel. From where she was laying, she could just spot Scott and Bodhi running through the water. Bodhi was giggling as Scott would dart in and out in an attempt to catch Bodhi, but Bodhi would always get away. Lily wondered if Scott was letting him, but she also knew Bodhi was getting pretty fast. She smiled and then picked up her book. She was having the most blissful week and really didn't want it to end.

It felt like hours later when shadows appeared above her. "Where's my towel, Mum?"

Lily rolled her eyes. "Your father is perfectly capable of getting you your towel, too, honey. 'Mum, Mum, Mum,'" she mimicked, laughing.

Scott shrugged. He was lucky to get away without Bodhi's constant nagging. Still, she couldn't complain—Scott was a great dad, and Bodhi was mostly an easy child, she knew.

"Last day today," Scott said, looking as disappointed as Lily felt. She nodded in response. She usually wasn't one to get Mondayitis or sad at the end of a holiday, but she wasn't looking forward to the next week with Bodhi starting back at school. Ugh, the school routine—making lunches, washing uniforms, and early bedtimes. They'd established a bit of a routine over their holiday, rising late, walking, returning and having breakfast, then relaxing by reading, watching TV, eating a light lunch, and heading to the beach or the pool til dinner time. They usually went out for dinner, but a couple of nights they'd done a poolside barbeque and board games. Bodhi had made a couple of young friends at the resort, and Lily and Scott had enjoyed watching him play with the other children. They now made a habit of annual beach holidays, and this trip, they'd discussed it might be important to return to the same resort each year to, hopefully, see some of the same children again.

Lily stopped pondering and glanced up at Scott, who was looking out at the ocean, wistfully. She smiled and caught sight of Bodhi, who was building a sandcastle nearby. He never stopped—not for a minute! She gestured to the bag and then said, "Shall we?" indicating to Scott that it might be time to pack up.

He understood immediately and nodded. "Yeah, I guess we better get organised to get on the road."

"We'll have lunch first though?" They'd changed up their routine on the last day in an effort to get on the road before too late.

"Yes, just something fast, and then we'll get in the car and go so we don't get home too late."

Lily nodded. That sounded like a good plan. The trio set about putting all their belongings into the car. By the time they were ready to go, their swimsuits had all dried. Lily had thrown a dress over the top of hers and decided they could just do the drive home that way. They grabbed sandwiches from a little café near their beach villa, and then made the two-hour drive home. On the way to the beach, Lily had given Bodhi a bunch of activities—never fun entertaining an active eight-year-old in the car—but he must have been exhausted because on the way home he happily put his iPod earphones in and relaxed, finally falling asleep. Lily smiled—she remembered back when he was young and would fall asleep in the car. She hadn't seen that for a long time.

"So back to school next week. I'm a little anxious. I always hate the start of a new school year."

Scott couldn't hide his amusement. "For you or him?"

Lily shrugged. "That's just the thing, isn't it? It's probably me!" She was fully aware that she was a little over the top. "But, hey, he's our only child."

"True. Do you know which teacher he has?"

"No, apparently he has someone new to the school this year. I forget her name. I hope she's nice. I really hoped he'd get Mr Stenlake. A nice male influence. He's one of the other grade three teachers."

"Oh! What am I if I'm not a nice male influence."

Lily said, "Okay, but you're his dad. You know what kids think of their parents."

Scott nodded. "I think I get what you mean."

*

A FEW EVENINGS later, Lily was anxiously packing Bodhi's school bag. His return to school also meant Lily's return to work, so she also planned her clothes out for the next morning. She always took the entire summer holiday period off work, and she wasn't excited to get back into the swing of things for herself, either—rushed mornings, packing lunches, planning her wardrobe—but deep down she knew that once they got into it again, it would all be fine. She really valued the flexibility her job and financial situation provided, but she also knew she wouldn't want to be at home full time now that Bodhi was at school. When he was younger, it was different. He had really needed her, and Lily had been a stay-at-home mum the whole time. Once he'd started at school, she had been excited about having something outside of the family. Something for her. Toward the end of that period, she'd almost been counting down the days, so she knew she shouldn't begrudge the fact that she was working now.

When she woke up, she could hear Bodhi talking to Scott in the kitchen. Lily slipped out. "Hey," she said, rubbing her eyes. "Oh, good, you're having breakfast."

"Yeah, Dad made me toast and cheese," Bodhi said.

"How are you going?" Scott asked, smiling kindly. "Did you sleep okay? You were up pretty late."

"Good, once I finally went to sleep, I was out like a light." Lily added, "I'll have a shower, get ready for the day. Back to the grindstone!"

Lily was acting like the return to work was awful, but she actually did love her work. She'd carved out an opportunity that worked perfectly for her, though the return to the routine was always a reality hit! When Lily had been ready to return to work, she'd spoken to her sister Jacqui about lots of different options. Should she manage an office, work in admin, work in sales? She didn't really know what she felt like doing. Maybe she could train to become a florist or cake maker. Maybe she should study to become a psychologist—she did love people. There were plenty of options.

Jacqui was in marketing, and always had good ideas, so she wanted to pick her brains. Not once had it occurred to her to start her own business, but one of the ideas Jacqui had had stuck with Lily—they could create a local magazine for parents, with a large section at the back for discounts. Lily loved writing and networking and thought the service for parents would be a great idea. She got to work creating a business plan, and when she presented it to Jacqui, Jacqui was just as keen to set it up. "If we're successful, I could work part-time and do the business the rest of the time," Jacqui had said, excitedly considering the possibilities. "And if we're super successful, I could give up my job and work with you full-time!"

That was all the motivation Lily needed to make this work. She got advertisers from all over Canberra. Each ad was linked to at least one discount voucher, and about half the readers bought the magazine just for the discounts. The others loved the articles, and Lily tasked people from all over the world to submit articles each month. Soon enough the magazine was successful enough that Jacqui could reduce her hours at work. The beauty of that was that Jacqui could cover all the summer months, and Lily would be a stay-at-home mum for Bodhi during the summer.

Jacqui's kids were older and a lot more independent than Bodhi. Jacqui constantly said to her little sister, "Enjoy Bodhi wanting you around because it doesn't last forever." Her three girls seemed to want to do their own thing all summer long, so Jacqui enjoyed pumping out the work to get the first issue of each year on to the shelves. In the last year, Jacqui had resigned from her job completely, and now they had the pressure to really make it work. Jacqui was already considering new options to expand the business. She was the creative brains behind the business, while Lily was all about implementing, connecting people with the right project. It seemed to work really well.

It was forecast to be such a hot day and Lily had a few meetings lined up already, so she threw a red dress on, heels, and brushed her long dark hair. After she spritzed some perfume on and completed the look with vibrant red lipstick, she felt ready for both the return to the school gate and to the office. She went downstairs where Scott and Bodhi were now watching cartoons, breakfast over. "Kettle's still hot," Scott called. "I didn't make you a cup. I wasn't sure how long you'd be, but the tea bag's in your mug."

"No worries, thank you!" Lily was so lucky to have Scott. He was really considerate of things like that. She had just popped bread in the toaster when he called out again, "I put Bodhi's lunchbox in his bag and got the drink bottle out of the fridge. Is that all he needed?"

"Oh, I wanted to give him one of the yoghurts from the top of the fridge."

Lily heard Scott say, "Bodhi, go grab a yoghurt for Mum." She spread peanut butter thickly on her toast and sat at the table munching on it while flicking through her phone. She glanced at her text messages—she had a few. Her parents, wishing Bodhi well; Jacqui, saying how excited she was to have her co-worker back; and one from one of the school mums saying she hoped Lily's morning was going better than her own, and she would see her at school.

They travelled to school in two cars, Bodhi opting to drive with his father. It was a bit more of a novelty, Lily supposed, as she did most of the school runs in the morning. Scott worked in the public service and usually preferred to start early and finish in time to pick Bodhi up from school. This meant that Lily didn't have to rush home, but she did have the flexibility if it was ever required. Lily preferred to do all the school pick-ups the first week back to school, to get to know who was in the new class, chat with the teacher, and get a feel for things. Then she'd relax into her more normal routine.

Each year, the school seemed to trial different strategies for managing the bottleneck of parents eager to see their little babies off on the first day. The year before, they'd all had to say goodbye in the playground. This year, parents were encouraged to visit their child's classroom, greet the teacher, deposit school bags, hear any instructions, and then leave. Bodhi led the way to the grade three section. They walked past Mr Stenlake's classroom, and Lily glanced in, a little sad to see that Mr Stenlake had the kids of some of her friends. She'd heard he was an amazing teacher, and as she'd said to Scott, she thought a male teacher would be good. On the other side of the hall, Miss Williams was setting up. Bodhi had Miss Kelly Williams back in grade one, and then she'd become a grade three teacher.

She popped out to say hello. "Does Bodhi have Ms Parker? Or Mr Stenlake?" Miss Williams asked.

"Not Mr Stenlake. He has the new teacher?"

"Yeah, Ms Parker. She's really nice."

"Oh, good. I always get anxious about new teachers."

"I think you'll be fine with her. She seems to know her stuff. I've just had a week of planning days with her, and we've had a ball."

"Oh. That's good to know." Lily really valued Kelly's opinion—she'd been impressed with her as Bodhi's teacher. Scott then spoke up. "Should we go meet the teacher then?" He half smiled, clearly thinking they were spending too much time talking *about* the new teacher when they could be talking *to* the new teacher. Ever the pragmatist!

They made their way to the next classroom, and there was a crowd of parents and children placing bags down, claiming desks, and just making general, noisy chaos. Lily always hated this part of the return to school. Bodhi found a bag hook with his name on it and hung his school bag up. He took out his books. Lily noticed a tray of gleaming laptops with a sign for each child to claim one and place a name sticker on it—their device for the year. Lily had been involved in the P&C fundraiser to get enough money, along with a government grant, for each child to have their own device to use. She felt pretty proud to see them there for the kids. The bell rang, and each child took their seat at their desk. The parents moved to the sides of the room, and Lily looked up to get a glimpse of the teacher. Never in her wildest dreams had she expected to see Parker at the front of the class!

Chapter Six

PARKER

"HI, GRADE THREE. I'm Ms Parker and, parents, you can just call me Parker. That's my preferred name. I'm new to South Canberra Primary, and I'm very excited to get to know you all! The grade three team, which includes Ms Williams and Mr Stenlake and myself, have been working together to create some wonderful activities. We'll be working together sometimes, and as individual classes other times. Today, I want you to spend a lot of time reflecting on your summer holidays, so we'll be doing some sharing—talking, writing, drawing, reading books about summer." Parker nervously looked down and then wrapped up. "Parents, please feel free to come up and say hello; otherwise, I'll meet you over the course of the next week or so. Please pick your children up from the classroom at 3:00 pm, or at the school gate. If they go to after-school care, someone will come to get them in the first week. It's all about the new routine and getting everyone comfortable. I look forward to getting to know you and your child during the year."

With that, Parker started to move around the room. She met a few of the lingering parents while noticing others had opted to leave the room to not compete with the crowd. From experience, she knew she'd meet them over the next week or two. She was standing talking to a curly haired mother who was explaining how her daughter's reading had improved, when she noticed someone she recognised at the door of the room—Lily, the woman from the bar the year before. Lily, the woman she'd had an amazingly passionate night with and then wondered about for months. Lily, the woman she'd seen naked and raw. Surely she wasn't a parent? Lily had never mentioned having a child—she would have remembered if she had. Maybe she was there with a friend or her sister. She noticed a tall, dark-haired man standing beside her and frowned.

The curly haired woman had asked her a question she hadn't heard, but she was clearly waiting for an answer. Parker improvised, and hoped for the best, saying, "Well, let's just see how her reading goes over the first term, and we can always meet to address it." The curly hair woman beamed, so clearly Parker's answer had been an appropriate response to the question. Who was the man standing beside Lily? She made a beeline for Lily although didn't know what to say. "Err, hello," she managed to say.

Lily seemed momentarily shocked but then smiled. "Hello. This is Bodhi," she said, "and I'm Lily." The smile hadn't reached her eyes.

Parker nodded. She wanted to say, "We met last year," or even ask, "How can you not remember me?" but glancing at the man next to her and having noticed the fear that had briefly crossed Lily's face moments before, she didn't say anything. To say her heart wasn't pounding, though, would have been a complete understatement. In that one moment, she'd felt excited to see Lily again and smashed back down to earth with three little words—"and I'm Lily." What was going on there? Whatever it was, she clearly hadn't told the man next to her that she knew Bodhi's teacher. Perhaps she hadn't even remembered her.

Ever the professional, she temporarily shook it off and crouched down to address Bodhi. "Hello. What did you say your name was?"

"I'm Bodhi, and this is my mum, and this is my dad."

She took a step back. The man next to Lily was Bodhi's father, and Lily was Bodhi's mother. So that meant…what? They were a couple? But…how on earth? Were they were divorced? Parker was really confused now.

"I'm Scott," the man said and shook Parker's hand. Parker glanced at Lily, but she gave nothing away. She seemed to be looking at her feet.

"Nice to meet you, Scott. I look forward to getting to know Bodhi over the next few weeks. Anything in particular you'd like me to know to focus on?" She had addressed her question to the man, but Lily stepped in and responded.

"Nothing, really. Nothing I can think of. Bodhi is doing well at school, mostly. We'd like to see a few more social connections established this year, but we can work on that." She glanced at Scott for confirmation that what she'd said was correct. He nodded in agreement.

"Thanks, Ms Parker," he said, clearly indicating they were happy for her to move on to the next child.

"Oh, please, just call me Parker." Parker couldn't recall for certain but was fairly confident she hadn't told Lily that Parker was her surname because it was really the only name she ever used.

Lily smiled. "Thanks Parker." She looked nervous, and Parker suspected that was due to the man she was looking mighty comfortable next to.

*

AT THE END of the day, Nathan grabbed Parker in the staff room. "How was your day?"

Parker was frazzled—it had been a huge day, but mostly it was her interaction with Lily and Scott that morning that was still nagging at her. She shrugged and glanced around the staff room. "I know you're probably exhausted, but fancy a coffee or something stronger when we get out of here? I'd love to debrief."

"Sure," Nathan said and went to pack up. Within thirty minutes, they were sitting across one another at a local coffee shop sipping lattes. "So you're happy? Enjoyed the new school? Must be a big change after so long."

Parker nodded. "Yeah, it's a bit of a blur, getting to know all the kids, meeting the new parents. But do you know a Bodhi Delaney-Jones?"

Nathan nodded. "Yeah, I know him. Not well, I've never taught him or anything, but the school's small enough that most of us know each of the kids. Is he a troublemaker?" Nathan squinted.

"No, he seems really well behaved so far."

Nathan was clearly wondering why Parker was singling him out if there were no concerns, so she explained, "I met his mother before."

"Oh, yeah." Nathan appeared confused, clearly not picking up anything.

"Remember about a year ago, we went out, and I met a woman while you were off shagging that flight attendant?"

Nathan grinned impishly. "That was a good night," he recalled, momentarily lost in his thoughts. Then he looked back at Parker, and his brow creased. "You're not saying… Mrs Delaney-Jones…?" He raised his eyebrows and grinned as he spoke.

Parker didn't return his smile but nodded. "That's exactly what I'm saying. So, she is a Mrs? They *are* married?"

Nathan looked apologetic. "Like I said, I don't know the family well. I've seen them around the school—both of them. I've definitely seen the dad before, so they're both involved with the kid, but I don't really know their circumstances. Can't you get Bodhi to tell you? Do an activity like a who-lives-in-your-house drawing or something. Maybe they've divorced?"

"Not a bad idea. Maybe I could link it into 'What did you do during summer holidays?'"

"Yup. But chin up, Parker. At the end of the day, who cares if she had a fling and cheated on her husband? Not your worry."

Parker was silent. Nathan was right, it was just a fling—Lily had told her she couldn't offer anything more than one night. *Oh, God.* That was the classic sign she had a husband, wasn't it? But she was fairly sure Lily had told her she was gay that night. Labels didn't worry her, but gay didn't usually mean you had a husband you looked pretty happy next to, did it? Parker screwed her face up, and Nathan looked at her sadly.

"This is why us guys have it easy. I don't care what the flight attendant is doing, or who he is doing. You look so miserable."

"The problem is that we had an incredible night. We had the most amazing connection both in and out of bed. You remember me going on about her back then?"

Nathan waved his hand as if to dismiss her. "Oh yes, I do recall you going on and on about something. It was just nice to hear you'd got some action. I didn't care so much for the details." Nathan screwed up his face in disgust, which made Parker laugh.

"Well, it was incredible, and I couldn't help wanting more at the time. And seeing her today—" Parker shook her head. "—I don't know. I need to know her situation."

Nathan cringed. "You're her son's teacher. Just let it go. Do some internet dating, or go to the club and pick up, but do *not* screw the crew."

"I'm not going to 'screw the crew'. God, that sounds crass, Nath. I just want to know what that night was."

Nathan gave her a look. "That night was a fun night. A year ago. Let it go. Especially now you're teaching her son." It wasn't like Nathan to deter any flings, so Parker nodded and figured the case was closed.

"Okay, but do you think there's a way of finding out the parents' surnames? Or whether they live together?" Parker didn't know why she needed to know. Nathan was right—it was better to just let it go.

Nathan nodded. "It's on his file, but you have to get through Elizabeth, the dragon in the front office, to get to that. Have you met her yet?"

Parker nodded and had to agree with him.

Nathan continued. "I say you've got no chance. Do the summer vacation activity."

That's how Parker found herself in class the next day trying to do her sleuthing. Each child was asked to draw a picture of their summer holiday—whatever they got up to—and then tell a story. It wasn't completely self-indulgent. It was a typical activity that Parker ran at the return to school after the summer. It allowed them to use art to tell a story and to share verbally with the class. It also gave Parker the opportunity to get to know her new students a little more. The fact that she had an ulterior motive this time was simply extra motivation to run the activity. The children were excited to have some time to play with pencils and crayons and chatter to their friends. Parker slowly made her way around the classroom, crouching beside each child to ask them questions about their picture.

When she got to Bodhi's table, she noticed his picture had three people in it, and what looked like a sun in the corner and the ocean. "Did you go to the beach, Bodhi?" Parker asked.

"Yes," Bodhi grinned.

"What else is in your picture? Who did you go to the beach with?"

"This is Mum. This is Dad. This is me. We went to the beach for nearly two weeks. We also did other stuff in the holidays, but I loved our beach trip."

Parker nodded and smiled at the picture. "And that was Mum who dropped you to school today? And Dad who came with Mum yesterday?" Parker had seen Lily from a distance that morning but didn't think she had seen her.

Bodhi smiled and nodded in response. "Yes."

"Do you have brothers or sisters?" Bodhi shook his head in response.

Parker felt she'd exhausted all her questions, so moved on to the next child, but more questions were swirling in her mind.

*

LATER THAT AFTERNOON when Parker had a short break, she took the opportunity to go to the front office. Being so new, she didn't want to overstep any lines, but she thought it could be good to get some answers. "Hi,

Elizabeth. I just wanted to get phone numbers of a couple of the mums. They had mentioned to me they might be interested in volunteering in the classroom." Parker rattled off three surnames to Elizabeth, who busied herself grabbing folders out of the filing cabinet. It wasn't a total lie, two of the mums had said that, but Lily wasn't one of them. Elizabeth placed the three files on the desk, and opened one, writing down the phone number of the first mother. Just before she opened Bodhi's file, there was a commotion down the hall.

Elizabeth swung into action, turning to Parker starting with "Excuse me!" before running out of the front office, calling, "Michael Davies, if I see you with that one more time…!"

With a pen in her hand, Parker opened Bodhi's file. She skimmed the front page, but wrote the phone number down—for authenticity if nothing else. She then noticed that the file clearly stated '*Mother: Mrs Lily Delaney-Jones; Father: Mr Scott Delaney-Jones*'. She glanced down the page further and saw that the address listed for both parents was the same.

Hmm, what a cosy little family, Parker thought, frowning. None of it made sense—especially not their night of passion. All she could assume was that Lily was a curious, married woman who had lied to her to get a fling. But that didn't make sense because Parker had pursued Lily. Lily had just been friendly—she certainly wasn't looking for something that night. And their night together didn't scream of experimentation or first-time nerves, and there were no signs that there was a straight woman in the room that night. In fact, Lily had appeared to be very much into Parker. It felt like she couldn't get enough of it…until it was over, and then she'd bolted. Maybe they were in an open marriage? Maybe she returned home to Mr Delaney-Jones and told him stories of what she got up to, and that was part of their game. It would explain a lot—her lack of nerves, her interest in women, but also her desire to leave. To rush home to her happy family. Parker had no idea. It was impossible to know what was going on.

Elizabeth returned. "Oh, you wrote them down?" she pointed in the direction of paper in front of Parker.

Parker nodded. "I did, thank you."

Elizabeth shook her head. "I swear, that Michael Davies in grade six! You're lucky you'll never teach him, such a difficult child. Always pushing our buttons. He'll be graduating at the end of the year. In theory, anyway. If he keeps carrying on, we might need to suspend him." Elizabeth chuckled.

Parker knew it wasn't up to the front office lady at all, but obviously she could make a complaint to the principal about the behaviour of a child. Parker smiled politely, obviously not knowing Michael to make a comment, but she ended up commiserating with Elizabeth about difficult students she had experienced in her time. Nathan might consider her a dragon, but Parker figured that made it even more important to get her on her side. Nathan preferred to avoid her, but Parker felt getting to know her would be the safest bet.

Chapter Seven

LILY

Scott came into the kitchen just as Lily and Bodhi were sitting down to breakfast. He looked at his watch. "I'm a bit late going this morning. Not used to this routine."

"It's a shock to the system, isn't it? Oh well, we'll quickly get used to it."

Scott agreed. "I've had brekky, so I'll get on the road, go to work."

"Just remember I can pick Bodhi up this afternoon—I've told Jacqui I wanted to ease back in—so if you being late for work is an issue, I can do it."

"Thanks." Scott grinned at her, and she smiled back at him.

"Maybe we could go for dinner tonight? Middle of the week, could trick us into thinking we're on vacation again just for an hour," she suggested. As Scott nodded, she turned to Bodhi. "Would you like to go for dinner tonight? Just the three of us?"

"Yeah, I guess so," Bodhi said.

"Where do you want to go?" Scott asked, directing the question to both of them.

"The Noodle House?" Bodhi piped up.

"Oh, nice pick," Lily said happily. Cheap, cheerful, and great food.

"Reckon we need a booking?" Scott asked, and Lily said she'd do it. "Sounds great," he said, and then gave Bodhi a kiss goodbye.

An hour later, Lily walked Bodhi to the school gate and into the schoolyard, where Bodhi found a friend and raced off to follow him. She stood watching as the two boys went running toward the play area. She looked into the distance as she saw Parker walking with Mr Stenlake around the schoolyard. One of them was probably on playground duty, and the other was keeping them company.

Lily sighed. Of all the schools in Canberra, she couldn't believe Parker had wound up there, teaching her son. She didn't know how she'd be able to survive the school year, but she had no other option. What was the alternative? Changing schools? She couldn't imagine telling Scott and Bodhi that they had to leave Bodhi's beloved school, and Canberra South was a really great school. She shook her head; no, she'd just have to pull on her big-girl panties and deal with it. She didn't even know if Parker recognised her. She just wished she didn't feel that unsettling sensation whenever she was around her. Just as she glanced at her one last time, Parker looked up, and their eyes met. Lily instinctively looked away, but not before noticing her penetrating gaze.

*

JACQUI WALKED INTO the office. "Have you had breakfast? Hope not. I had an early meeting with a bakery and they gave me croissants!" she called out cheerfully.

Lily was working on some new advertising packages but struggling to focus, so she welcomed the interruption. "Oh, yum. I had a very healthy muesli for breakfast, so I'm more than happy to ruin that by stuffing my face with pastries and jam."

"Jam, good point." Jacqui went to the office pantry and pulled out a jar of raspberry jam and then went to the fridge for butter. She quickly put the kettle on and made two coffees, taking the steaming mugs to the desk. Getting some plates together, she sat down at Lily's desk with the croissants, and the two of them got busy doctoring their baked goods.

Biting into them, they were silent for some time before Jacqui finally spoke up. "How are things?"

"Good," Lily said, not giving anything away.

That wasn't good enough for Jacqui, who shook her head and responded. "Are you struggling, being back at work? Or is it something else?"

"Nothing's wrong," Lily said, her voice a little too high.

"Oh, come on, you haven't been yourself for days. What is it?" Jacqui pressed. She used her fingers to count off options. "Back to school? Back to work? New routine? Scott? Or Valentine's Day coming up?"

Lily looked up as her sister said that. "I hadn't even thought about Valentine's Day."

"You will," Jacqui said knowingly with compassion.

Lily smiled, but her tone was sad. "Yeah, I will."

"So, if it's not that, is it one of the others? Bodhi back at school? Or problems with Scott?"

Lily shook her head and wondered whether to confide in Jacqui. "Scott's great, as always. He's perfect. I'm so lucky to have him."

"Yes, but he's lucky to have you too."

Lily nodded. "Yeah, but he's great with Bodhi. It's a huge help."

Jacqui rolled her eyes. "He's his dad. Dads should be good with their kids."

"You know what I mean. Look, I'll tell you what's up, but you have to promise to never mention it again."

Jacqui looked surprised but agreed, licking the jam off her fingers. "Sure, fire away."

"The issue is Bodhi's teacher. She's new to the school."

"Okay, you're three days into the term. What has she possibly done?"

"Nothing. I'm sure she's fine. It's just… I've met her before."

"Okay," Jacqui said, looking at Lily like she was going mad. "Typical in Canberra."

Lily didn't know how to say it without sounding crass. Finally, she just bit the bullet. "I've slept with her."

Jacqui practically choked on her coffee as she spluttered, "You slept with Bodhi's teacher? When?"

Lily blushed but laughed a little at her sister's response. "Last year."

"You slept with a woman last year!" Jacqui's eyes widened. "What?"

"Well, don't look so surprised." Lily was offended that Jacqui thought the idea was so unexpected.

"I am surprised. I didn't realise there had been any women since Megan."

Lily looked down and rubbed her forehead in her hand. "There hadn't been. Until Parker that night. Or Ms Parker as she's called at the school. I'm really unsure if Parker's her first name or her surname, but I knew her as Parker. And there's been no one since."

"Does Scott know?"

Lily shook her head and said, "No way. It would break his heart. Of course not. Only Maree knew."

Jacqui nodded and Lily continued, "It was an incredible night. Totally unexpected but amazing. And I bolted out of there so fast in the end. It was so wrong. So perfect…and so wrong. I felt like the worst person in the world. I didn't stop thinking about it for months afterwards. I figured it could just be my dirty little secret, and then suddenly I see her in our son's classroom." Lily had tears in her eyes.

Jacqui shook her head and gave her a sad look. "Oh, Lily." She moved around the desk and put her arms around her sister, who fell into the embrace and cried. Lily was pleased it was finally out in the open.

"I feel like I've been walking on eggshells at home. Like what if somehow Parker lets Scott know?"

"Is that such a bad thing?" Jacqui asked. "Would it be so awful if he knew?"

"I think it would break his heart."

Jacqui considered it. "I don't think Megan would want you living like this, Lily. And I'm sure if you talked to Scott, he would agree."

"He's living like it too."

"Yes, I suppose so," Jacqui pondered aloud.

"He hasn't dated in a long time either."

"I think it's just an excuse for him. It's just easier to play the role of co-parent, career dad, that type of thing. I don't think he's not dating because of Megan, is he?"

Lily shrugged. "Hard to say why he doesn't date, but he doesn't, and I feel bad if I…"

Jacqui gave her sister a look. "You can't live your life in honour of your dead wife, honey. You need to live too. Maybe Ms Parker is the woman for you."

"Even if Ms Parker is the woman for me, she's now Bodhi's school teacher, so…"

Jacqui grinned, displaying her amusement about the situation Lily had found herself in. "It's a bit complicated, isn't it? So maybe it's not Ms Parker, but maybe this is the push you need to get back out there. Go online. Go to the club. Find someone."

Lily was pensive. "I don't know about that," she said. "Nothing's actually changed."

"Nothing other than the fact you suddenly have an opportunity with the woman who apparently rocked your world a year ago." Jacqui shrugged. "Anyway, I have a bone to pick with you. Why didn't you tell me back then?"

"It's complicated, of course. I didn't feel great about what happened. I felt like I was cheating on Megan."

Jacqui looked sadly at Lily. "Like I've always said, I can't pretend to understand what you've been going through these past six years, but I know Megan would have wanted you and Bodhi to be as happy as possible. And that could mean meeting someone and becoming a family."

"We are happy. We are a family. Our little trio has just as much love as any normal family without the romance!"

Jacqui agreed and then took the plates from Lily's desk, signalling that it was time to get a move on back to work.

"You're right though," Lily said. "Megan would want me to be happy, I know, but I just don't feel right yet. And I don't want Scott knowing."

Jacqui nodded. "Yep. I get it."

Lily knew she really didn't.

Chapter Eight

PARKER

Parker couldn't concentrate on her lesson plans, so instead she was flicking through educational magazines hoping inspiration would strike. She didn't know why she was letting the situation with the Delaney-Jones family get to her so much. She'd had flings before, and no doubt even had flings with married women before. Until she'd moved schools, she hadn't anticipated seeing Lily again, and although she'd absolutely loved their night together and thought they had a strong connection, she hadn't exactly been pining for Lily.

But her reaction to seeing Lily was not her normal response. Seeing Lily had really unsettled her. Whenever she'd imagined running into Lily, it was at the bar or at a party with friends, certainly not at her workplace. Of course, she hadn't known Lily had a child, so she couldn't have expected to ever run into her at a school. And now, she was the teacher of Lily's child, and it turned out that Lily was married. Parker sighed. This was definitely not what she'd pictured when she'd fantasised about the possibility of running into her.

Deciding that it was fruitless trying to work that evening, Parker packed her bag and flicked the television on. She stared mindlessly at that for about an hour, before finally heading to shower before bed. She wondered if a debrief with Nathan would help her get back on track, but she was concerned because he'd basically told her to stop—she was Bodhi's teacher after all, and he wanted her to be professional. Wise advice, really, given she was five minutes into her new job. It was exactly the same advice she would offer someone in her situation. She didn't want Nathan thinking she was losing control, particularly after he'd recommended her to the school principal. Both her reputation and his were on the line if she did the wrong thing.

And Nathan wouldn't expect she would. Pining after a woman was not really standard Parker behaviour, after all. She couldn't even remember the last time a woman had gotten under her skin like this. She didn't know if she was reeling because of a connection with Lily and true attraction, or if she was bothered that Lily had lied to her. She had certainly presented as a single woman—albeit a single woman who hadn't wanted anything more than one night—but she was clearly anything but. No, Mrs Delaney-Jones had really thrown her for six.

She shook her head. She had to focus on this new job. She wanted to impress the principal and connect with the other grade three teacher, Kelly. She wanted to show them they'd made the right choice in hiring her and that she was going to make a positive impact at this school. She'd built a very solid reputation at her last school, with everyone—parents, children, and the school team. She was determined to use her years of experience and natural talent for making a difference to children's learning to really make an impact. She needed to build her reputation at the new school, and now was not the time to lose focus. She certainly wasn't going to let some fling with a married woman a year ago interfere with the career she'd worked so hard at.

It wasn't Bodhi's fault that his mother had lied to Parker and possibly cheated on her husband. Obviously, they could have an open marriage. Parker would never know what had happened, but she knew she would treat Bodhi just as well as she treated any other child in her class. With love, compassion, and an eagerness to get the best outcomes for the individual child. She just hoped she didn't have to come across his mother much during the year ahead. Though, she had to admit, the prospect of engaging with his father didn't really excite her either. How could she have authentic conversations with him about his son's progress and any needs he might have while knowing she'd seen his wife naked? This was not the ideal scenario at all, but she had to accept it, move on, and put her best in at work, otherwise the job change would have been completely pointless.

Secretly, Parker had ambitions to get into school leadership. She'd built a really good reputation at her last school but was overlooked for leadership opportunities. She felt that starting fresh at a new school, with years of experience behind her, would be beneficial. She believed she would come to the school confident, full of ability, and surprise them in a way she couldn't do at her old school. She was also attracted by the much shorter commute and the fact that she would be working with Nathan. Although change was always hard, she had known she had to make the big leap. But, after over a decade at one school, it hadn't been easy to leave. She just kept anticipating the future. She'd thought about her new job for the past few months, but never in her wildest dreams had she imagined teaching the son of a fling!

On Friday, Kelly was in a great mood, and that rubbed off on Parker. They had a fun day with the children and enjoyed cracking jokes together in the staff room at lunch time. Nathan clearly approved of the two of them getting along, joining them when a meeting he had was over. He smiled at Parker, and Parker assumed he was happy to see her in a much lighter mood. "We should go for Friday drinks after work," he suggested, and Kelly and Parker agreed.

"Let's have a big night. Let's go home, get dressed, and do it properly," Kelly said. "Let's have dinner then go to the casino to dance."

Nathan shook his head. "I'm not sure I'm up for a big night. I was thinking more like an after-school cocktail."

Kelly pouted. "I really feel like dancing. Besides, what else do you have planned this weekend?"

Nathan shrugged. "Nothing, really. I have some washing to do."

Kelly playfully whacked him. "I feel like we need to do a proper welcome to Parker, and an 'after-school cocktail'," she said, using air quotes to emphasise it, "just doesn't seem like a proper welcome."

"Fine. Fine! What do you think, Parker?"

Parker shrugged. "I'm not a big night-out person, but this weekend I have absolutely nothing planned. I kept it free specifically because it was the first week back," she clarified. She didn't want Kelly thinking she was dull.

"Okay, Kelly, we're in. As long as we can go to the Palace for a jig too."

Parker rolled her eyes—trust Nathan to want to go to the gay club. Kelly was excited to go. She said she preferred it to many of the other clubs in town, which seemed to be increasingly typical of gay clubs around the world. Parker saw this as both beneficial—supportive, and nice to have allies—but also challenging to have a space where you feel completely free to meet people. Nevertheless, Parker wasn't really keen to meet anyone. She'd tried internet dating for a while, and she'd been introduced to people, but no one had really excited her. Until she'd met Lily, that was, but Lily had made it clear she couldn't have a relationship. Why hadn't Parker questioned that more? But she knew the answer—she had been so attracted to Lily that it hadn't mattered at the time.

Hours later, they were at a small Italian bistro sharing a pizza and chugging beer, chatting about the different people at school. "Have you met the PE teacher, Adam? Well, he's had an affair with a preschool teacher, Donna, but then Donna and her husband got back together, and now you just see Adam shoot longing looks at her whenever she walks past him. Athletics carnivals are a riot."

"I don't really believe that. I think it was speculation," Nathan said. "Besides, I always thought Adam played on my team."

"Maybe he plays on your team in football or something, but when it comes to dating, he definitely chases women. He's even flirted with me," Kelly said. "I reckon I had a chance for about five minutes, but I guess I was too available for his liking. Turns out he likes his women married."

Parker blushed—that was not how she liked her women, but the comment certainly reminded her of Lily. She craved a sounding board, and Nathan had said her case was closed. She wondered about using the fun evening as an opportunity to get some advice. Kelly seemed the type who would find the conversation fascinating. But Parker had to remember she'd just started at the school, and she wanted to get into a leadership position, so she had to remain professional. Friendly with Kelly, yes, but she didn't need Kelly sharing this 'rumour' on the next girls' night with another group of teachers. Parker resolved to keep this to discuss with Nathan when they had a moment alone.

"Do you like Adam?" Nathan asked Kelly.

"I used to think he was cute. He has a body to die for," Kelly quipped. "But the more I get to know him, the more I realise he's not my type. And now I can't get him and Donna out of my head anyway."

Nathan paused. "Yeah, I wouldn't have picked him as your type."

"Probably not," Kelly shrugged. She certainly didn't seem bothered either way. Parker was beginning to realise that was Kelly's style. "This pizza is amazing," Kelly added.

"Yeah, I bet you're glad you let me talk you into getting the olives on it," Nathan said, grinning.

"I don't know if you've noticed, but the olives have all been safely peeled off and placed on the side. But the meat, the feta, and the sauce are great."

"I love it too," Parker said. "I love the olives and feta cheese with it though. I'm a real Mediterranean girl!"

"So, the plan is casino first and then Palace?"

Everyone nodded, and they started to make their way to the Casino. Kelly had dressed to the nines; in a short satin dress and black heels, she was ready to kick up on the dance floor. Nathan was in skintight jeans and a blue fitted shirt—he looked great. Parker was wearing black jeans and a white linen shirt over a fitted black T-shirt. It was a hot night, but she felt good anyway. If it got too hot, she could always pull off the white shirt. The Casino played 80s music, so Kelly and Nathan made a beeline to the dancefloor.

While they danced, Parker grabbed a beer and enjoyed watching the crowd. She liked to analyse the relationships between groups of friends or people enjoying a date. *Family or friends? Were they a long established couple, or was it a first date? Were they friends and had suddenly connected romantically?* She'd never know the answer, but she could amuse herself for hours with her natural curiosity for people.

Her desire to people watch and wonder about their stories was exactly what confused her about Lily. Lily hadn't told her much about herself that evening, but she'd certainly presented as a single woman. And Parker had assumed, incorrectly, that she didn't have a child. In her experience, most parents generally brought up their children in conversation. Didn't they? Parker and Lily had discussed what she did for a living, for example, although, in hindsight, she didn't think Lily told her about her work. Parker couldn't believe she didn't ask more questions. Her natural fascination for people's stories meant that she was curious about Lily. That, and the fact that she was a gorgeous woman Parker was incredibly attracted to.

She needed a distraction, so she made a pact to herself. She would talk to the first woman to catch her eye that evening. Scanning the room, she hoped someone would appeal so she could at least give it a go. She was willing to try anything. The song that was playing ended, and Kelly and Nathan came over to Parker.

"I'm pooped," Kelly said, then added, "We should go to the Palace soon. A group of school mums just walked in." She pointed her head towards the left to indicate where the women were.

"Oh, seriously, not grade three mums I hope?" Nathan whined. Parker wasn't too concerned because she was so new to the school anyway, but she figured they'd move on to the Palace where school mums were unlikely to be.

"Actually, they are grade three mums," Kelly said, groaning. "Bianca, Amber." She squinted through the crowd. "Lily and Caroline. Bloody hell."

At Lily's name, Parker and Nathan both turned and peered through the crowd. Parker caught sight of Lily, who was standing in a fitted, purple dress, with a light, black cardigan over the top. Her long, dark hair was tied back in a tight ponytail, a look Parker hadn't seen on her before. She looked amazing. Realising she was the first woman to catch her eye, Parker wondered if she had to stick to her pact to talk to her. *Why not?* "Maybe I'll go say hello."

Kelly shook her head and stage whispered to Nathan. "I don't think Parker understands the efforts we go to to avoid school mums in the real world."

Nathan stage whispered back. "True. Maybe Parker is trying to make the 'old' teachers look bad as they hide from the school parents. Maybe it's a gleaming 'new' teacher thing to do."

Parker chuckled. "I'm just trying to get to know them all. Their kids are all in my class, aren't they?" She actually had no idea, but she had to justify why she wanted to say hello. And Nathan knew the real reason, anyway, so it was all for Kelly's benefit.

"You don't have Amber's kid in your class. He's in my class," Kelly said, "but the others are all yours. Amber's son, Christopher, we're trialling separating from his friends. I get the joy of him! And I'd prefer to avoid

Amber as much as I can." Kelly smiled good-naturedly. "But you go say hi. You'll earn some brownie points."

"Actually, we can escape, meet you at the Palace?" Nathan fixed his eyes on Parker.

"Great idea," Kelly enthused. She was definitely keen not to ruin her night off with school business. Parker agreed it made sense and then made a beeline for the group.

"Oh, Parker!" Bianca said as she noticed her. "Everyone, this is Parker, the grade three teacher." Bianca was clearly the parent ringleader. She was the president of the P&C Committee and seemed to know everything that was going on in the school. She'd spent quite a lot of time talking to Parker already.

"Hey, I just wanted to come and say hello. I saw you all from over there."

"Are you here with friends?"

"I was, but they've gone. I'll meet up with them later," she said. "They've just gone somewhere else." She didn't want to tell them she'd been out with other teachers who'd rushed off to a gay bar when they saw school mums. She was concerned that might give Bianca a heart attack, judging by how uptight she appeared. Lily smiled at her, and Parker was unsettled once again. How was it that one smile from that woman was enough to throw her off course? Parker couldn't look away from her, although she had every warning bell whirring in her head to back away, head to the Palace, and forget about Mrs Lily Delaney-Jones.

"Big night?" Lily focused her question on Parker.

Parker shook her head. "I really hope not. Grade three has worn me out this week, but it will entirely depend on my friends. Anyway, I hope you have a lovely night. I better be off."

The group of mothers nodded, and Lily turned to the group. "I might just head to the loo, maybe get some fresh air too." Everyone carried on chatting like it was no big deal, but Parker wondered what she was playing at. Surely she wasn't using a trip to the bathroom as an excuse to talk to her. Parker didn't dare hope. So far Lily hadn't even acknowledged she remembered Parker, though she clearly did. Sure enough, as Parker walked toward the door of the club, Lily followed.

"Parker," she said, "I just wanted to say hi."

Parker nodded. "Hi." The mood was awkward between them.

"We didn't get a chance to talk the other day with Scott and Bodhi there," Lily started, and Parker frowned. She wondered how Lily was going to tackle this. "I just wanted to say it was a surprise to see you at the school. I didn't expect that."

"I didn't expect it either. I didn't even know you were a mum."

Lily nodded. "Sorry about all of that. I really just wanted to check in and see if we were cool with each other, given you're teaching my son." Lily looked nervous as she spoke, and Parker nodded coolly.

"Of course, we're cool. I'm your son's teacher, and nothing will interfere with my professionalism." She smiled at Lily to reassure her a little.

"Thanks, but you don't need to be just professional. Hopefully, we can be friendly too."

Parker gave Lily a small smile. "Sure." Inside she felt like screaming at Lily, asking her for an explanation, but ultimately Lily didn't owe her that. She returned to the professional teacher talking to school mother role and said, "I hope Bodhi is enjoying grade three so far."

"Oh, he's loving it. He thinks you're awesome." Lily's eyes twinkled.

"I had really wanted Mr Stenlake for Bodhi this year." She looked a bit bashful as she spoke. "Nathan. But I think Bodhi couldn't be any more thrilled with the teacher he got. Nathan—he's your friend, isn't he?" The penny had just dropped for Lily. "The one you were out with that night we met?"

Parker smiled. "The one and only. Actually, I'm out with him now, but please don't tell the other school mothers. Nathan and Kelly made a quick exit and I'd like to too!"

Lily made a gesture of zipping her lips. "Kelly Williams?"

"Yeah, I've only just met her, but I've known Nathan for years."

"Is Nathan the reason you moved schools?"

"Nathan, the commute, needing a fresh start. It was just time for me. Of all the schools in Canberra…" She shrugged and laughed and Lily shared an amused smile with her.

"I better get back to my friends. You have a good night, hey?"

Parker smiled. No matter how frustrated and confused she was about the situation, there was something that still warmed her to Lily. She was nice to be around, and Parker felt drawn to her. She decided her mantra around Lily needed to be "professionalism". Plus, she had no idea what her status was—traditional marriage, open marriage, or what? Either way, she wasn't going to get involved. She was going to steer clear of Lily. That was all she could control.

"Yeah, you too" was all Parker said. Then she left and walked toward the Palace, reeling from their exchange. Lily had admitted she remembered their evening together, so that was a bonus, but she still had a husband, didn't she?

The rest of the evening was a blur. Kelly was fun to be around, and she was easy to get along with, but Parker secretly hoped that now they were working as a trio wouldn't stop their 'bestie' evenings out. The conversation flowed differently with Kelly around. Still fun, but different. A little more reserved, a little more polite. Parker would absolutely do it again, though—that wasn't in question. She was having fun.

Every time the conversation lulled, or Nathan and Kelly got engrossed in something, Parker's mind would wander. *What was Lily thinking after their exchange? Would she end up back at the Palace that evening?* Parker had deliberately not told her they were going to the Palace—not because she didn't want to see her again, but because Nathan and Kelly had made it very clear they were in hiding from the school mums. She hadn't wanted Lily to return to her friends and they make a beeline toward the very place the teachers were using as their hideout.

Besides, a gay bar is a kind of sacred space, and although straight people—women in particular—go there all the time for the good music, atmosphere, and the lack of sleezy men hitting on straight women, it wasn't Parker's place to out Nathan. Nathan wasn't really closeted at work, but he wasn't out either. Parker was sure that if he was asked directly, he'd answer, but otherwise he'd likely avoid any questions. "Do you have a wife?" or "Are you married?" would probably be answered with "No" rather than "No, I'm gay." Parker assumed everyone could read that she was gay just by looking at her, so never felt closeted in any way. It was always more surprising to her when someone—usually a little old lady—asked her about her husband or anything else to imply she'd been read in any way other than gay. Hell, some women even looked twice at her in a women's bathroom!

As the evening wrapped up, the trio made plans to do it again some time. "Soon," Kelly had insisted, and Parker could tell she'd be the type of person who would hold her to it. "See you Monday," they all said, as they farewelled one another.

Chapter Nine

LILY

Seeing Parker had really thrown Lily—she had expected to go out with the school mums, have a quiet evening talking about their children's milestones, compare notes on the new school year and the routine, and maybe exchange some recommendations for books, movies, and recipes. That was generally the way these evenings went. Lily had become friends with the school mums back when Bodhi was in kindy, and they were all very supportive, but underlying that was the competition that mothers often shared. Lily didn't buy into any of it so usually just listened. If she did find herself in a competition with another mother trying to prove she'd done better, Lily wouldn't let it affect her at all. None of her life had turned out how she'd planned it, so she no longer benchmarked her success or lack of success as a mother against other mothers. She supposed she never really had.

Ever since Bodhi was born, Lily had known her path to motherhood was not going to be what she had planned. She had realised there was no point in planning at all—you know what they say about making plans. Megan, the love of her life, was not going to be by her side parenting with her. Nothing had gone to plan.

By now, Lily had imagined she'd have two or three children. She and Megan might have taken turns carrying the kids, or maybe Megan would have carried them all. Lily hadn't known how she'd feel. Her plan, before Megan's diagnosis, was to wait and see how Megan felt after the pregnancy and birth. If Megan wanted to carry them all, Lily wanted to give her that. But, at seven months pregnant, during a routine ultrasound, they were shocked to learn that Megan had ovarian cancer. It was very rare to be picked up during pregnancy apparently. They delivered Bodhi a month early—by C-section at thirty-six weeks—and got Megan straight into treatment.

It was clearly too late, although they did have two wonderful years together after Megan's diagnosis. Well, at least that was the line Lily used when she didn't want to upset the person she was talking to. The truth was, they were the hardest two years of Lily's life. Welcoming a newborn and all that came with the start of a new life, while fighting with everything you had for life, was the hardest contradiction one could imagine. Lily tried to protect Megan as much as she could from the sleepless nights, but Megan wanted to participate in it all. "I don't want to miss a minute," Megan would often say, smiling sadly. Lily wanted her to conserve her energy in some hope that a full night's sleep would somehow fight the cancer the team of specialists were unable to fight.

Despite how ill and exhausted she was, Megan was a hands-on

mother. She built a beautiful relationship with Bodhi. He was talking well by his second birthday—better than most other two-year-olds—and would point things out to Megan all the time. Lily loved watching them together, and Megan said she loved watching Bodhi and Lily together too. But, to Lily, it was more important to give Megan and Bodhi special moments together, knowing they would never be forever. She sat back as much as she could for the beautiful moments, while doing as much of the physical work of parenting—changing sheets, preparing food, dressing the active toddler, and getting up during the night.

Megan kept trying to raise the future with Lily, but Lily couldn't bear it, for so many reasons. Not only was she losing the love of her life, she was losing the person she had planned a future with. The person she had planned to co-parent with. Bodhi was losing his other parent. One evening, Megan turned to Lily in bed, and suggested the donor take more of an active role. Lily was confused. When they'd discussed the donor arrangement, they'd always agreed Scott was to play an 'uncle' type of role in the children's lives.

"What if he becomes 'Dad'?" Megan had suggested. Lily had been absolutely opposed to the idea. She was worried that if she agreed to it, Megan might relax, let go, and lose her fight to survive. "Think about it, please" Megan pleaded.

"I can do it on my own," Lily had protested. "I don't want to," she had said, tears streaming down her face, "but I can."

Megan shook her head. "I have no doubt. But I know you hate asking for help—even getting a babysitter so you could have an evening out will be nearly impossible for you. I want you to enjoy parenting, and I never want you to feel like it's a chore. I want you to have support. The support I would have provided you if I were by your side. Scott would do that. You know he would."

Lily nodded slowly. She had a million questions for her but didn't ask them that night. She waited, and she questioned Megan over the next few months. *What did Megan really want? What would make her feel comfortable?* Megan managed to convince her that Scott loved Bodhi just as much as they did, and having him step into a parental role made a lot of sense. The more love for Bodhi the better, as Lily knew her life ahead was going to become impossibly hard—both emotionally and in the day to day.

When Lily had finally agreed, she'd closed her eyes and said to Megan, "Let's talk to Scott." It was like she couldn't bear to look into Megan's eyes as she admitted she was ready to start making plans for a future without her wife.

From her bed, Megan had summonsed Scott over. Megan and Scott had been inseparable best friends since childhood—their mothers were close friends and they'd met before their second birthdays. Scott was devastated at what he was losing, but when Megan suggested he take a more active role with Bodhi, he was delighted. "What are you thinking?" he asked Megan, but she had gestured toward Lily, indicating that she had to be the one to set the parameters. "It's up to the boss," Megan had laughed, and Lily had joined in, shaking her head. Everyone knew Lily was not the boss, but in Megan's mind, it had to be Lily's decision. Megan was becoming at peace with the fact that they she would no longer have control over the future. Her time was coming.

Lily and Scott chatted, while Megan watched, holding sleeping Bodhi in her arms. Lily noticed the tears trickling down her cheeks as they discussed different possibilities, from 50/50 custody (Lily did not want this), through to him just being on-call, and finally agreeing that eventually he would move in with Lily and Bodhi.

"I love that idea," Megan had said, and Lily was relieved. She had been a little worried Megan would think it was too much. "Don't wait though. Move in now."

"No," Scott protested. "I don't want to intrude on your time together." He had gestured between the three of them.

"Move in now, and I can take my wife on a date," Megan had said, grinning at Lily, "or lots of dates." And he did, and they did. The beauty of him moving in meant Megan got to take some control of the process, directing where he placed particular items from her armchair. "Stop calling him Scott," Megan said to Lily one evening at the dinner table. "Call him Dad so Bodhi gets used to it."

"Oh my God," Lily had said in disgust. "Pass the salt, Daddy!" she had said in a silly voice. They erupted in giggles at how crazy it sounded.

Lily and Megan had a gourmet meal at one of the fanciest restaurants in town. They lingered for hours, reminiscing about all of their favourite memories of their fifteen-year relationship. It had been just in time before Megan's health went downhill. She declined quickly, and within months, Lily, Scott, Bodhi, and Megan's parents and siblings were by her side having last moments with her.

Lily couldn't believe she had to farewell Megan. In farewelling Megan, she also farewelled all of her hopes and dreams for the future. Megan had told her she and Scott should think about having another baby, but Lily couldn't imagine doing it all again without Megan. She couldn't imagine planning and dreaming of a future without her, even with Scott playing an active role. Lily never regretted not having another baby. It was too hard.

Life was no longer what she'd planned.

Through their grief, Lily and Scott worked very hard to become a family, to give Bodhi the most normal upbringing possible. He had three loving parents, although only two present, and he never missed out on anything he needed. He had love, affection, and support. For Lily though, it gave her a perspective that was different from the other mothers, and that was why she didn't buy into the 'who is better than who' parenting battles that some other mothers seemed to partake in. She just enjoyed their company and support and didn't worry too much about whose kid was doing better, or whose relationship was stronger. None of that mattered to her. None of it should matter to anyone because what really mattered was love and life. Living. Health. None of that was guaranteed.

That didn't mean she hadn't established some lovely friendships with some women from mothers' group and school over the years. She had connected with a number of the mums, and some connections were superficial, like making small talk at the school gate, while others were a lot closer. This particular evening had been heart-warming. She was enjoying the company of the women around her. But then she'd seen Parker. Parker had walked over to the group of mums, and Lily wondered if she was making a point to her that she was there. Or could it just be Parker's way of connecting with the mothers, given she was at a new school? She wasn't sure. She couldn't even begin to imagine what Parker thought of her, or whether Parker just thought it was a one-night fling that was over and done with now. Maybe she did that type of thing all the time, and a year later, that night would just be a distant memory for her.

As Parker started to leave, Lily decided she had to talk to her—it felt inappropriate to talk at the school in their role as teacher and school mum, so she took the opportunity to talk in a public space. She felt brave and silly all at the same time, but Parker was kind and gentle, and those eyes took her back to her moment in time with her a year ago. It was a moment she had replayed over and over in her mind ever since. She couldn't keep her eyes off Parker's lips as she spoke, remembering how remarkable that kiss had been.

Kissing another woman, after Megan, was something she'd both anticipated and feared for such a long time. Meeting Parker was a completely unexpected moment.

Parker couldn't have been any more different to Megan if she had tried. While Megan was petite, feminine, with curves in all the right places, big brown eyes, and long rusty brown curls, Parker was tall, slim, and muscular, masculine, with piercing light-blue eyes, a distinct contrast against her olive skin and short crop of dark hair. Lily had been incredibly attracted to Megan and would have said that a woman like Parker was not her type until she met her. All the women she'd tried to date before Parker had been feminine women. They'd all been more like Megan, and yet, she was not at all attracted to them. Was her attraction to Parker because she was so different, and Megan was not on her mind when she was with her? Or was her attraction to Parker just something that couldn't be explained?

Parker oozed sex appeal. She was a real stud, and ever since she had first met Parker, Lily had noticed more butch women out and about. They intrigued her; they turned her head like they never had before, but no one had attracted her the way Parker had. Her attraction to Parker had been instant—like some kind of uncontrollable force pushing them together. It was so out of character for her to go home with someone, particularly after losing Megan, and yet it had felt so right. So perfect. Afterwards, she'd thought of Parker constantly. Sometimes she felt incredibly guilty, and other times she felt incredibly stupid for not seeing whether there was really something there. Seeing her in her son's classroom had made her numb. She didn't know what to say or do. She couldn't even recall their discussion.

At the Casino, Lily barely registered the women's chatter. She couldn't get Parker out of her mind. She hated that she had that effect on her. She had expected that no one but Megan would ever have that effect on her. Bianca turned toward her, and Lily snapped out of it, realising she was being asked a direct question. "You are coming, aren't you?"

"Coming where?"

A look of disappointment crossed Caroline's face. "The trivia night. Only what we've been talking about for the past thirty minutes."

"Oh, of course." Lily couldn't even remember that there was a trivia night. She assumed it was a school thing, given Bianca's focus on the event, but she didn't recall a note being sent home yet or anything. "When is it, again?"

Bianca frowned. "You are on the Facebook group, aren't you?" She shook her head and sighed. "I asked Katie to put all of the helpers on there. I'm assuming you're helping." Katie was the P&C vice-president, but she had to do much more implementation than leading. Bianca certainly enjoyed doing the leadership. Over the years, Lily and the other mothers had been roped in to do various fundraisers and so on, but Lily did not recall agreeing to a trivia night. In fact, she generally found trivia nights dull, so was fairly certain she would have remembered that. "I'll check when I get home, but when's the trivia night?"

Bianca was speechless, so Caroline piped up. "It's another six weeks away. Bianca was just saying that Katie was meant to send notes out last week, but didn't, and so they were seeking helpers through Facebook." Caroline shrugged. "I didn't know about it either. My newsfeed is so clogged with random stuff."

Lily gave an apologetic look. "Sorry. I don't know how much help I can be, with work. Also, the new school year is always tough on Bodhi, but I'll do my best. Even if you need a helper on the night."

Bianca waved her hand as if she were brushing the idea away. "Sure, talk to Katie about what you can do. She's keeping a list. We'll start selling tickets this week. The objective of the event is to fundraise and give the mums a good night out."

"And dads," Amber added.

"True," Bianca agreed. "But we all know that the mums usually come to these things. It's a fun mum's night out."

Lily rolled her eyes at the gendered assumptions being thrown around, and also the expectation that it would be a fun opportunity for the mums to get some time out. Lily could think of a million things she'd rather do than a trivia night. She wondered if she should ask Scott to do this one. That was one interesting thing Lily had noticed—as part of what appeared to be a nuclear family to the outside world, different expectations were placed on both of them, as mother and father. She often wondered what parenting a school-age child would have been like with Megan by her side, two mums navigating the school expectations together. As a mother and father duo that tried to share the load, she noticed how often Scott got accolades for doing less than she did. "Oh, Scott is always so present at the school," women would say. "You're so lucky." It made Lily sick.

Lily and Scott didn't publicly share their relationship, so many people assumed they were a couple; however a few of their closer friends knew.

Certainly, Caroline and Amber knew, as Lily had confided in them early on. Although she wouldn't say she was particularly close to Bianca, she knew, too, just from their evenings out, but Bianca was so self-absorbed, it hadn't really made any impact on her. Bianca was certainly not Lily's favourite person, but she adored Amber, and she seemed to really like Bianca. Once, Amber had said, "Keep your friends close and your frenemies closer" and then laughed, but she didn't really think Amber felt that way about Bianca.

Of course, Bianca was totally fine—in small doses—she just took the P&C committee a little too seriously. She was the kind of mum that Lily hadn't anticipated having much to do with at the onset of their parenting journey. Lily and Megan hadn't talked much about school days when they were becoming parents—so much of that discussion focused on conception, then pregnancy, birth and then baby milestones, before turning to end-of-life conversations. Because Megan had known the end was coming, she had shared her dreams, but she was very clear her dreams were simply that Bodhi would grow up to be resilient, confident, and follow his passions. She was never prescriptive. She told Lily and Scott that she was confident Bohdi would be okay with them looking out for him. Lily still remembered her sitting on the couch, eyes large. She had calmly said to Lily, "I wouldn't have done this with you if I didn't think you'd be an amazing mother. I have complete faith you can do this without me. Don't ever doubt yourself."

Lily was not so certain. She wouldn't have done it alone, and she wasn't sure she could. But Megan's complete faith in her gave her confidence, and Scott's involvement helped a lot. It made the really hard days possible. In the end, they built some kind of modern family.

Committed, in principle at least, to everyone finding out more about the trivia night and seeing where they could help, Bianca was happy. Her job seemed to be complete. Lily smiled at her friends. It seemed that the night had reached a point of conclusion, at this club at least. Lily wondered if they would move on to somewhere else. "Are you planning a late night, or finishing up earlier?"

Amber shrugged. "We have a big day tomorrow, a birthday party and a christening. I think I should probably call it a night."

The other women nodded. "Yes, me too, I guess," Caroline agreed.

Lily found herself a little disappointed. Although Scott was always happy to look after Bodhi, Lily rarely took him up on it, so an evening out was not a frequent event. She figured an early night wouldn't harm her, but while walking toward her car, she felt a small tug to head toward the Palace—the place she assumed Parker and Nathan would be. She didn't know Kelly's situation, but from what she did know about Kelly, she assumed she'd be up for a good time regardless of where they went.

Lily shook her head—she couldn't believe herself. Analysing the social lives of a group of teachers at her son's school! Of course, if she was completely honest, there was only one teacher she was remotely concerned about, and she knew she had to stop that line of thinking completely. If only the other mothers there that night realised what she'd been thinking about while they'd been debating trivia night questions and other fundraisers. She'd been picturing Parker's muscular torso, her strong shoulders, and her incredible ass. When she was being chastised for not listening, she'd been thinking of Parker kissing her neck in the most passionate way.

It was a heart-warming thought until she remembered she was remembering Bodhi's teacher naked. And it had been a nice thought until she remembered Megan.

*

ONE THING THAT hadn't occurred to Lily, when Bodhi had started school, was the amount of Valentine's Day craft that Bodhi brought home. For the week leading up to Valentine's Day, ever since kindergarten, Bodhi had brought home heart cards, and drawings, and small gifts wrapped in red paper. Valentine's Day wasn't easy for Lily since Megan had passed away. Valentine's Day was the day she and Megan had first started dating. It had seemed remarkably romantic for their whole relationship, but now was an awful reminder of everything she had lost. Usually, Lily wrote off most of February as being a depressing reminder of everything. This year, for the first time, she felt less depressed. This year she wondered if she'd see Parker.

Chapter Ten

PARKER

On Valentine's Day, Parker was packing away the stacks of home reading books when she caught movement out of the corner of her eye. She glanced up and noticed Lily in a black skirt suit and heels bending down at the school bag storage talking to Bodhi. Parker couldn't look away, and thankfully neither Lily nor Bodhi had noticed her. Lily gave Bodhi a kiss goodbye and stood up. At that moment, she caught Parker's eye and smiled, then pivoted and walked away.

It was unusual but not unheard of for grade three parents to bring their child into the classroom each morning, and Parker both enjoyed seeing Lily and felt unsettled by her presence. She would love to take the opportunity to talk to her more, like they had started to do at the Casino on the weekend, but she got the sense that Lily was very much putting a barrier up between them at the classroom. She guessed that was to do with both Lily's husband and Bodhi. Parker needed to listen to Nathan—move on, be professional, and treat her no differently to any other school parent, but it was so hard when her heart raced at the sight of her. This wasn't normal for Parker.

*

THE DAY WAS exhausting, so Parker was thrilled to slump into the chair she'd already identified as 'her' chair in the staff room at lunch time. She was thankful she'd packed a chicken salad and didn't need to queue for one of the two microwaves that always seemed to be in high demand.

"How are you?" Nathan asked as he made his way over with a Tupperware container of stir-fried noodles, vegetables, and some kind of meat. Beef, maybe?

"Exhausted." Parker rolled her eyes. It was unusual for them not to catch up during the day—they often did whole grade activities, which gave them a chance to catch up while the children were otherwise occupied, but they hadn't had a moment to chat that day. "The kids have been so full-on today, and of course it's the day I've started the new maths module."

"Must be something in the air. My class are the same. At least we've finished the Valentine's Day craft! Have you got a lot planned after lunch?"

Parker shook her head. "I did, but I think I'll shelve it. Not sure what to do now."

"Let's let them run on the oval. Let off steam til home time. Some races and obstacle courses. We can see if Kelly wants to join us too."

"Love it! We must do that."

*

PARKER GOT THE children to take their bags to the oval, so when school was over for the day, she walked them up toward the large outdoor area where they waited for their parents to pick them up. Some children made their way to after-school care. Bodhi called out "Hi!" and Parker glanced up, wondering if Lily was picking him up. She noticed Scott, Bodhi's dad.

"Hey, bud," Scott said, giving Bodhi a kiss.

"How was your day, Dad?" Bodhi asked.

Parker pretended to look at something in the distance, but she listened to them chat about their day. She wanted to know what Scott was like. Was he the kind of man who treated Lily horribly, and that's why she cheated on him? Or was he the type of guy that allowed his wife the opportunity to date women, in some kind of open marriage? Or did he, himself, have an open marriage? Did they swing together? Parker shook her head. She guessed she'd never know, although she'd love to know to understand what had happened between them that night and why she was thinking about Lily so long afterwards. Lily had seemed so genuine that night. Parker looked at Bodhi and his dad as they walked happily together, and his dad asked him questions about school. He seemed like a nice guy.

As they started to walk away, Nathan walked over to Parker, clearly having noticed her looking at them. "That's the kid, isn't it? The one whose mother you…err…met?"

"I've met a lot of mothers. It kind of happens in this job," Parker said, grinning, "but, yes, that's the one I…err…met."

Nathan looked far more coy than usual and Parker teased him about it. "C'mon. It's not like you to be so bashful, Nath. What's going on?"

He shrugged and looked around, then stage whispered, "I'm trying to be professional. Which, you'll remember, I told you to be!"

Parker nodded. "And I have been. Uber professional!"

"Great stuff," Nathan responded. "Keep it that way. That's his dad, isn't it? He's the one I've seen before." By now, Bodhi and Scott were nearly at the school gate, walking toward their car.

She nodded. "Mr Delaney-Jones."

"He's a good looking guy," Nathan said, and she rolled her eyes in response. Then he changed the subject, and Parker was grateful. "Did you have a better afternoon? I enjoyed it."

"I did. It was a great idea."

Kelly came over to them then. "Are we setting up a junior school teacher table for the trivia night?"

"A what?" Parker was baffled.

Nathan groaned. "Every year the darn P&C run this trivia night, and teachers are encouraged to support it. Last year I took vodka in a drink bottle and added it to my juice."

"There's no alcohol served?" Parker frowned. "I knew it was coming up, but I admit it hasn't been on my radar. I've been handing out notes about it for weeks."

"They have beer and wine you can buy, but the wine is awful, and I generally need something stronger to get through the night of Bianca and her cronies."

Kelly playfully whacked him. "He's being overly dramatic. Sure, it's not fun to give up your Saturday night, but it ends up being a laugh between the teachers, and it's a great fundraiser for the school. Last year they raised enough to play for a whole cupboard full of play equipment!"

Parker nodded. "It sounds like something we should be at." She poked Nathan for being difficult.

"I'll be there, but I tell you, there isn't enough vodka in the world for it."

"Well, I've never heard you complain about it before, so I'm inclined to think Kelly's right and you're being melodramatic for the sake of it."

Kelly smiled. "Exactly."

"You women ganging up on me. It's not fair, being the minority sex around here," Nathan said, sulking.

The trivia night was only a few weeks away, which explained Kelly's eagerness to finalise their table. "Perfect. I'll just lock a few others in. Is anyone bringing partners?"

Now it was Nathan's turn to laugh. "Nooo."

Parker grinned. "No partner for me." Of course, Kelly would have already known this from their evening out at the Palace. Kelly shrugged. "So just the grade three trio. We really want a table of eight, but ten can help us get the answers right."

"The pressure is on for the teachers to win, or at least not fail in any major way. We don't want to look like losers," Nathan stated as if he were informing Parker of something critical.

Kelly nodded, deadpan. "Absolutely. It was difficult to rebuild our reputations after the trivia night two years ago."

"Which does beg the question," Nathan added, "of why we bother. But we do." He sighed audibly. "Vodka does take the edge off." Parker decided to make certain she'd have enough cash in her wallet for the promised beer on the night.

*

IT HADN'T EVEN occurred to Parker that Lily would be at the trivia night. Stupid, really, because of course she was obviously friendly with Bianca and the other P&C mums, but she just hadn't thought about it. She'd been so busy getting coached about stupid trivia questions—which ended up being useless—by Nathan and Kelly. They were clearly very competitive. The teacher table did not win, but they weren't the major losers, either, so they were relieved.

For Parker, the trivia didn't matter. She walked in and laid eyes on Lily immediately. She looked amazing in black skinny jeans, black singlet, denim jacket, and casual sneakers. She looked more casual than Parker had ever seen her. Every time Parker had seen her, she'd seemed to rush in ready for work—often in a suit or dress and heels. She always looked amazing dressed to the nines, but she looked adorable in her more casual attire. And once the questions started being fired to the crowd, Lily was flustered. She clearly wanted to win, and she was debating with her table.

Parker had to really struggle to take her eyes off her, but she knew she had to before anyone noticed. Every so often she'd glance in the direction of the table and would meet Lily's eye. Parker couldn't believe how attracted to her she was—Parker was hardly short of female attention, so why was Lily the one she wanted? It was way too complicated, for millions of reasons. At least her husband wasn't with her, but it was still far too complicated for Parker's liking.

"Drink up, we're clearly not going to win!" Nathan had said, about three quarters of the way through the night. He sipped his glass of juice that Parker knew had vodka in it.

She raised her beer, downed it, and went to the bar to get another one. And another one. By the end of the night, she was feeling the effects of the alcohol. "It was a great night," she said, grinning. "I'm glad we came."

Kelly shook her head. "Even if we shamed the teachers once again by losing to the parents?"

Parker shrugged. "We didn't come last though."

They made their way down to the car park and kept talking. Kelly offered Nathan and Parker a lift, but Nathan's ride share arrived to take him to the Palace to extend his Saturday evening. Parker said she would prefer to quietly stroll down the road to home, and although Kelly protested, she finally gave in and drove off. Parker started to walk down the driveway. She didn't feel like meeting Nathan at the Palace, but she didn't really feel like going home to an empty house either. She really would have preferred to sit, chatting. She probably should have tried to talk Kelly and Nathan into chatting at the bar.

"Waiting for a cab?" A voice interrupted her thoughts.

Parker was startled, and even more so when she turned and realised it was Lily. She shook her head in response. "I don't live far from here. I was thinking about walking home, but really, I don't feel like going home alone."

"Are you propositioning me?" Lily smiled cheekily.

"What? No!" Parker quickly replied. "Why did you think I was?"

"Oh, I don't know," she said, grinning. "Saying you don't feel like going home alone."

Parker frowned. "I'm sorry if I gave you the wrong idea." She was really worried, now that they were in the teacher-parent dynamic, that she might have offended Lily.

But Lily didn't look offended. She looked flirtatious. "That's a shame," Lily said, raising an eyebrow, but still grinning ever so slightly.

"Well, it's a very bad idea," Parker said, more so as a reminder to herself if nothing else.

Lily nodded, but she looked disappointed. "What about just some company, then? You don't want to go home alone, and I don't want the evening to end either."

Parker looked at Lily, wondering why she wasn't hanging out with her P&C friends. Finally she spoke up, "Aren't there some school mums keen to continue the evening?"

"Nope," Lily said, shrugging. "They always rush home early. Believe me, I'd be talking their ear off if they were hanging around. I feel like some adult company this evening myself. I don't get a hall pass that often." Parker wondered what her husband was up to for her to be craving the company of another adult so much. "So…what do you think?"

Parker wasn't thinking—that was the problem. Parker was feeling. She was feeling incredibly attracted to Lily. She was feeling happy to be talking to Lily and figured that taking her home and having a chat might help her to get the attraction off her mind and get to know her as a friend. Was it potentially dangerous? Parker didn't know. If she was unmarried then yes, but Lily had made it clear over a year ago she didn't want anything more than just the one night, and Parker now knew why.

Besides, Parker had been cheated on by her partner years ago. She was hardly about to knowingly participate in Lily cheating on Scott. It was the most heartbreaking and deplorable thing that could happen to a person. It had taken her years to recover, and she wasn't going to do that to him. She needed to get Lily out of her head, and perhaps the best way was a chat over coffee, talking about her life as wife and mother.

Parker finally shrugged. "Okay, come over to my place. We can have a drink, a chat…"

Lily grinned. "Great. Lead the way." She gestured in a forward motion, and Parker led them to her house.

*

AS THEY ENTERED the house, Lily glanced around. "I remember this place," she sighed lightly.

Parker cringed. "Want a cup of tea or coffee? I remember you had coffee at the coffee shop, but I didn't make you anything."

Lily blushed a little. "No, we didn't make it that far last time."

Parker was quite certain she was blushing, too, but thankfully the lights were dim enough that Lily wouldn't have noticed. "Coffee, then? Or something alcoholic?"

Lily pondered for a moment, then answered, "Do you have wine?"

Parker busied herself in the fridge, digging for a bottle of white wine. She then went to her wine rack and grabbed a bottle of red. Placing both on the kitchen counter, she presented them to Lily with a silent question. Lily pointed to the red, and Parker filled two large glasses of red wine. They took a seat on the couch.

"Nathan brought vodka to the trivia night," Parker blurted out unnecessarily, and then laughed in a moment of self-consciousness. Thankfully, Lily laughed with her. Parker paused for a moment and added, "You know, any teacher secrets I share, especially under the influence, cannot be shared with the other parents." She was only half joking.

Thankfully, Lily seemed to understand. "Of course! I'll stay silent.

What other secrets do you have?"

"You'd have to give me another glass of wine for that. I've known Nathan for twenty years. There are many stories."

"Must be nice to have a friend like that!"

Already the wine was going to Parker's head, and seeing Lily relaxed was nice. She decided to change the flow of conversation. "What do you do for work, Lily? I don't remember ever discussing it, but I see you rushing off from school in your suits."

Lily nodded. "Yes, I don't think we discussed it. My sister and I run a business, actually."

"Oh, really?" Parker was impressed.

"*Kidzine?* Do you know it?"

Parker shook her head, so Lily explained the magazine.

"So, regular free discount vouchers, advertisers, articles? Gosh, it must be busy!"

"It's busy, but I'm really proud of it. We hear from families all the time that they've had family outings because of us, and the businesses love the clientele. It's a great way for them to promote what they do. I really feel like we're making a difference, and that's so important to me in my job. My sister, Jacqui, is the brains behind it."

"I'm sure she couldn't do it without you."

Lily agreed. "It is a joint effort, that's true. And it's so nice working with her. It's not what I expected doing, but it gives me a chance to spend more time with Bodhi. I have flexibility to work from home, if I need to, without having to justify to a boss. And I have the entire summer off."

"Do you? That's nice. Just like a teacher."

"Yes, without the kids." Lily poured herself another glass of wine and gestured toward Parker's glass. Parker nodded, although she knew she shouldn't. She was enjoying Lily's company, but the beer from earlier, and now the wine, were certainly going to her head.

Lily moved closer to Parker on the couch. "This is a nice red," she said, "and I'm so pleased I could come by. This is all very strange for me—you being Bodhi's teacher, but…" Parker was wondering where Lily was headed with her speech, but then Lily didn't continue.

Finally, after an awkward silence, Parker spoke up, "Yes, it was a little strange, but we can just be professional about it all. I like getting to know the parents of my students."

Lily raised her eyebrows.

Parker blushed again. "You know what I mean," Parker said and couldn't believe the innuendo. "I wasn't meaning…"

"It's okay," Lily said, placing her hand on Parker's leg. "It's fine."

Parker couldn't believe the heat on her leg with Lily's hand on it. There was something about this woman that sent her crazy. Lily must have clearly felt whatever it was, too, because she looked at Parker in such a way that showed her interest. It was interest, wasn't it? It seemed they were both attracted to each other, but both were trying to run from whatever it was that was drawing them toward each other. And yet, here they were having wine in Parker's home. *A stupid move.* Crazy of her to have entertained the idea. She would never do this with any other school parent, and it was especially crazy after their night together last year. *Madness, really.*

Yet, she couldn't tear herself away. Was it the wine? Would she be looking at Lily like she was if she hadn't had a few drinks?

"It's nice though, hanging out," Lily finally spoke up. "I know it's probably different from what you normally do with school parents, but it's still nice. Isn't it?"

Parker remained silent. Of course it was different from other school parents. She'd never had a school parent at her house, for starters, but the heat between them when Lily had reached out to her was something she hadn't felt in a long time.

"Is everything okay?" Lily seemed oblivious to how Parker was feeling.

Parker nodded. "Fine, yes." Her mouth suddenly seemed dry, so she reached for her wine glass, which Lily had filled up again. She took a sip, then looked at Lily, contemplating the mood between them. It had gotten serious, rather than flirty, and Parker was feeling uncomfortable. She shifted away from Lily a little. "Would you like something to eat?" she asked, ready to get busy in the kitchen.

"No, I'm good," Lily said. "I had dinner before the trivia night, and then we had chips and dips and stuff at the event."

Parker smiled. "Nice."

"Bianca's idea." Lily shrugged.

"Of course."

Lily sipped her wine and moved forward to place her glass down, brushing Parker's arm with her own. As if sensing the heat between them, she looked up, and Parker noticed Lily's eyes were focused on her lips. In return, Parker looked at Lily's lips, and then told the voice in her head to not even entertain the idea. *Too late.* It was difficult to say who had started the kiss, but they were drawn to each other, and it was impossible to stop.

Parker's body responded instantly, and finally, when they broke away, she said, "This is a very bad idea."

Lily grinned cheekily—and in a sexy tone said, "Mmm, yes, bad, but so good too." She reached forward, playfully kissing Parker. Parker knew it was a bad idea—for more than one reason!—but the wine, the beer, and her body were all screaming "Yes!" As Lily managed to reduce all of Parker's protests through her kisses, Parker willingly became a total participant in the process, finally leading Lily toward the bedroom.

Remembering their amazing night a year ago, Parker was already turned on at what this night would bring. Lily tugged her jeans down, then threw her top over her head the moment they hit the bed, and Parker's eyebrows raised—both at her enthusiasm and also at her body, in her black lace lingerie. "Wow," she said, tracing her fingers across Lily's shoulders and down into her cleavage nestled tightly in her bra.

Lily grinned. "Want me to unclip it?"

Parker shook her head, unclipping it herself in one swift movement. They were sitting on the bed, and Parker moved her hand over Lily's amazing breasts—the breasts she had remembered for the better part of a year. She licked Lily's curves, outlining one breast with her tongue, without a thought other than being in the moment. Lily was passionately kissing Parker's neck, which was sending her wild. For a moment, there was no one else in Parker's world. They were so in tune with each other, and every touch, every lick, every moan brought them closer and closer, and soon the two became one.

Hands and tongues were everywhere, and they climaxed together the first time, then Parker spent considerable time going down on Lily while Lily responded over and over again.

"You're a master at that," Lily marvelled after she'd finally calmed down. "You're amazing."

Parker grinned cheekily. "Thank you."

Lily hadn't finished with Parker and now used her hands to bring her pleasure. Parker was incredibly wet and responded quickly. Lily raised an eyebrow at Parker's enthusiasm, moaning slightly herself as Parker came.

"Wowwww," Parker said and lay with Lily in her arms. "Shit." She shook her head in relaxed happiness about the moment. Lily lay in silence, tracing her fingers over Parker's shoulders, neck, and torso. Parker shut her eyes, relaxed, happy, and enjoying the sensation of Lily's gentle fingers.

Everything felt perfect, but suddenly, her mood came crashing down as she remembered why this was so wrong—she was Bodhi's teacher, and there was the not so little matter of cheating on Scott, and if all that wasn't enough, there was the fact that Lily hadn't wanted anything more than a one-off. Already they'd broken that rule, and how on earth would she face Lily on Monday morning? And what if Lily gossiped with the other parents? Lily didn't seem the gossipy type, and already Parker had found herself sharing thoughts with her that she wouldn't dare share with any other school parent, but it didn't change the fact that this seemed highly dangerous.

"What's your name?" Lily asked.

"My name?" Parker raised an eyebrow. "I'm sorry?"

"Well, you're Ms Parker. Is Parker your surname? Or are you like Madonna, just a first name?" Lily must have also been thinking about their roles as teacher and parent to be analysing her teaching name of Ms Parker.

Parker sighed but answered her. "Louise."

"Louise?" Lily's eyebrows raised in surprise. "Your name is Louise? Wow. I do not see you as a Louise." She smiled, but clearly tried to bite it down.

"I know, right? Thanks Mum and Dad." She shrugged. "I've been

Parker since I was about ten."

"Oh, wow. Do your parents call you Louise?"

Parker shook her head. "No, not since I was about twenty. It got too confusing for them when all my friends called me Parker, but they didn't. I hated being called Louise at home. *Hated* it. Or Lou, or any other variation. I'd tried them all, but none felt right. My Nan called me Louise til she passed a couple of years ago. Somehow, I tolerated it from her because she never meant it badly. To her, I was always Louise. My parents are lovely too. They took a while to accept my sexuality and also my name. I guess because they have Parker as their surname, they didn't seem to get me using it as my first name."

"Did you ever think about a different name? Because you'd have to go by Louise Parker on forms and stuff, but you could be 'something else' Parker if you changed your first name."

Parker shrugged. "As a ten-year-old, that clearly wasn't on my radar, and Parker is just right for me now. I can't imagine being anything else."

"True." Lily seemed to really understand.

Parker couldn't believe how much she was confiding in this woman, a very dangerous idea indeed. "I think this was a bad idea," she said, finally speaking her thoughts.

Lily looked hurt momentarily and then said, "You're probably right. I hadn't intended this when I wanted to come over. I promise. I honestly just came for a drink."

Parker wasn't sure she believed her, but also felt she had no reason to not be truthful, so she just nodded. "It was amazing, but I think we really can't do it again." Parker couldn't believe Lily hadn't said it already. She didn't know what Lily wanted—a repeat performance?—but she wasn't going to put pressure on Lily if she didn't want anything more. Besides, there was Scott to think about, and Parker was not going to be the one to cause a rift in their marriage. Perhaps Scott and Lily had an arrangement, but that wasn't for Parker to determine. She felt awful enough that she'd now been intimate twice with Lily, once knowingly. She could only put it down to the magnetic attraction between them—and the boozed-up evening—and she had to be certain they were never alone again.

"Oh." Lily looked surprised. "Because you're Bodhi's teacher?"

Parker nodded. "That's just one reason."

Lily pulled her underwear back on and then slid her clothes over the top. She put her shoes back on and looked at Parker while fumbling for her phone. "Okay, I'll be honest. I really like being with you."

Parker laughed wryly. "Oh, Lily, if things were different, you're just my type."

Lily smiled sadly. "I've booked a cab. It will be here soon, so I'll go wait out front."

"Let me come with you." Parker quickly threw pyjama pants and a T-shirt on, some old slip-on shoes, and ran her fingers through her messy, gelled-up hair. The cab pulled up fairly quickly, and Lily gave Parker an awkward hug goodbye. "See you Monday."

Parker smiled. "Have a good Sunday. I hope everything is okay for you at home."

"Thanks," Lily said, her voice flat. The cab drove off into the darkness.

Chapter Eleven

LILY

Lily was baffled. She'd had a fun evening with her friends at trivia, but the night greatly improved once she caught up with Parker in the car park. She wasn't sure if Parker had noticed, but Lily hadn't been able to keep her eyes off her the entire night. It had made concentrating on the trivia hard, though their team had still done very well, coming in at second place. The alcohol had given her confidence, though truthfully, she really hadn't intended for things to progress beyond a chat, perhaps an innocent, flirty kiss at most. She wasn't ready for a relationship and didn't want to send mixed messages to Parker, but once they were at her house, she just couldn't stop looking at her, feeling drawn to her. Megan's passing had taught her so much, and one thing was that life was short. It was too short to sit there and wonder, so against her better judgement, she'd leant forward and kissed her. It was so out of character for Lily, but felt so perfect.

Parker had eventually led them to the bedroom. She guessed neither of them were thinking. Parker obviously had her reasons for thinking it was the wrong thing to do. Was it just her job? She had said that was just one of the reasons, hadn't she? Was she really not interested in Lily in that way? Lily sighed, and the taxi pulled up outside her house. She paid and made her way in, being especially quiet to avoid waking Scott or Bodhi. It was the early hours of the morning, and Scott would have expected her home hours ago. Then again, he'd probably gone to bed around eleven pm and hadn't thought twice about her. If he had, he would have expected her to go out to a bar with the girls, rather than going home with one girl in particular. She made her way to her bedroom, pulled her clothes off, and climbed into bed, naked, falling asleep within minutes but thinking of Parker through all her semi-conscious thoughts all night.

*

"HAVE YOU GOT your bag, Bodhi?" Lily looked in the rear-view mirror.

Bodhi nodded. "Yes, Mum!" She opened her car door, smoothing down her chocolate brown pantsuit as she did. "Today we're going to do science experiments!"

Lily grinned at Bodhi who looked excited—she knew he loved science, and she was thrilled for him. "You take after your mama," she said, referring to Megan. She had been a self-professed 'science nerd'.

Bodhi grinned at her. "I hope we get to do some crazy stuff today!" He laughed, and Lily joined in. She was always happiest when he was laughing.

*

WALKING INTO THE classroom, she noticed Parker in jeans and a jumper that was more fitted than she usually wore. She felt a stirring inside as she looked at her broad shoulders and remembered caressing them on Saturday night. Parker was strong, but such a soft, gentle person. Lily loved the contrast. Parker's naked body was impressive and highlighted the contrast even more, with her gentle caresses and care for Lily's emotions. But this was at odds with her practically kicking Lily out the moment they'd finished. This was the moment Lily had pondered all day on Sunday—over and over, torturing herself, wondering why on earth Parker had shoved her out of the house. She didn't look much better herself—she looked pale and exhausted.

*

FIFTEEN MINUTES LATER, Lily stepped into the office. "Good, you're here on time. I got you a coffee." Jacqui handed her sister a latte, which was still piping hot.

She put it down and sank into her office chair. "Thanks. I need it!"

"Bad morning with Bodhi?"

She shook her head in response, picked up her coffee and upon sipping it, burnt her tongue. She placed it down again and decided to talk to her sister instead of attempting to drink the coffee. "Remember Bodhi's teacher?"

Jacqui grinned instantly at the reminder but tried not to look too excited at what she clearly anticipated was gossip. "I sure do! What's up?" Jacqui would understand Lily's mixed emotions, but she was also clearly excited to see the topic wasn't over yet.

"Well, I saw her on Saturday night. The trivia night." Jacqui simply nodded, indicating she needed more to go on. "And by seeing her, I mean, I went home with her after trivia."

Jacqui choked on her own coffee. "You dark horse," she said in response. "Next time you pick up someone, can you invite me over for brunch and debrief or something the next day? At least phone me. Bloody hell. I mean, none of this waiting to tell me business."

Lily smiled and shook her head. "I don't know what's wrong with me. It's like I can't help myself around her."

"That's great," Jacqui said. "God, I need to live vicariously through you. An ageing husband isn't all it's cracked up to be! So, when you say you went home with her…?"

"It was my idea." Lily looked surprised. "So not like me, I know. But I suggested it, and we did, and it was really just meant to be a coffee or a glass of wine. I opted for the wine, that was my first mistake."

"Or not mistake," Jacqui said, delight in her tone.

"We had a few glasses of wine. I kept filling our glasses." Lily had replayed that moment over and over. She'd probably filled the glasses three or four times. At some point, they'd opened another bottle. "And then I kissed her." Jacqui looked elated, and Lily didn't know whether to blush or laugh with her sister. "I kissed my son's teacher." She cringed. "You're laughing; you should be judging me."

Jacqui shooed her away. "You're not the teacher. You've done nothing wrong."

"I seduced my son's teacher, Jacqui. Like, shit! I like that school. Bodhi loves the school, and now we're going to have to move schools. How do I explain that to Scott?"

Jacqui couldn't hide her laughter now and put on a voice mimicking Lily. "Sorry, Scott. We have to change our son's school because I couldn't stop hitting on his teacher. Oops."

Lily tried not to laugh, but Jacqui always managed to make her laugh. "You're no help. I should catch up with Maree and confide in her instead of my big sister."

"Oh yeah, because Maree is a good example of restraining herself when it comes to women." Jacqui was laughing even harder now.

"True." Lily bit her lip and then picked up the coffee, sipping it slowly.

"So, you just kissed her?"

Lily raised her eyebrows, bit her lip again, and shook her head. "Oh, no. That would have been a good place to stop, hey? But it wasn't where we stopped. Noooo. Not at all."

Jacqui tried to hide it, but she was grinning like she'd won the lottery. At Lily's stern look, she responded, "I'm sorry. I'm just happy to see you living. Having fun. Enjoying yourself. Following your heart. Megan would have wanted it."

"I feel awful for Megan. I also feel awful because it's Bodhi's teacher. And I feel awful because she kicked me out."

"Okay, back up. What? She actually kicked you out?"

"Well, no, but she said it was a bad idea, and we can't do it again."

"She said that? Not you?"

Lily nodded. "Exactly. I said it last year. It was me. And now she's the one practically shoving me out the door."

"How did you get home?" Jacqui was always the concerned older sister.

"I caught a cab. She waited with me, so it wasn't like she'd actually kicked me out, but it sure felt that way." Lily shook her head, feeling a mixture of embarrassment and disappointment. "And then I saw her this morning, and she looked awful. Stressed, exhausted, pale…"

Jacqui raised an eyebrow. "That could be a good sign. She's been thinking about it."

"Thinking about it and feeling ill. Great."

"Thinking about it and torturing herself that she basically kicked you out, maybe? What do you think?"

"I don't dare even hope. But she's right. It's messy. If she hadn't said it probably shouldn't happen again, then I probably would have said it anyway. I'm all sulky because she said it first."

"Did it feel wrong?"

Lily closed her eyes for a second and then looked at her sister. "It didn't feel wrong. It felt perfect."

She shrugged. "I'm sure there's a way around the teacher-parent thing, isn't there? Don't some teachers even teach their own kid?"

Lily stood and took her coffee cup to the kitchen sink to rinse it out. She hoped her movement away from where they were sitting would put an end to the conversation, but Jacqui persisted. "Maybe you should talk to her?"

"I went home with her, thinking we'd chat. I think talking to her is dangerous. I can't stop myself."

"I don't think you take someone home to chat at eleven pm or whenever it was, after you'd both been drinking, then having more to drink. Maybe you hadn't realised it, but deep down you had an ulterior motive."

Lily groaned. Jacqui tapped some papers on her desk. "You know, this could be a good thing, this little fling with the teaching staff at the school."

"Teaching staff! It was one teacher—" Lily grinned. "—not several."

Jacqui nodded. "I've had a new idea. I want to run parenting workshops at schools. We can reach our target market, support parents, sell the magazine. Maybe set a small fee for the workshops. Some guest speakers or a panel. We just need to start with one school and get some testimonials, and then we can start a proper promotional campaign. We'll probably need to hire an event planner if this takes off. What do you think?"

Lily was impressed. Jacqui was very creative. "It's a great idea, except I don't think Bodhi's school is the first school we should try—for obvious reasons. Why don't we try your girls' school?"

"We could. I just thought Ms Parker might be our in."

Lily shook her head. She wasn't even going to ask her.

"For a high school, we'd need to think about what to cover. Cyber bullying, resilience, or something else?"

"Resilience is good—it's a positive start. I like that. Do you have a speaker?"

Jacqui had a psychology professor contact she knew that would be ideal, so they spent the morning planning things out. Never one to waste time, Lily made a few phone calls while Jacqui went into her office to work on the magazine. "Okay, I've organised us a meeting on Friday morning at the school. They seem keen enough. We need to determine our price point though. They asked, and I said we'd have it all sorted by Friday."

"Great. In the meantime, if you happen to know any teachers, you could ask them for advice on how to get the school on board." Jacqui raised her eyebrows as she spoke.

Lily shrugged and smiled. "I don't know any teachers. Not well, anyway."

Jacqui winked at her. "I think you might know one fairly well."

Lily was so relieved that Jacqui had presented a new idea. Sitting working on the magazine all day was not going to take her mind off things, but by late afternoon, she realised she'd been so engrossed in planning out workshops she had barely thought of Parker. Her only wish was that Jacqui's plan hadn't involved schools and teachers—every so often her mind would turn to Parker because of it, but otherwise she was too occupied with the planning.

Jacqui was definitely the ideas woman of the pair, but Lily was the planner. The one who sat down and worked out the details to determine if it was feasible, and she was the one who jumped on things to put them into action. Left to Jacqui, and an idea might have been parked for years before she got around to thinking about it in any practical terms. Because of that, Lily had told Jacqui to tell her all of her ideas—even the dumb ones—and Lily would do a feasibility assessment to determine if it was worth proceeding. Lily was determined that all business initiatives had to align to their mission—to support families or foster fun for families—so it meant some ideas got discarded because, while they could be profitable, they didn't align with their core objective. That was the most important thing for Lily.

By the time Lily walked out of work that afternoon, she was pleased with what she'd achieved that day—unexpectedly at that—and was keen to spend some time relaxing with Bodhi and Scott.

Scott was cooking a barbeque when she arrived home, taking advantage of the last few weeks of the warmer weather, before it turned cold and dark. They ate in the backyard, relaxing and talking about their day.

*

THE NEXT MORNING, Bodhi was hyperactive and annoying Lily as she dressed for work. She put on green capri pants and a green-and-white blouse, brushed her hair, and added some light makeup. She grabbed a pair of black flats and went into the kitchen to make breakfast and Bodhi's lunch, with him trailing behind her.

"I want a hazlenut sandwich today," he said. The nutty chocolate spread was his favourite.

"You can't have nuts at school. You know that. What else would you like?"

"Peanut butter?" Bodhi's cheeky smile showed her that he knew he couldn't have peanut butter either. He was a smart boy, so he was clearly testing the boundaries.

She rolled her eyes. "So you want Vegemite?"

"Yes, please," he said.

Thank goodness he'd finally agreed to something. Sometimes when he got in these moods he could argue back and forth many times. Lily buttered the bread and did a thin spread of Vegemite, then wrapped the sandwich. She grabbed him a homemade muffin, an apple, a packet of crisps, and some cheese and crackers.

"Here's your lunch," she said, even though he hadn't left her side all morning and knew it was ready. She finally sat down with a cup of tea and a slice of toast and avocado, reading emails on her phone while Bodhi somersaulted in the lounge room.

"You better get that out of your system before you go to class! Your teacher won't be happy to see you so crazy," Lily warned him. At the mention of his teacher, though, she felt a flutter inside. Picturing Parker's tight butt and broad shoulders gave her a shiver. That woman turned Lily on like she'd never imagined anyone could.

As soon as that thought crossed her mind, she sent a silent apology to Megan. Megan had turned her on, but in a different way. Lily and Megan made love in a way that expressed their feelings for each other. It was nice, beautiful, and even exciting. It brought them together, and they communicated through touch. But being with Parker was different. Maybe it had been different with Megan in the early days. She couldn't really remember. Or maybe it was always just an expression of their love, rather than raw passion. With Parker, a magnet drew them together. A very scary magnet, given the circumstances.

Parker was the tall, dark, and handsome type: muscular and slender. Megan was more like Lily—curvy, petite, long hair, and ultra-feminine. If someone had asked Lily's type two years ago, she'd have simply said she was into feminine women, but Parker had changed that. Parker oozed sex appeal—she was hot, and Lily appreciated every single inch of her.

Bodhi's annoying behaviour that morning, combined with her thoughts of Parker, reminded her of the contrast between her role as single mother and single woman. Part of the reason she hadn't really dated since Megan had passed was that her focus was on Bodhi. It was hard to switch gears. To feel sexy and attractive when you're kid-wrangling and exhausted, constantly being needed by someone, wasn't the easiest to switch on.

And there was Megan, and somehow Lily felt like she was betraying Megan by wanting to date again. It didn't help that Scott didn't date—he grieved incredibly hard when Megan died and lost part of himself in the process. Scott and Lily had put on a good act for Bodhi, and perhaps for each other, trying to remain positive and upbeat, but the truth was both of them were lost without her. They'd connected through Megan, and though they had a lot of mutual respect and affection for each other, without Megan there to connect them, they lost their connection for a while. They had a polite relationship, rather than a close relationship. It had taken them quite a long time to learn to be friends without Megan, but over the past couple of years they *had* become friends, instead of just co-parents. But he still hadn't started dating, and he hadn't even been in a relationship with Megan. Lily felt guilty for potentially moving on sooner than Scott.

Before she died, Megan had told Lily she should date after she passed. She was too young to stay single forever. She had talked to both Scott and Lily and said they needed to talk openly about new relationships—now, while it was a hypothetical—if they were going to have a good arrangement as co-parents, friends, and housemates.

"Would you want to continue living together if both of you got new partners? Or how would you co-parent if you didn't?" Megan had pressed one evening. Lily and Scott had looked at each other as if they couldn't possibly begin to answer that question. Lily kept telling Megan she couldn't imagine ever living with anyone romantically other than Megan, but Megan told her she had to consider the possibility and talk openly with Scott. "I don't want you to not have a relationship because of us," Megan had said. "Please jump in when you find the woman that lights your fire."

"You light my fire," Lily had said. "I want to be with you."

Megan had nodded sadly and ran her fingers through Lily's hair. "I know, and I'm so grateful we had that together. But, you have time to meet someone else," she had said. "And you need to think about how things will work with Scott now that he's Dad and not just donor." Lily had understood, but the hypothetical had just been that, and it hadn't seemed important to her at all.

*

BODHI JUMPED IN the car and was bouncing around talking the whole way to school. "I pity your poor teacher today," Lily said, laughing. "You've been so hyper this morning."

"I'm excited. Today we're finishing our science experiment and practicing the dance for the assembly."

"Oh, good! You'll have a nice day, then."

When they got to the classroom, Lily noticed Parker talking to Nathan in the corner of the room. They seemed to be talking quietly, but Parker met her eye. Lily waved and smiled, and Parker waved back. Nathan responded by waving as well. She left the classroom and walked toward the car park.

"Lily."

She heard a voice and turned to see Parker. She frowned and Parker glanced around. "I'm going home unwell. I'd love to have a chat if you want to? Maybe a coffee if you have time?"

Lily nodded slowly, wondering what Parker wanted to talk about. Her stomach was doing somersaults.

"It's not contagious," Parker added, and Lily smiled. She wondered whether Jacqui could manage without her and mentally went through her calendar before realising she had nothing critical on.

"The Bean Sprout?" She suggested a coffee shop at the nearby shops.

Parker shook her head. "Can we get away from where the school parents catch up?" She suggested a coffee shop about fifteen minutes away, and they both got into their cars and drove there. She first rang Jacqui and told her she wouldn't be coming in.

"Are you okay?" Jacqui asked.

"Yes," she said, "Parker wants a coffee. To chat…"

"Some coffee to be missing work for. Totally understandable. Have fun!"

There were definitely some benefits to being her own boss. "Wait," Jacqui said. "Is Parker missing school for this coffee?"

"Apparently she's unwell, but it's not contagious."

"I wonder what she needs to talk to you about."

And that's exactly what Lily wondered the whole way to the coffee shop. What was she going to talk about? Why, if she was unwell, did she want to catch up for a coffee? Why did Lily so readily agree and ditch work for this coffee? And perhaps most importantly, why was she so drawn to her? Why did she want to be with her, by her side, regardless of what it was about?

Chapter Twelve

PARKER

"Hey," Parker said, smiling as she saw Lily. She half wondered if she was mad catching up with her, but she'd felt awful ever since Lily had left her house early Sunday morning. She'd spent all of Sunday and Monday analysing things, and finally did a class handover that morning so she could have a day off work to hopefully catch up on some sleep. She hadn't planned for it, and in fact had turned up to work ready for the day, but suddenly realised she wasn't really *there* for her students, and the best thing to do would be to take a day's break.

She certainly hadn't planned on asking Lily for a coffee—that wasn't the goal of the day off—so she didn't really know what she wanted to say. She just knew that the moment she saw her walk into the classroom, they had to talk. It was too awkward to just let the whole thing go, especially when they had to deal with each other for the whole year.

As they grabbed a table in the back corner, Parker mentally rehearsed how to start discussing any of it. She sighed audibly once they sat, and Lily gave her a bemused smile, or perhaps a confused smile. Parker made a big deal out of picking up the menu and going through each item line by line. Lily looked impatient, but she still hadn't worked out what to say. Finally, they ordered their drinks, and Parker sighed again.

"Sorry for the impromptu coffee on a work day. I saw you come in this morning, and I was having the day off, and… I don't know what to say." Parker felt awkward and anxious, which was crazy given they'd been naked together. They weren't teacher and parent; they had been so vulnerable to each other. All she had to do was start talking openly. "Look, I guess I'll just say what's on my mind. I want you to know that I'm Bodhi's teacher before anything else. I'm professional, and I'll strive to do the best for Bodhi that I can this year. Like I would for any kid." Lily frowned but nodded, and Parker continued, "That aside, I'm super attracted to you, and I've never been in this position before. Obviously, I know we can't go anywhere, and we need to be careful not to be alone after today. I feel like an asshole, unless you have an 'arrangement'?"

Lily looked even more confused now, and Parker was wondering if she had to spell it out for her. Surely not. She continued, "Our two nights together were amazing, but I just can't do it."

Lily seemed relieved when the waiter turned up with their drinks. She made a big production out of stirring sugar into her coffee, then looked up at Parker and shook her head again. "I agree. I'm just not in the right place to date anyone."

Parker couldn't believe she was lying to her. Furious, she bit the bullet.

"Do you and your husband have an arrangement? Or is that the reason you're saying you're not in the right place?"

"My husband?" Lily asked. "Husband?" She gave Parker a look of disbelief. "There's no husband. There was a wife, but there's definitely no husband."

What the hell was she talking about? Parker pressed on. "Bodhi's dad?"

"Scott. He was our donor, initially, but now he plays the role of dad."

"Oh. Right." Parker didn't know if she was relieved or more confused than ever. "I'm confused."

"He lives with us." Lily smiled. "He's a big part of our lives."

Hmm. In what way? The normal way, or a co-parenting way?

"You mentioned a wife. Ex-wife? Bodhi doesn't have another mother, does he? I've never met her." Could she have done a runner? Or was Lily cheating on her? This was very confusing.

Lily looked down at the table and then looked Parker in the eye. "He did have another mother, my wife. She died. I'm a widow."

Oh shit. Parker said, "I'm so sorry. I didn't realise. Wow, that's awful. This whole thing is so…unexpected. I actually thought you were cheating on your husband."

Lily shook her head. "No, I'm definitely not cheating on my husband. Cheating on Megan is what it feels like." She smiled sadly.

"Megan is your wife who passed away?" Parker needed to be certain there wasn't someone else in the story.

Lily nodded. "She died when Bodhi was just two."

Parker nodded, but she thought it seemed like a long time to still feel like she was cheating on her wife. "You must have had a great connection."

Lily nodded and smiled. "She was my person. If I believe in soul-mates, she was my soulmate, one hundred per cent."

Parker sat back in her chair and searched Lily's face, looking for answers about her marriage and how things were for her now. "And how's life now…?"

Lily responded, "After Megan got sick, I gave up my job, and I became a stay-at-home mum for Bodhi. I never thought my life would go in that direction." Lily paused. "I enjoyed it, though, but once he started school, I was considering my options, and that's when Jacqui and I started our business—we started from nothing, and now we employ the two of us full time, and it looks like we'll get a third employee. Bodhi's doing well. I'm doing mostly well. Scott is doing well. Life is good."

Parker's heart lurched for Lily. Life might be working for her, but there was something missing. She was missing that connection with someone. She was holding herself back out of loyalty. Nevertheless, she said all the right things to Lily—congratulating her on her business and complimenting what a good boy Bodhi was and how successful she'd been at raising him so far—but then she asked the silly question that was on her mind. "Scott's your donor, but you have the same surname. Is he a relative?" She didn't know why she needed to know, but it felt like the missing piece of the puzzle.

Lily smiled. "No, he's not. He was Megan's best friend. His mum and Megan's mum were best friends—they met in mothers' group when the kids were two or something. They were family friends, and Scott and Megan went to school together and somehow became best friends along the way themselves."

"They never dated?" Parker couldn't help but be curious.

Lily shook her head. "He's gay too. He came out first. I think they were fifteen. Then Megan met some lesbians through him, and that prompted her own realisation and coming out. She saw something in them that she knew was in herself but hadn't had the words for. She was about seventeen when she came out, and I met her at nineteen. We met at university."

Parker smiled. "That's lovely." She couldn't believe Scott was gay, too, after all of this. Lily nodded.

"The surname? You have the same surname as him?" That part made no sense.

"His name was Scott Richards. Bodhi is Bodhi Richard Delaney-Jones. When Megan was dying, we asked Scott to play the role of dad, rather than donor. Scott jumped in, fully, and in fact he suggested he legally change his surname so that we all had the same name. Megan and I had changed our names legally when we'd had our commitment ceremony. I added Delaney to my name, Megan added Jones. We ended up legally marrying later, when that came in, but we already had our names by then. We knew we wanted children from the start, and they'd be Delaney-Jones. Well, we only had Bodhi in the end." Lily swallowed and then continued, "I never expected Scott to take on Delaney-Jones. It was beautiful that he wanted to though. A real signal that he was fully committed to us."

"Wow." Parker was practically speechless. Somehow, even though she wasn't causing Lily to cheat on Scott, she still felt like she'd intruded in on something really special between them.

"What Megan and Scott had…their friendship…" Lily shook her head. "Sometimes I felt like I was their third wheel. When Megan initially suggested he be our donor, I said no way. I didn't know what to do. And over time, I went with it, but there was a small part of me that was worried. Not that they'd run to the hills together or anything like that, but that I was a going to take a backstage role to their leading acts in raising our baby. As the non-bio mum, I think it can be common to worry about that, but then their friendship was so fierce, plus their families were so connected. In some ways, it was a little weird, like did everyone really see me as a valid parent?"

"You're the non-bio mum?" Parker hadn't even thought about that.

Lily nodded in response. "When we realised that Megan's days with Bodhi were numbered, I felt so guilty for all my thoughts. So guilty for ever worrying about my role in all of this, and ever being envious of what I had deemed Megan's 'leading role'. Shit, we were in it together the whole time, and Scott really was respectful. Megan and I were the parents. Even Megan and Scott's families were really great. But Megan got diagnosed during her pregnancy, and Scott stepped up from the start. If at the outset you'd told me I'd be living with Scott and Bodhi would call him Dad, I'd have run a mile. That wasn't what we wanted at all, but it has been perfect. All my fears about our donor selection were totally wrong—he couldn't have been more perfect for us, and he has helped us so much. I can't help but think it was meant to be."

Parker couldn't believe what Lily had been through, and what Bodhi had been through, over the years. The way Lily spoke, talking about Scott helping *us*, it almost sounded like she was including Megan in their present.

"I'm happy. Life is good. It's not what I expected my life to be, but Bodhi and I are good."

Parker nodded. Again, it might be good on the surface, but it still seemed like Lily was missing something in her life. Fun. Was that just parenting, or was she choosing to punish herself because of what happened to Megan?

"Lily, what happened between us…"

Lily smiled. "What happened between us was the first time…"

Parker's eyebrows raised. "The first time since Megan…?"

Lily nodded.

"Wow, I wouldn't have known you were out of practice," Parker said, trying to lighten the mood a little and inject some flirtation.

Lily blushed. "Thanks. You weren't so bad yourself."

"Not *so* bad, huh? Shit, I need to up my game."

Lily grinned, eyebrows raised. The mood had definitely become more flirtatious. "I had actually tried to do some online dating about two years ago. I met two women face to face, a heap online. The first one was desperate to become a co-parent. She wanted to be Bodhi's other mother immediately. *Grr*, it was awful. She was clearly dating me because I had a child. We hadn't even kissed! I ran a mile. When I returned to the site, I removed the fact I had a child from my profile. I met another woman, and it looked promising. Then I told her about Bodhi. This time *she* ran a mile! She had chosen me because she didn't think I had a kid. I couldn't win. If I ever do date someone, I want them to be accepting of Bodhi, but also happy to let their relationship evolve naturally." Lily shrugged. "If I meet someone, I want them to want me, and then accept my package deal. I don't want the package deal to be the lure or the turn-off. Maybe I'm asking for too much. I've decided not to date til Bodhi's much older now. I have too much to lose."

Parker looked at Lily, wondering what the future held for them.

As if reading her mind, Lily spoke up. "I'm not ready to date, and you're Bodhi's teacher. It's wrong for many reasons. I said to you when we first met I wasn't relationship material, and that hasn't changed. In fact, even more so now because you're Bodhi's teacher."

"From where I'm sitting, you do seem like relationship material. You were married."

Lily nodded. "Yes, you're right. You're very perceptive. I am relationship material, but my circumstances have changed. If I had my way, I'd be in a relationship. With Megan." Lily paused to make the point and then continued. "I don't need to bring that baggage into someone's life. Second-guessing where they stand in relation to my dead wife and all of that. Then there's the whole Bodhi thing, and being sure that whomever I date would be good with him, but not dating me because of him." She shook her head. "Plus, in terms of you… You're his teacher. Isn't there some kind of rule against that?"

"I don't actually know, and I don't know how I could find out."

"You don't need to find out." Lily smiled. "I meant what I said."

She nodded, but the disappointment hit her immediately. She felt sick to her stomach. She knew Lily was right—it was far too complicated—but she couldn't help the tugging at her heart and the pull she felt toward her. But Parker had too much pride to push, and she had to think of her job and the fact she was at a new school. She just nodded and grabbed her wallet off the table. "I suppose I should go home. I'm home sick today, after all."

"Sure," Lily agreed. "I'm sorry that…"

"Hey, I'm just pleased I wasn't somehow part of you cheating on your husband, Mr Delaney-Jones! I felt awful after Saturday night. I just hoped you had an open marriage, and it was above board."

Lily laughed in response and then rubbed her hand down Parker's arm. Parker stepped backwards, knowing that if she didn't, she'd melt into Lily's arms. She had too much respect for Lily already to push.

"Thanks, Parker. I don't usually talk about Megan. Everyone who knew me then knew the story, and now Megan's an old memory for them. Apparently, I'm meant to have moved on by now."

Parker couldn't imagine how that would feel. She shook her head. "Any time you want to talk…I'm happy to hear all about her."

"I'd love to take you up on that actually. Dinner out some night?"

Chapter Thirteen

LILY

"No, I need to know more. She thought you and Scott were married?" Jacqui thought it was hilarious, and Lily couldn't blame her.

"She did. She figured, I guess, that was why I couldn't date her."

"I'd like to know why you can't date her. She sounds lovely."

Lily nodded. "Yes, but aside from the fact she's Bodhi's teacher…there's Megan."

Jacqui shook her head. "I'm sorry, but there's not Megan. I love Megan, you know that, and I know you had something special, but she's not here. She wanted you to date someone."

"When I'm ready. She said that."

"Lily, it has been six years already."

Lily was annoyed. Jacqui couldn't possibly understand. Lily would have thought that herself if she was giving advice to someone. "Anyway, we're going for dinner Friday night."

"So, there's potential? Like a date?"

Lily shook her head. "There's no potential." She didn't tell Jacqui she couldn't get Parker out of her head, and that being with her made her happier than she'd felt in a long time. She certainly didn't tell Jacqui she was looking forward to their dinner on Friday night more than she'd looked forward to a dinner in over a decade. Jacqui was sulking and protesting, but Lily didn't need the pressure. She certainly didn't need Jacqui thinking there was a chance, when Lily knew that as attracted to Parker as she was, she wasn't going to replace Megan.

*

PARKER AND LILY read the menu in silence before sharing what they were ordering. "I'm getting fettucine carbonara," Parker said.

"Me too." Lily grinned. "It's my favourite."

They shared stories—small talk at first before discussing bigger topics—Megan, Bodhi's schooling, and then, finally, Lily asked Parker for her dating history.

"I had a wife too. Well, it was before it was legal, but we called each other wives after our commitment ceremony. Ebony. She ended up cheating on me—with a guy! I never saw that coming. I think that's why I felt so awful for your 'husband'." She smiled as she used air quotes around the word husband.

"How long were you together?" Parker's story made her hesitation around Scott much more understandable.

"Six years. Nothing compared to you and Megan, I suppose, but I still gave it my all."

"Of course," Lily said. Everything she knew of Parker showed she would be all in. She seemed loyal and considerate.

"I felt so betrayed, humiliated. We tried to make it work, but I could only picture her with him. Our relationship relied on trust—I suppose all relationships do—and she'd completely betrayed my trust. I no longer believed her about anything, from where she was after work, through to what money she was spending on what. It destroyed us. When we broke up, she ended up dating the guy she'd cheated on me with, so it wasn't just a fling. I think they were together a few years but eventually broke up."

"What's she doing now?" Lily wondered although she didn't know why.

"Last I heard she'd had a string of partners, and I think she's settled down with some guy now. I don't know." Parker shrugged, trying to downplay her feelings, but Lily could see the pain cross her face.

Once their food arrived, silence fell over the table as they practically inhaled their carbonara pasta. "Mmm," Lily expressed her appreciation for the warm bowl.

"It's great, hey." Parker took a momentary break from her food, dabbing at the sides of her mouth with a napkin. Lily nodded in response and returned to her bowl. Parker finished her food first, so started to talk. "I'm pleased I'm getting to know you. Meeting you last year was very unexpected. I knew I liked you, and not just like that. I know we had a fling, but I thought you were really cool even before that."

Lily smiled. "Me too. I think that's what made it so easy for me. We had talked at the Palace and then we went for coffee. You were easy to talk to. But I'm pleased to hear your story about your wife. It would have been really hard for you."

Parker nodded. "It was. I've moved on, I think. I've dated here and there. I'm not angry, or sad, so I've moved on from Ebony. There's a part of me that finds it hard to trust now, so I haven't really dated seriously since."

Lily nodded. "I am sure it would be hard to trust. But remember, she's only one person."

She pondered for a moment before responding, "She's one person, but she's someone I lived with. If she could pull the wool over my eyes, how do I ever trust my judgement again?"

"That definitely makes sense. So, will you date? Have you gone online or anything?" Lily didn't know why the answer to this question was so important to her, but it was. She hated that she cared, when she was the one telling Parker that they couldn't have a relationship.

"Like I said, I've dated here and there. Some of that was online. Mostly Nathan telling me to get back out there. He always says I need to find someone. I've dated online, which meets his approval, but I'm always second-guessing everything. I don't just allow myself to *feel* anymore. I'm constantly analysing."

Lily felt sad for Parker, but she understood why she'd feel that way. Part of her was relieved that it didn't sound like Parker was planning to rush out to meet someone any time soon.

"I might go back online soon though," Parker added, ruining Lily's moment of peace about it all.

They paid the bill and walked towards an ice cream shop that Parker recommended. Ordering large serves of ice cream, then sitting outside in the chilly air, they shared more stories—now, stories about Parker's work.

As they got up to walk toward the car park, Parker's hand grazed Lily's accidentally, and Lily instantly felt her whole body respond to the touch. She hated that her body betrayed her mind. She had hoped that getting to know Parker as a person would reduce some of the chemistry between them as their attraction morphed more into a friendship, but the opposite seemed to be happening—Lily was incredibly drawn to Parker. Parker's respect for her decision only drew her to her more.

At the car park, Parker stood by Lily's car and thanked her for dinner. "I'll see you Monday," she said and stood waiting for Lily to get into her car. It seemed like the weekend that stretched before them felt too long—she wanted to spend more time with Parker.

Lily got into her car but looked at Parker, standing waiting for her to start her car, and felt an overwhelming attraction for her. She got back out of the car, and Parker looked her in the eye.

"Everything okay? Is something wrong?" Parker asked.

Lily strode towards Parker, filled with confidence, nodding as she walked. "I missed my goodnight kiss." She reached up to Parker and kissed her.

Parker responded immediately. "Are you sure?"

Lily nodded. "I'm sure. I don't know what it means, but I'm sure." They kissed for what felt like both seconds and hours. It felt like a life changing kiss to Lily, and she hated that.

"Shit. Your kiss sends me wild," Parker said, clearly feeling the same. She glanced around the car park. "I don't usually kiss in public, being a teacher, but I can't help myself with you."

Lily smiled. "Let's go somewhere private, then. Can we go to your house?" She couldn't believe how brazen she was being. Parker nodded, groaning in anticipation a little. That little groan instantly turned Lily on, as she felt a tingle between her legs. She had to have Parker—now.

Having travelled in two cars, they drove separately, and then arrived one after the other at Parker's front door.

"Are you sure?" Parker asked her again.

Lily nodded. "Like I said, I don't know what it means, but I'm sure about tonight. I need you. Tonight."

Banishing all thoughts of Megan and Scott, and the fact that Parker was her son's teacher, Parker and Lily reunited and had one more incredible evening.

Afterwards, she lay in Parker's arms, tracing the muscles that turned her on so much.

"I wish I got a goodnight kiss every night," Parker said.

Lily was pleased to hear it and hated that she felt that way too. She was absolutely not ready for anything like that, and besides, Bodhi was in Parker's class. But Lily was incredibly turned on by Parker, and they connected in a way she hadn't felt in such a long time. She craved Parker. And, perhaps more dangerously, she loved her company.

"I want you to be honest," Lily said. "Please feel free to say no, if it's not your thing. Have you ever had an FWB?"

"FWB?" Parker frowned.

"Friend with benefits." Lily couldn't look Parker in the eyes as she proposed her idea. Instead she continued tracing Parker's body with her fingertips.

"I know the acronym. I'm just surprised to hear it from you, Mrs Delaney-Jones."

Lily laughed at the posh accent Parker put on whenever she said her name. "Well, I think we have something. But I'm not ready to have a relationship, and you don't trust women. Bodhi's your student, and Scott hasn't dated, and I'd hate to be the first. Those are just a few reasons why we can't be. But I love when we do…that." She blushed. "But if you're keen to do it, I don't want to stop you from meeting your Ms Right if she comes along. We need an agreement."

"What if I've already met her?" Parker looked intently at Lily.

"See, that's also what I'm afraid of. This is not to be misconstrued as meaning anything. This is not going to be a love story for us. We would be friends. With benefits." Lily shrugged. "You're free to keep dating, and the moment you meet someone, you tell me." Lily hated that deep down she didn't believe what she was saying to Parker, but she also knew she wasn't ready for a relationship, replacing Megan.

Parker considered for a moment, then finally spoke up, "Okay. Let's be completely honest. We're both free to date, but we catch up for fun times—benefits—and also catch up to be friends if you want."

"Dinner dates." Lily shrugged. "Movies?"

Parker nodded. "How often do we meet?"

"I don't know if we need to be prescriptive, but it would help with planning with Scott. Once a week?"

"Twice, and you have a deal." Parker raised an eyebrow.

The idea of twice a week really appealed to Lily, but she didn't know if she could arrange it with Scott without raising suspicion. She could finish work early once a week though. "What about one weekend night a week, and an afternoon after school? Scott picks Bodhi up, so I could get away with it. Be at your house by four?"

"Okay. It can't be Thursdays because I have duty roster. And we'll possibly have dinner dates Friday or Saturday nights. Wednesday? Or Tuesday?"

"Tuesday," Lily said excitedly. "That should space out nicely and give me my fix before the weekend." Lily raised her eyebrows and gave a cheeky look.

Parker grinned. "You're a little minx, aren't you?" She kissed Lily on the forehead and then on the lips, and suddenly, she trailed kisses all the way down her body, til they were moaning together again.

Chapter Fourteen

PARKER

The doorbell rang on a Tuesday afternoon a couple of weeks after their arrangement had commenced. Parker grinned. Quickly straightening her collar, she opened the door. Lily stood there in a wrap dress, which showed her curves off to perfection. Parker felt a stirring inside her and grabbed Lily by the hips. They started kissing before she'd even entered Parker's house. Finally, they broke apart.

"Hey," Lily said shyly, greeting Parker.

"Hi." Parker grinned at her.

They wasted no time talking, keeping their hands on each other and barely breaking their kisses. Lily took control, leading Parker to the bedroom herself this time. Continuing to kiss and break away, then return to each other, Parker sat back, taking the image in front of her in. She peeled the stretchy wrap dress over Lily's shoulders, and revealed her full breasts nestled in a red bra. She trailed kisses all over Lily's neck and down her chest.

Lily moaned. "Parker?" she asked breathlessly.

"Mmm?" Parker responded without breaking away from what she was doing. She was enjoying herself too much, and from the way Lily's hips were already bucking and her breathlessness, it sounded like Lily was too.

"I have a question for you. I'm a little embarrassed."

Parker frowned, wondering what Lily wanted to ask, and why now. As if reading her mind, she added, "I probably shouldn't be asking a question right at this point, but it does to pertain to all this."

Parker sighed and silently wished Lily would just ask whatever was on her mind before the mood was completely killed. Perhaps she needed some encouragement. "Don't be embarrassed, Lily. You can ask me anything."

"Do you…do you ever use a strap on?"

Parker hadn't expected that question, but she liked that it was. She grinned at Lily, probably blushing a little. "I certainly do. Are you keen to…?"

Lily nodded. "I'm curious. I need you…in me. I want it if you do too."

She certainly did want it. She'd thought about it and wondered if they would introduce toys but felt it was too early to address. She was grateful that Lily was on the same wavelength. She'd clearly never tried it, and Parker was excited to be her first.

She excused herself and got organised, returning with a pair of stretched boxer shorts over the top. It always felt a bit awkward to start, but

Parker knew it would be worthwhile. Lily giggled and blushed, but soon, Parker was kissing her again and was pleased the moment wasn't lost. Kissing her soon had her sighing with soft, gentle moans, and Parker knew Lily was back in the mood. Reaching between her legs confirmed it—Lily was slick with anticipation, and Parker was more turned on than ever.

"We can use lubricant?" she asked, but Lily shook her head.

"I don't think I need it."

Parker agreed and rubbed her with her index finger, enjoying the wetness.

Lily moaned harder, bucking her hips upwards to meet the palm of Parker's hand. "Please. I need you."

"You've got me," Parker said. There was no place she'd rather be.

"I need you inside me. Fuck me. Please. Please fuck me, Parker."

Parker raised her eyebrows in surprise. She'd never heard Lily swear, and her begging to be fucked turned her on so much, she kept rubbing with one hand while struggling to remove her boxer shorts with the other.

"I hope you're ready for me," Parker said gruffly, and Lily nodded, smiling. She spread her legs wider.

"Please," Lily pleaded again. Parker took her time, enjoying that Lily was on the edge. Finally, she inserted the tip of the strap on in her. She was so wet and welcoming. Parker felt arms around her ass, pushing her forwards. She grinned at Lily, surprised by how desperate she seemed to have her push further.

Finally, Parker pushed all the way into her, and for a moment, they melted together, eyes closed, silent and still. Gently, Parker started to buck her hips. Lily kept her arms around her, holding tight. They were one. Over time, she picked up the pace, thrusting into her while Lily's hips bucked back and forth. She moaned into Parker's ear, exploding against her and crying out in pleasure. It was hot, and Parker's newest favourite sound. Picking up the pace, Parker continued, aiming for a second explosion. As she did, the friction caused her to shudder, and soon, the two of them were orgasming together. A third explosion soon followed before they stopped, worn out.

"Oh my God," Lily said as they slowed afterwards, lying still connected, but still.

Parker gave her a lazy, exhausted, but very satisfied grin. "Mmm," she responded.

"Shit, that was amazing," Lily shook her head. "I feel…done."

Parker nodded in full agreement.

"I didn't think you'd come from that. It's not in you, and it's not part of you."

"It turns me on so much." She shrugged. "I can feel you on me. I feel connected, and that…that gets me going!"

Lily nodded. "That makes sense."

"It might not be part of me, but it feels like part of me. You were so hot."

"Thank you." Lily grinned at her. "But I think all credit goes to you."

Parker was delighted and was quietly confident they'd try again some time.

Chapter Fifteen

LILY

Lily wasn't usually one to kiss and tell, but this time she wanted to talk about her catch-up with Parker for no real reason. She just felt compelled to. She arranged to meet Maree for dinner on the Saturday. When Maree breezed in, they ordered their dinner and settled in for an evening catch-up.

"I feel like I haven't seen you for ages. Any news?"

Maree shook her head. "Not really. I'm not dating anyone at the moment. Work's been super busy, but I'm going to try for a holiday once the school holidays are finished. I don't want to travel with all the families." She screwed up her face.

"I'm counting down til the school holidays, although I'll be working some of it anyway."

"Are you doing anything fun?"

Lily shook her head. "Not anything remarkable, I don't think. It'll just be nice to have a change in pace." Lily and Maree's friendship had commenced long before Lily became a mother, but it hadn't been impacted by parenting. They didn't catch up frequently, and rarely included Bodhi and Scott in their catch-ups.

"So neither of us have news. How dull."

Lily knew there was a twinkle in her eye as she grinned. "I didn't say I didn't have news."

Maree raised an eyebrow. "Do tell."

"I'm seeing someone."

This was a turnaround for the books. Maree was always full of dating and fling stories, but Lily never had anything much to share. Sure, she'd tried to date a couple of times after Megan, but it hadn't worked out, and Maree certainly wouldn't have been expecting this news. She looked intrigued, so Lily continued. "We're not a couple. I still don't feel ready for a life partner."

"Who said anything about life partner?" Maree was clearly amused. "Are you shagging her?"

Lily nodded slowly. "That's about it, though. A friends with benefits arrangement."

"Right." Maree's forehead creased in confusion. "How do you know her?"

Lily blushed and bit her lip, buying herself some time. She wondered whether to mention meeting her last year, or the fact that she was Bodhi's teacher, or both. In the end, she told her that she was Bodhi's teacher. This titillated Maree.

"Wow! How does *that* happen?"

Lily blushed. "Let's just say we had some unfinished business." Maree looked baffled and had questions for Lily, so she finally explained that she was the woman she'd 'hooked up' with the year prior.

"Oh, wow. Seriously?"

Lily nodded in response. "And…last night we used a strap on. It was my first time."

Maree grinned. She loved sex talk, but Lily never usually shared anything. "Mmm?"

Lily shrugged. "It was incredible. I felt so close to her. I can't believe I've never done that before. What do you think of it?" Lily was certain Maree had mentioned using one before. Plus, Maree, being Maree, had tried everything.

Maree shook her head. "It isn't for me, actually. Not my idea of a good time. I don't love it. Many other things I'd rather do."

Lily nodded. "Fair enough."

She was a little surprised, and that must have shown to Maree because Maree felt the need to justify herself. "I've tried it a few times, with a few different people, so it's not just a one-off. And you know I'm not a prude."

"I absolutely know you're not a prude!"

"I just prefer fingers and tongues to toys…" Maree justified.

"It's okay. All I'm saying is it was hot. In my case."

"So, is it just physical stuff? You and this woman? Hot physical stuff?" Maree grinned but was clearly curious.

Lily shrugged and the confusion was apparent on her face. "I don't know. In theory, yes. In reality, we seem to have feelings, and I don't want them." Lily was letting down her guard about this in a way she hadn't ever done with anyone. Maree was thoughtful enough to not try to encourage her to just go for it like others might. A look crossed her face, and Lily wondered what it meant. Did Maree think she should go for it? Or was Maree surprised it had even got this far? After all, Maree had known how devastated she had been when Megan died.

"Ugh, you probably think I'm awful."

Maree was surprised by this. "Hey, you know I think pleasure in life is underrated, not overrated. If you're enjoying being with her, I absolutely think you should do it."

"But there's Megan."

Maree nodded. She had spent enough hours supporting Lily during her darkest days. She understood. "I can't say I'm not surprised, but I was just as surprised when you told me last year. It doesn't change your love for, or devotion to, Megan. How you feel about Megan is clear to anyone who knew you, and probably anyone you chat to today."

Lily was grateful, but it didn't change her discomfort at moving on. She still felt guilty. Plus there was Scott… "Please don't tell anyone. I really don't want Scott and Bodhi knowing."

"I won't. I promise. I love a bit of gossip, but not this, and not at your expense." Lily was certain Maree would be true to her word, which was the only reason she'd confided in her in the first place.

Once they'd finished eating, they ordered drinks and soon ended up hugging large, steaming mugs of Italian hot chocolate. Italian hot chocolate is so rich that it would take them plenty more time to get through it, which Lily was grateful for. It meant more talking time. Now, they talked business and family, rather than dating. Once they'd paid the bill, Maree suggested they go dancing. She'd already suggested this when they'd made the plan to catch up, so it wasn't overly surprising. Lily felt torn—she wasn't sure she felt like dancing but was happy to go out with her friend if she really wanted her there. She'd been a little antisocial lately, so maybe it would be wise. Besides, she figured that, ultimately, Maree would catch someone's eye, and Lily would be free to leave early.

Chapter Sixteen

PARKER

"Bowling? I haven't bowled in years, but I'll give it a go," the text message read.

Parker grinned. She was happy Lily was going to give it a go and thought it could be fun to try something other than a dinner date. Now they were catching up once a week on weekends, working around Scott's schedule. Their dates always ended up with them in bed together, and sometimes, when pushed for time, they skipped the date part entirely.

But this particular Sunday afternoon, they intended to spend some time bowling, and Parker couldn't be more excited. She found it particularly interesting that she was so eager to spend time with Lily out of the bedroom. Parker had deliberately picked a bowling alley on the other side of town so they would be less likely to run into families or teachers from the school. In some ways, she felt she was in hiding, always working through their dates in her mind to determine if they were *safe*. Most of the time they avoided touching in public, but sometimes it got the better of them. Parker couldn't help thinking that the fear of getting caught added to the excitement in some ways, but they weren't hiding an illicit affair—just a FWB situation between a commitment-shy widow and a teacher. Parker sighed. It really was complex. And yet, when they were together, it didn't feel difficult. It felt enjoyable, light, fun, and certainly very sexy.

*

ON SUNDAY AFTERNOON, Parker picked Lily up from outside her house.

"Hi." Lily grinned as she jumped in the car.

Parker eyed her appreciatively—she was wearing jeans, and a low-cut, green top showing off her generous cleavage. Parker grinned, knowing that later that afternoon, back at her house, she'd be able to show Lily her appreciation. They gave each other a lingering peck—Lily was always too anxious to properly kiss outside the house—and drove towards the bowling alley. "How has your week been?"

"Great, Bodhi is doing well, work has been busy. Scott's fine." Lily shrugged. "Jacqui has been having some kind of drama with her middle daughter, but everything else is going well. She's been a bit preoccupied at work, but I've been putting the finishing touches on our workshops, so I haven't really needed her to be there. I went out for dinner and drinks with Maree last night. We went dancing."

Parker couldn't help wishing she'd been there with her but was relieved when Lily admitted they'd had an early night. "It was fun, but once Maree got dancing with some woman, I went home. I was tucked up in bed by ten thirty! What about you? How have things been since I saw you on Tuesday?"

"I'm counting down the days til the holidays, to be honest!" Parker shrugged. "I don't usually say that to a school mum! I'm looking forward to a few days of rest, and I will visit my parents in Sydney. My sister is visiting for a weekend too."

"Tired?"

Parker nodded. "A little tired but not too tired for some Sunday afternoon fun!"

Lily gave Parker a cheeky smile, which sent tingles through Parker's body. As they drove, they kept chatting about their week and upcoming plans.

Their arrangement to see each other on Tuesdays and weekends was working beautifully. Tuesdays were simply an opportunity to spend time enjoying the 'benefit' side of the friendship, while weekends were more for the 'friendship' side. Tuesday afternoon catch-ups were fast, sexy, and left little time to talk. Jacqui thought Lily was leaving the office early for something to do with Bodhi's school, and Scott thought Lily was just in the office. "I hope they never talk to each other on a Tuesday," Lily had once said, laughing.

As they got close to the bowling alley, Lily put her hand on Parker's knee. Parker smiled. She felt so relaxed around her. They arrived at the bowling centre, hired shoes, and began their game. About halfway through, Lily came up as Parker went to bowl and held her from behind.

"Err, what are you doing there? Trying to get me off my game?" Parker protested although she was enjoying Lily's touch. "You're just upset that I'm about to beat you."

"Beat me? You're losing, baby. You can't recover now."

"I might just get a strike this very turn. And then I'll be very close to you."

Lily shook her head. "Face facts. Let's just call it a win for Lily, and we can head back to your place immediately."

Parker had to admit, the idea was very tempting indeed, especially now Lily's arms were around her, but she was far too competitive to let it go. While Lily's arms remained around her, she turned her body, so they were now pressed up against each other.

"You can't win me over that way," Parker said. "Not when I still have an opportunity to beat you. But, we will have time to go home and take advantage of this. Thank God, because…" Lily silenced her with a kiss, and Parker's body pressed harder into Lily's. She moaned into her mouth. "Oh my God."

Lily nodded while they were kissing, and Parker sensed a smile. "Fine," she said. "Let me just see if I get a strike in this go, and then let's rush straight home." She bowled the ball down the alley, getting it into the gutter.

"Point proven, baby. It's time to go."

Parker concurred, and they returned their shoes, then walked to the car hand in hand.

"Oh my God, I need you now," Parker said.

"Good things come to those who wait."

Parker waited, and good things definitely did come her way.

*

ON TUESDAY AFTERNOON, Parker lay with Lily in bed after they'd spent the afternoon enjoying each other. "Hey," she said, "I have an idea. But it might be crazy."

Lily smiled indulgently at Parker. "Give it to me."

"Sometimes I feel like I'd like to spend more time with you out of the bedroom. And I want to know you in your normal life. Would you ever want to do something with Bodhi in the holidays? The three of us? Or maybe I come over and hang with you and Scott."

Lily was silent as she considered it, and then she shook her head. "I don't think we should."

"Why?"

"FWB, this is what we do." Lily gestured around the bedroom, and to their naked bodies.

"You're forgetting the F part though."

"We went bowling on the weekend. Next weekend we'll go to dinner or something." Lily shrugged. "That's F."

Parker was disappointed but didn't want to let it show. Lily must have realised. "Besides, you're Bodhi's teacher, and Scott and Megan were so close. It's just harder than a usual friends with benefits situation."

"We don't have to tell them. I won't kiss you in front of them." Parker realised she was protesting too much. This really hadn't gone to plan.

Lily spoke after a pause. "I'm open to considering it, but it would need to be like a barbeque or something. I don't know. Scott and I don't have a lot of friends over. Maree, now and again, but that's usually if I'm going out. My family visit, but I'm more likely to visit them, and Scott usually sees his friends out of the house."

"Is that how you want to live?"

"None of this is how I anticipated living," Lily said sadly. "None of it. I never expected to have a housemate like I do with Scott. It's a little strange. I'll be honest."

Parker nodded. She wanted to understand the dynamic between Lily and Scott, but it seemed that sometimes they were really close and other times they just tolerated each other as housemates.

"Do you like him?"

"Scott's great and I've come to really appreciate him. He's always happy to look after Bodhi so we can both have a life outside of parenting. He's quiet, a bit of an old man sometimes." She paused. "We spent so long grieving Megan that our house was depressing for a while there. I think we reminded each other of her, and it was really hard. At one point, I thought about suggesting he move out, but I knew I couldn't share custody of Bodhi, and I wouldn't want Bodhi to live without him either. Over the past two years, our lives have moved on a little, and we're injecting more fun. Megan wanted us to have another baby, and sometimes I thought that would have been good, for Bodhi at least, but I don't think Scott or I could have done it. It just wasn't what we'd planned at the outset, and it was all too hard. And now Bodhi is eight, so I think that ship's sailed."

Parker felt an emotional tugging inside, imagining how Lily's life had gone off course when her wife had died. It seemed that she really planned things out, and to have life change direction so suddenly would have been really hard for her. She tried to be upbeat for Lily, rather than drag her down. It seemed she had enough of that in her life, so after saying how hard it must have been for her, she finally raised the topic of fun. "Injecting more fun? It's still warm, but it will get cold in a matter of weeks. Why don't we go to the beach one day in the holidays? We could go in a group?" Parker thought it was exactly the sort of thing that Lily needed to do.

Lily pondered and then asked, "Are you thinking of inviting Bodhi and Scott?"

"I'd love to get to know Scott more. Maybe you could invite Jacqui, and the kids. C'mon, school holidays next week, so we need to enjoy them."

"Isn't this verging on relationship stuff?" Lily was worried.

"This is merely the friends part of our FWB arrangement. I promise. I won't do anything to worry you in front of Scott. I understand how important it all is for you."

Lily nodded. "Thank you. Let me talk to Scott and Bodhi and see. Bodhi will think it's so cool to go to the beach with his teacher."

Parker cringed. "Do you think it's okay?"

"Look, I know plenty of school mums who are friends with teachers, usually friendships formed before they were at the school. I just don't know any that are sleeping with their kid's teacher."

Parker gave her a look, and Lily continued.

"There really are so many teachers with kids at the school. I've been to parties of teachers' kids, and teachers have dropped their kid to my house. It's weird to go to the beach together, but it's not crazy. I just wish I'd told Scott I knew you when you first became Bodhi's teacher. That would make things easier to explain."

Parker gave Lily a look of curiosity. "At the time, I wasn't even sure if you remembered me…the way you just pretended like I was just the new teacher."

"How could I forget you?" Lily grinned, raising her eyebrows.

Chapter Seventeen

LILY

"Middle of the week! We've got so much to get done today, Lily."

"Ugh, at least let me get a coffee," Lily said, laughing.

"I already got you one." Jacqui handed her sister a takeaway coffee purchased from the café down on the corner.

"Thank you." Lily grinned in appreciation. "You're a gem."

Jacqui smiled. "Our first interview is ten thirty." They were interviewing for a part-time assistant to really help out with the education program, but they could also assist on the magazine.

"Is that the student? I like the sound of her."

"Erin. And then we've got Barbara, the semi-retiree. And Alex, the token male."

Lily chuckled. "It does feel like that when you advertise for an assistant role, doesn't it?"

"He seemed good though. Setting up his own business on the side."

Lily nodded. "We were just a bit anxious about that—like whether he'd really be devoted to our work."

"We could be mentors to him, in a way," Jacqui pondered out loud. "We could help him with some of his business ideas."

Lily agreed. "Let's just go into it with an open mind. All three have something to offer us."

The interviews themselves were really enjoyable, so even though it was a long day, Lily was very content.

"I can't actually decide. I loved Alex, and I think you'd really enjoy mentoring him." Lily knew Jacqui loved taking younger people under her wing and supporting them. "But Erin seemed like a good fit for us, studying marketing and all of that. You decide."

"What about two days a week for each of them?" It seemed they both agreed not to hire Barbara, which Lily felt a little bad about. She was a lovely lady, but the other two aligned with their objectives more. Lily frowned. "Could we actually do that?"

"Well, like Erin said, one day a week could be her internship for the university this semester. Then after that, hopefully. If not, we'd possibly have to reconsider, but we're working on some big projects, so we should be able to afford it then. But we could definitely make three days' work between them." Jacqui looked upwards, clearly doing calculations in her head, so Lily stayed silent. "Yes, I think it's doable, if you're happy. It'd mean we wouldn't take a pay rise in June, but we just had one in December," Jacqui said.

"To be honest, the help across four days a week would be better for me than a pay rise," Lily stated.

Jacqui nodded in agreement.

"Okay, let's do it."

After Alex and Erin got the good news, Jacqui and Lily sat and chatted for a while. "I should head home soon," Lily said, looking at her watch. "I've barely been home lately." Between dinner out with Maree Saturday night, then bowling with Parker on Sunday, and getting home late on Tuesday night, Scott had been carrying the heavier load.

Jacqui frowned. "You went home early yesterday. After school?"

Lily always forgot the lie she told her sister about Tuesdays.

"Ah, yes, Tuesdays," was all she said in response. Tuesdays were quickly becoming her favourite day of the week. Lily continued, "Speaking of Tuesday…next week want to take a day off and head to the beach." Parker had suggested Tuesday, and Lily was happy with that, too, providing it worked with Scott and Jacqui.

"Take a day off and go to the beach?" Jacqui was surprised, and Lily couldn't blame her—she was rarely one to suggest a fun activity like that. Lily just shrugged in response.

"Why do you want to go to the beach? And with whom? With the kids? I doubt Rebecca would come." Jacqui mentioned her eldest but clearly assumed Penny and Isabelle, the middle and youngest daughters, would come.

"I'll ask Scott, and Bodhi, of course. He'll enjoy some time-off vacation care. Parker is keen."

"Parker, as in Bodhi's teacher, Parker?" Jacqui's mouth twitched upwards, but she tried to hide her budding smile. Lily nodded, and tried to hide her smile too.

Jacqui shook her head. "I'm sorry. I need to know more."

"There's nothing to know. I just caught up with her, and…" Lily looked away, then added, "she suggested some fun at the beach."

"Fun at the beach. Sounds lovely, darling." Jacqui put on a posh accent as she spoke, and then her tone turned serious. "How often do you spend school holidays with your kid's teacher?" The twitching mouth was back.

"Shut up," Lily pouted.

"You have a thing?" Jacqui wasn't getting the details she clearly wanted.

"We don't have a *thing*." Jacqui looked like she didn't believe her. Lily could never hide what was going on from her sister. "Fine, we might have a teeny thing. Like this big." She used her thumb and finger to show a small gap. "It's not even a thing though."

Jacqui nodded. "Where were you when she asked about going to the beach?"

"In bed," Lily muttered and then cursed herself for answering honestly.

"I'm sorry. You mumbled. Where were you? What did you say?"

Lily playfully whacked Jacqui. "I'm not repeating it."

"You really did mumble, but did I hear you say in bed? In bed with Bodhi's teacher? Was that what you said?"

Lily glared at Jacqui but remained silent.

Jacqui grinned. "Oh, Lily, this is great news."

"This is not great news, Jacqui. I feel like the worst woman on earth."

Jacqui shook her head. "Megan wanted you to have fun. Gosh, it has been six years. This is great. Is it good? The…y'know?" She gyrated to indicate what she thought went on in the bedroom. Lily raised her eyebrows in disgust.

"Thank God lesbians don't do anything like what you were just miming. That looked repulsive."

Jacqui roared with laughter. "Who cares what you do? Is it good? Actually, tell me what you do too."

"She's amazing, and I hate that she is. I'm addicted."

"So, it's happened a few times?"

Lily bit down a grin. "Every Tuesday afternoon."

"No way!" Jacqui said, looking both horrified and delighted that her sister hadn't been truthful with her about her Tuesday afternoons. "Here I was thinking you were going to some boring parenting seminar or hanging out with Bodhi or something dull. You were always vague about what you got up to."

"Yeah, well I didn't want questions. I'm trying to hide it from Scott and Bodhi, so we catch up Tuesdays and then on weekends."

Jacqui blew out in surprise. "Wow, so that's why you've barely been home! You dirty little minx!"

"That's what Parker called me." Lily gave a cheeky look, blushing as she said it.

"A dirty minx? Oh my God! It sounds like you're having *fun*!"

"Well she didn't say dirty. That's clearly just how my delightful big sister feels about me."

Jacqui smiled. "I'm really happy for you. I was worried you weren't having enough fun."

"Well, I'm having fun in the bedroom now, but I think Parker's worried I'm not having enough fun *out* of the bedroom, so she has made it her mission to change that. She suggested we have fun at the beach."

"I like her already," Jacqui said. "So, is she your girlfriend?"

"Oh, God, no. She's a friend with benefits. That's it. We aren't telling anyone. Clearly, I failed at that. But I can't tell anyone else—there's too much to lose."

Jacqui nodded again. "I won't say anything. Let me know if the beach is on. Chat to Scott and let me know. I'll go along, make up the numbers. I'm looking forward to meeting her."

"Just remember it's top secret."

Jacqui rolled her eyes. "You do know you're free to date, don't you?"

"Thanks for the constant reminder. As I keep telling you, I'm not quite ready to replace Megan."

"It's not replacing her though." Lily could tell Jacqui was exasperated, but no one who hadn't been through this themselves could understand. "Besides, you've been having your Tuesday catch-ups…"

"Yes, and I felt guilty for that as it was, but I've worked through it. I can't quite stop myself when it comes to that with her. But that doesn't mean I need people to know about it, especially Bodhi and Scott. I feel awful, but there's no way I need anyone thinking she's my girlfriend, and there's no way I want Bodhi wondering anything. You need to be discrete."

Jacqui nodded. "Okay, I get it."

Lily very much hoped she did.

Chapter Eighteen

PARKER

Parker was thrilled when Nathan agreed to come to the beach. She figured part of it was curiosity, but he had been happy to come. She had wondered for a minute about inviting Kelly, too, but then thought that was too risky. Nathan loved her completely and supported her regardless of the situation. Kelly, on the other hand, she was still getting to know. She only knew Kelly in a professional capacity, and so wasn't certain if inviting her to a catch-up with a school mum was appropriate. Would it set tongues wagging? Perhaps.

To say Nathan had been surprised when Parker had asked him would be an understatement at best. "Wait a minute, she's married, isn't she?" was the first thing he'd said.

Parker had filled him in.

"Why do they have the same surname then?" he'd asked suspiciously.

"Oh wow, that's beautiful." He'd been quite moved by the story.

"But, Scott hasn't dated, and somehow Lily has in her head that she won't date til he does. I think she's worried about their living arrangement and doesn't want to change things or show Scott she's not loyal to her wife in any way."

"Wow." Nathan shook his head. "So you and her…?" He wiggled his fingers between her and an open space, as if to indicate there was something going on.

Parker shook her head and then shrugged. "We're friends. With benefits. I'm Bodhi's teacher. It's complicated, but we're definitely not dating."

"Not dating, but you're…you're sleeping together?"

Parker blushed and whacked Nathan. "You know we did." He raised his eyebrows in response and gave her a stern look, but she knew him enough to know he would be okay with the truth.

"I ask in the present tense. Not last year."

She nodded but remained silent in response and then glanced around the empty classroom they were in. She picked up a few items to put away and then looked up at him again. "So, you'll come to the beach?"

"With bells on! I wouldn't miss this."

Parker shook her head again and grabbed a pile of books to put away. "Okay, then. Just please…be discrete. She really doesn't want anyone to know. I don't think she's told anyone. And I have a lot to lose too. Mainly her."

Parker noticed Nathan looked worried during the whole conversation but even more concerned once she had revealed her true feelings.

*

ON THE WEEKEND, Parker and Lily each had dinner at home and then met for dessert at a coffee shop prior to heading back to Parker's place.

"I'm sorry we caught up so late. We took Bodhi to Scott's parents' place for a late lunch, and I didn't want to rush off for dinner the moment we got home. So I made us toasted sandwiches for a light dinner after a big roast lunch."

"Are you close to Scott's family?"

Lily nodded. "They were so close to Megan and her family, of course, so I met them all early on in our relationship. And once she was sick, as I said before, they were really supportive of us as a family. I've become closer to them over the last six years. Often Scott takes Bodhi alone, but sometimes we go together. I enjoy seeing them dote on Bodhi. Occasionally Megan's parents come along too. Bodhi has three sets of grandparents, and sometimes he's lucky enough to see them all together."

Lily smiled wistfully, and for the first time, Parker felt a little jealous about Lily's bond with Megan, and all their connections. She had been determined not to be jealous of Megan. After all, it sounded like if all had gone to plan, Lily and Megan would still be together today, perhaps with another child or two. It wasn't a competition, and yet hearing about the bonds she had with Megan's family and family friends made her feel unsettled. "He's lucky," was all she said.

Lily's eyes sparkled. "We all are. I've been so lucky, other than losing my wife. I won the in-law lottery with both Megan and Scott's families." The fact that Lily saw Scott's family as her 'in-laws' rattled Parker. Scott wasn't her lover, and yet she saw his family as her in-laws. Perhaps Parker would never really understand the bond Megan, and then Lily, had with Scott.

That night, they talked. They didn't make love, and strangely, that alone felt more intimate to Parker than having sex. Holding each other, talking openly, and just being together made her think that Lily was there for more than the sexual encounters. Parker went to sleep that night with a grin on her face, wondering who on earth she'd become. The old Parker would never have such a sexy woman visit and happily not try anything!

*

ON TUESDAY, THEY all left early to arrive at the beach by ten. Parker didn't know what to expect. On the one hand, she was concerned it was a little couply and that everyone there would read it that way. On the other hand, she really wanted Lily to have more fun in her life and to see her in a different environment. She didn't know if she'd made the right move, and as she and Nathan drove together, she couldn't help expressing her anxiety.

"This is a bit stupid to do this, isn't it?"

Nathan shook his head. "Stupid is shagging your student's parent. Going to the beach…meh…" He shrugged. Parker couldn't help wondering if he was right. She could tell that Nathan was teasing her, even if he was being deadpan, but it still concerned her to hear him say it out loud.

"There is no rule against it though. Is there? I mean, if we had a relationship—if I were Bodhi's stepmum—I could still teach him. I'd just have to let the school know. Right?"

Nathan paused for a moment, then spoke. "I believe so. I don't know if there's a rule book, but I'm sure sneaking around having a fling with a parent is possibly a no-go. I am no expert though."

Parker groaned and felt turmoil in the pit of her stomach. Lily wasn't ready for a relationship, and Parker was falling deep for her—admittedly it had been Lily's fear, but she'd promised her she wouldn't. And, yet, here she was.

As if sensing her fear, Nathan spoke up. "Let's just have a good day today, hey? Don't panic about things. Have the fun you're here to have. We can sort feelings out later. Feelings always get in the way." He waved flippantly, and she was surprised at how dismissive he was being. And he was being comical. That was just Nathan's style, pretending he didn't do feelings, when she knew, even if he didn't admit it to himself, he'd love to settle down.

By the time they'd arrived at the beach, Parker had been forced to endure Nathan's awful hip-hop music. She'd kept turning it down to talk, but whenever there was a conversation lull, he'd turn it back up. "Remind me to bring my car next time," she'd joked, and he'd pretended to be really insulted.

*

"OVER THERE. THERE she is," Nathan said, glancing over in the direction of a small group. Parker smiled and tried to stride confidently toward Lily and her gang. It surprised her how nervous she was—she'd been naked with the woman many times! But seeing her with her sister, her co-parent, and her nieces made Parker feel much more vulnerable. Being Bodhi's teacher made it harder.

Lily was right—there were plenty of friendships between teachers and parents, so it wasn't completely out of the ordinary to be *friends*. Just friends that is. Parker had to focus on the friendship part of their FWB relationship because the benefits part was totally irrelevant to their day at the beach.

In theory.

Separating the two wasn't as easy in practice.

She couldn't help but wonder if there was a chance of something—at the end of the school year, and once Lily felt ready… But Lily seemed so adamant that she wasn't ready. Given it had taken her six years to get to this point, it was probably going to take another six years for her to be ready for an actual relationship—in public.

"Hey," Lily said.

The woman that Parker assumed to be Jacqui turned her head instantly, eyeing Parker up and down and then turning to Lily. An intriguing look crossed her face, but Parker couldn't read it.

"Hello, I'm Parker," she said to Jacqui as she reached out to shake Jacqui's hand. "You must be Lily's sister, Jacqui. You look just like her!"

"I am indeed Lily's big sister, Jacqui!" She grinned, and Parker smiled in response. Lily's eyes twinkled as she watched their exchange.

"Hey, Bodhi, how are you, mate?"

"Good, thank you, Ms Parker! I'm excited to go swimming today."

"Well, that depends on whether it warms up a little." Lily pulled her cardigan close as if to indicate the breeze was bothering her—perhaps as a subliminal message to Bodhi. "It's a little cold, isn't it?" She instinctively turned to Scott for input. He nodded at Bodhi.

"Swimming season may be over, Bodhi, but we'll see. As Mum said, it might warm up."

Parker tried to hide an amused smile. Hearing Scott call Lily mum seemed strange. "Well at least it's not too cold for fish and chips on the grass, and maybe some cricket?" She grinned.

Jacqui turned towards her daughters. "Parker, this is Penny, here, and

Isabelle, my daughters."

Parker greeted them and then turned to Nathan. "This is Nathan. He's another teacher at Bodhi's school."

Scott looked quizzically at Nathan, obviously trying to place him. Nathan smiled and said hello. Scott then turned and quietly said something to Lily. "He's the one you wanted for Bodhi?"

Lily nodded in response. "Yes, but I think Parker's perfect." She blushed as she said it, and Parker looked down to the ground, afraid she would show her reaction to what was meant to be a private exchange between Lily and Scott. She was also grinning at Lily's response to Scott—which couldn't have been more perfect —and didn't want to share her smile with the group.

Finally, Parker put her sunglasses on and faced the crowd. "So, are we going to stand here all day, or who wants to hit the beach? Sandcastle competition?" She raised her eyebrows as if to entice them. Penny nodded enthusiastically. "Well, at least I have one taker."

"I'll do it, if Mum and Dad say I really can't swim," Bodhi said, grinning.

"Excellent. Well let's make our way down there. We have a couple of hours before lunch."

"I brought snacks!" Jacqui said. "So anyone not building sandcastle can have chips, dips, and carrot sticks. Anyone touching sand needs to stay away from my snacks, I'm afraid, but we can do you a little plate." She looked apologetically at Parker, who laughed it off.

"I'm not hungry. I'm trying to build up my appetite for greasy fish and chips at twelve!"

Chapter Nineteen

LILY

As Parker and Nathan raced off with the children, Jacqui turned to Lily. "I like her."

Lily shot an anxious look toward Scott, but he was silently staring toward the beach.

"What, I'm not allowed to like someone?" Jacqui gave Lily an annoyed look, and Lily shook her head. She couldn't believe her sister wasn't being as discreet as she'd asked her to be. Actually, scrap that—she could believe it. Jacqui wasn't known for being discreet, but Lily would never learn, and always confided in her. She valued her input, even if her secrecy was not ideal.

Scott turned toward the two sisters. "Are you putting those snacks out any time soon? I want to go join the sandcastle competition, but I'm scared of missing out."

Jacqui grinned and opened up her plastic dip platter, which had sections for carrot sticks, raw broccoli and crackers, with a dip in the middle. She then opened up another container which had two other dips. Scott took some crackers loaded with dip and ate them, returning for a handful of carrot sticks topped with dip. He smiled in appreciation but kept eating and walked toward the sandcastle builders.

"She's different from your usual type, but I can see the appeal," Jacqui said, taking the opportunity of being alone to talk more. "She's a great looking girl."

"Different from my usual type? You mean different from Megan?"

Jacqui looked down at the ground, clearly trying to determine her next move. Lily hated that talk of Megan often resulted in silence, but she also couldn't blame her family and friends when she brought her up at every opportunity. Sometimes it was simply so that Megan continued to be discussed, but other times she worried if she was just being contrary.

"Sorry, I shouldn't have said that," Lily apologised.

"It's okay. Yes, she's different from Megan, but she's different from other women that I've thought you've liked over the years. The few girls before Megan, and any that have turned your head since Megan. Or even while you were with her."

Lily gasped. "No one turned my head when I was with Megan!"

Jacqui rolled her eyes. "Not in the chase them down the street way. But I've seen you look twice at a person. Lil, you're only human. Shit, I adore John, and I look at guys all the time."

"You're a perve."

"I am a proud perve. You don't need to be a nun, just because you're married. Shit, you certainly don't have to be a nun if you're a widow."

"Yeah, I'm hardly being a nun!" Lily glanced toward Parker.

"Well, don't be so sensitive. I like her and she's hot, but she's different from what I thought was your type."

Lily nodded. Jacqui was right, she was being overly sensitive, and she didn't really know why. "You're right, I've never dated a woman like Parker before, but oh my God, she's so hot."

Jacqui looked elated. "You said dated!"

Lily rolled her eyes, playfully punching Jacqui, who had picked up the snacks.

"Watch it," Jacqui said, pointing her forehead toward the dip platter. "You knock these out of my hand and your life won't be worth living." She handed one container to Lily. "Now, come and offer these folks some food."

*

WITH PLATES LOADED with fish, chips, and potato scallops, they all claimed a patch of grass overlooking the water. Lily was seated next to Nathan on one side of her and Scott on the other. Bodhi was sitting with his cousins.

"How's your class going?" Lily asked Nathan. She didn't know him very well at all, so thought it might be a nice opportunity to get to know him. Small talk wasn't her favourite thing, but Parker clearly adored Nathan, so Lily figured that after some small talk, they could become friends themselves.

Nathan finished chewing his mouthful of food, then spoke up, "Really good, but I was so pleased to have these holidays. I think everyone seemed a little exhausted by the last week of school."

"Bodhi was," Scott chimed in. "He started having a few meltdowns, unexpectedly."

Nathan smiled in understanding. "Yes, it's typical of the last couple of weeks of school. I think they're just exhausted, and they know the end is near. He's a good kid though."

Lily nodded. "Most of the time."

"He can push us, but he's a beautiful kid, kind-hearted, and I'm always learning from him." Scott smiled, reflecting on his son.

"I love this age," Nathan said, gesturing toward Bodhi. "They're becoming independent thinkers. They don't need us to remind them to go to the toilet, but they're not as jaded as the older grades. I prefer teaching this grade."

"I take my hat off to you. I find one child hard enough; I don't think I'd survive twenty of them!" Scott said.

"I think your own kid is always going to be harder than a class full of kids."

"True, I certainly couldn't teach Bodhi," Lily responded.

"Have you taught other grades, Nathan?" Scott asked.

"Yes, I started as a grade six teacher, and then they turned me into a grade one teacher. Worst year of my life."

Scott cracked up in response as if it was the funniest thing he'd ever heard. Lily was surprised at how much the two men were carrying the conversation without her. She shot a bemused look toward Parker and Jacqui, but they were engrossed in conversation themselves.

Too full to finish her plate, Lily sighed audibly. "Wow, I'm stuffed."

Scott looked down at his platter. "I better eat up." Lily looked at him in surprise—it wasn't like Scott to talk so much and not eat! She briefly wondered if there was an attraction between the two men, or if that was too cliched. If it were a movie script, the guys would fall in love, and Parker and Lily and Scott and Nathan would all live together, parenting Bodhi as one big happy family…but it wasn't a movie script… Lily shook her head at herself for daydreaming like this! She glanced over in Parker's direction again, and this time caught her eye. They exchanged a quick smile at each other, Parker's eyes glinting as she grinned. That smile. That smile could melt her. It was dazzling. But…she was hardly about to risk everything just because of some minor attraction. Right?

But then there was that look. Parker was so striking.

*

"ISN'T THIS NICE?" Jacqui stretched her legs out in the sun and looked around the group. "I'm never one to take a mid-week day off work, but this is so refreshing." Everyone nodded.

"Gotta love school holidays," Nathan said.

"I wish I had school holidays," Scott agreed. "Lily and I usually divide up being home with Bodhi, except during the summers, which Lil takes off completely."

"Yeah? That sounds great. It must be so hard for parents to juggle it all if they don't have flexibility."

"You don't have kids?" Scott asked Nathan, and he shook his head in response.

"I don't either," Parker chimed in. "Sometimes people are surprised that teachers don't have kids. Sometimes I think it makes it easier to front up and teach each day."

Nathan nodded. "I agree. Sometimes after a really hard day, I don't know how my colleagues with kids juggle it all. It's exhausting."

Lily nodded. "And having kids is exhausting. And we only have one."

"I just let my three run wild together when they were young," Jacqui joked, but Lily shook her head and told them that wasn't really true. Jacqui was always a very organised and in control parent.

"So, what's next?" Jacqui asked. "A couple more hours before we should hit the road home?"

Parker nodded. "Let's go for a long walk along the beach, and then we will end up at the ice cream shop, return back to the cars, and go." Lily loved that she had it all planned out, making it a fun day for everyone.

As they walked, people moved in various combinations for chatting—Bodhi initially talked to Parker and Lily for a while, then walked forward to chat with his dad and eventually his cousins. Lily stayed by Parker's side, chatting, and when Bodhi joined his cousins, Jacqui stepped back to join Lily and Parker.

"This has been a great day, Lily!" Jacqui said, once she caught up with them.

"Thanks, but so much of the planning has been thanks to Parker."

Parker nodded. "I do like to get away now and again. Usually I like to stay a few nights at the coast, but Nathan and I are heading home this afternoon too. I've always liked the beach though."

"Me too," Jacqui sighed wistfully. "Sometimes I wonder why I don't move to a seaside town, but I love having family around me."

"We could run our business anywhere, though, couldn't we?" Lily knew they'd never move away, but Jacqui often dreamed, and Lily usually joined in.

"We could. I suppose you could teach anywhere?"

Parker nodded. "I could. I moved to Canberra to study at uni, and Nathan and I became close friends, and so I stayed for a while. I was going to go back to Sydney, but it grew on me. And now, all these years later, I can't imagine leaving."

"Do you have brothers and sisters?"

"I have a brother and a sister. We're close, but I don't think I'm as close to them as you and Lily seem to be. It's nice."

Jacqui shrugged. "She annoys me, but she's good. We've always been pretty close, but we did become closer when Megan got sick, I think."

Lily nodded. "I guess so. And even more recently, working together." They'd always been close, particularly growing up, but once Jacqui and John married and then started having babies, Lily had felt there was some distance between them. They spent time together—movie nights and family dinners, and Lily often babysat the girls—but their lives felt so different. Then, once Megan was pregnant, Jacqui gave Lily tons of advice. It all felt quite hypothetical.

When Megan had been diagnosed, Jacqui was the first person Lily had told. She'd wanted to hide her own sadness from Megan. She'd wanted to be strong and supportive, but she'd sobbed and sobbed at Jacqui's house. Jacqui would sit there in silence, and just her presence was supportive. Every so often she'd say something—something wise, and sometimes just something like "I wish I knew what to say." And somehow that was comforting to hear. There were no answers.

All through Megan's illness, Jacqui showed up. And Scott showed up. All of their families showed up. They supported them through it—who knows how Lily would have coped without them?—and then when Megan had passed away, everyone still showed up, repeatedly. But over time, people returned to their normal lives, and Scott and Jacqui had remained constantly by her side. They'd held her up when she hadn't been able to. They'd helped her parent Bodhi when she'd not been certain she had the motivation to even get out of bed. Then, Jacqui and Lily had set up their business together and were now practically inseparable.

"It's just up here." Parker gestured forward, toward the ice cream shop. "There are two, but I like the first one better."

"Me too," Jacqui said. "John and I often take the kids if we come on holidays."

"Bodhi loves ice cream, so I know he's excited," Lily said.

The group went inside to the quiet store, where the overwhelmed staff member seemed surprised by the sudden arrival of a group of eight. She quickly got busy giving them taste tests, and then preparing their ice creams. The walk back after the ice cream was cheerful, but it had been a long day, and the group were keen to get on the road to get home. Just before leaving, Lily managed to steal a moment alone with Parker. "Let me know if you get time this week, and we'll catch up," she said.

Parker grinned. "I will. I've found it so hard not to kiss you today; it's sweet torture."

Lily felt herself melt inside a little, and even more so when Parker winked at her.

She blushed and smiled. "Drive safely."

"You too."

Chapter Twenty

PARKER

"Please tell me he's gay."

"You tell me." Parker shrugged. "Don't you have gaydar?"

"I do. I think he's gay. The whole dad thing is throwing me off the scent."

"You know he was the donor, though, right? He didn't do it the traditional way." Parker gave him a look. "Hang on, why are you asking?"

Nathan just shrugged, but Parker knew. "No! No way! You are NOT going to do your thing with my pseudo-girlfriend's housemate and co-parent. The parents of a kid at our school. Back away now."

"I'm an adult; he's an adult. You can't tell me who I can and cannot date."

"No, you're right. I cannot, but I can make a request that you please,

please, please leave him alone." Parker sounded whiny and she knew it. It wasn't her usual style, but she knew Nathan's style, so she had to make an appeal.

"Don't let it stress you out. He might not be interested. But…he's gay?"

Parker shook her head but decided to not to tell him that Scott was gay. She certainly wasn't going to mention that given how much time they'd spent together at the beach, she suspected Scott would be interested. She didn't want to encourage Nathan.

"He's a great guy. I can't believe I've never noticed him at the school. Admittedly, I don't usually check out the school dads. Parents are usually off-limits for me. Not off-limits for everyone, but for me…"

Parker ignored his dig and muttered, "Yeah, well let's just keep it that way."

Thankfully, Nathan kept his eyes on the road as he drove because Parker didn't want him to see how anxious she was about all of this. She knew Nathan's mode of operation, and she didn't want to get between what could be something very promising between her and Lily through his short-term fling. "I mean there are plenty of other guys around."

"Okay," Nathan responded, and Parker could tell he was annoyed at her. "Let's just leave it be. So, did you enjoy today?"

"I did. I enjoyed seeing Lily let down her hair a bit."

"Oh, and you haven't seen that in your twice weekly dates?" Nathan's smile was cheeky, and Parker was relieved he didn't seem to be annoyed with her anymore.

"Well, yeah, but that's…different." Parker looked down at her shoe to avoid catching Nathan's eye. As open as they were about their lives, they never went into details about their sex lives. Sometimes Nathan tried, and

Parker would generally cover her ears and say "Enough!"

"I love Jacqui. She's great. And Scott seemed great, too. More chatty than I expected."

"Yeah? Does Lily say he's quiet?"

Parker shrugged. "Not exactly. I just get the sense they co-exist beside one another. Taking shifts as parents. Living together, but not necessarily by choice?"

"They don't get along?"

"Well, they do, and they did choose to live together, but it wouldn't have happened if Megan hadn't died. I don't know, it sounds complicated, and a bit depressing. So, it was nice to see them happy together, and to see that Jacqui clearly loves Scott too. I suppose today painted a picture of a happier family than I had expected."

Nathan remained silent as he took it in. "Will they live together forever?"

She shrugged in response. "I have no idea. I think that's the plan. I think they'd both struggle to not have Bodhi full time. That's part of the reason she's not ready for a relationship though."

He nodded. "Must be so complicated, going into something expecting one thing and getting something entirely different. Must be hard for both of them."

Parker hadn't actually thought of it from Scott's perspective. From the image she'd had of him in her head, she hadn't really expected to like him, but she got to know him a bit at the beach and had been pleasantly surprised. Lily was right. He was clearly a good person, and very committed to their family. He'd set out to donate sperm to a couple and ended up becoming a full-time, live-in dad. He seemed like a good dad too.

Chapter Twenty-One

LILY

"Great day," Scott said on the way home.

Lily nodded. "I enjoyed it."

"I hadn't realised you and Bodhi's teacher had become so close."

Lily was suddenly relieved that Bodhi had travelled back with his cousins in Jacqui's car. "Did I tell you I met her last year at some event I went to?"

"No." Scott seemed surprised but not suspicious at all.

"Just the once, and then I wondered if I knew her when we met her at the start of the year. Well, we got talking and realised we did know each other. She's great."

"She's nice. She's clearly gay."

Lily nodded. "Clearly."

Scott was silent, and then finally spoke. "Are you attracted to her?"

"She's Bodhi's teacher," Lily said as if that answered the question.

"But…?"

Lily couldn't believe he was asking. In the six years since Megan had died, relationships simply hadn't been discussed between them. Megan had been the one to make them talk about it constantly, as uncomfortable as it had been at the time, talking about some hypothetical new relationship before they'd even grieved her loss. But now, out of the blue, Scott was asking. She didn't know whether to tell him the truth or just play innocent. Finally, she spoke up with what she hoped would be enough. "She's an attractive woman. I'll say that."

He nodded but then added, "You're not answering the question."

"Well, yes, I guess I think she's attractive. I don't know what you're asking. She's attractive." Lily fumbled over her words, wishing she could hide away in a hole for the duration of this conversation. "I'm not looking for a relationship if that's what you're asking."

Scott nodded and didn't speak for quite some time. When he did, Lily was relieved that he discussed the song on the stereo and moved on to what they were going to have for dinner that evening. Safe topics. Lily and Scott conversation topics. It made Lily feel much more settled to return to normal.

*

AS SHE WAS dishing up slices of pizza for dinner, Scott walked past the kitchen and said one more thing to suggest the topic wasn't entirely closed. "I'm pleased you've been going out a little more lately. It's nice to see you socialising."

Lily stuffed a small bit of pizza in her mouth and smiled. "Mmm" was all she said in response, and he shook his head. She hated that she was not responding to him attempting to open up lines of conversation. She just hadn't been prepared for it, and she wondered if he suspected something. Finally, she spoke, "It's nice going out a little. You should too. It's good to have some fun outside of work and parenting."

He nodded. "Good point. It's nice to have the balance. I might try it too."

She called Bodhi to the kitchen and handed Scott a plate. "Thanks, this looks good," he said.

*

SCOTT HAD TAKEN most of the first week of holidays off work to spend time with Bodhi, so Lily went to the office. Jacqui went home early on Thursday afternoon, so Lily had taken the opportunity to invite Parker to the office to explore. Their new staff were commencing in about ten days, so Lily wanted to use the opportunity to show it off to Parker while she had a vacant office—something that would become harder in the days to come.

When Lily opened the door to Parker, she was impressed. Parker stood there in fitted black jeans, a black V-neck shirt, and a denim jacket. White sneakers and spiky hair complimented the look, but it was her cheeky smile that melted Lily. Lily grinned, shook her head, and pulled her inside into an embrace, then, ultimately, a passionate kiss.

"Well, that's one way to say hello," Parker said, grinning once they broke away. "I could get used to this kind of greeting. So, tell me about the place."

Lily gestured around the room, now feeling silly that she'd invited Parker to the office. She hoped Parker wasn't expecting something more impressive. It had felt important to share her workplace, but now that Parker was here, she wondered if it was a crazy idea—they weren't in a relationship, for starters, and secondly, it was hardly an impressive top floor on a city skyscraper. No, it was just an office space. Sure, it was an office space she was damn proud of, having worked very hard to get to this point in her business, but how did it look to an outsider? "Well, there's not much to tell." She shrugged. "This is the space, but for some reason, I wanted you to see it."

"I love the feel of it!" Parker said, and that got Lily more enthused again.

"Really?"

"Yes, the wooden floorboards, the red accents all around, and I love all the posters." Lily had decorated the office space with childlike posters, due to the nature of their business. Although Lily and Jacqui were more likely to go out for meetings, whenever they did have an advertiser come into the building, she wanted them to walk away with a sense of fun and happiness. She'd colour themed red, black, and white as much as she could with vases, posters of *The Little Mermaid* and *Bambi*, and some old advertisements on the walls. The old ads were more Jacqui's thing, but Lily loved them too. They depicted an image of a simpler family life. On one long wall, they had framed some of their favourite magazine covers.

Parker's eye finally rested on this wall, a wall Lily was most proud of. She stepped forward. "Wow, are these your magazine covers?"

Lily nodded, grinning. Parker did a short walking tour, reading the headlines of each one. "This is great. I've seen it before but never bought one."

"We're so lucky to have the support of so many newsagencies and stores."

Parker kept looking at one of the covers as she spoke, "I don't think it's luck, Lil. Why wouldn't they want to sell your magazine? You're offering a great service to local families."

"Thanks." Sometimes Lily thought their business was just a business, and other times, she felt the same as Parker had said—that they were really offering a service. When she was proud of her business like that, she could work for hours and hours without feeling like it was a chore.

"You really are impressive," Parker said, now shifting her gaze from the posters to Lily. "Sometimes you act like this business is just a little thing, but it's pretty big, isn't it?"

"I'm so excited that we have our first employees starting in just over a week." Deep down, she hadn't really thought she was successful before Jacqui had given up her job. Once she had, she started to wonder if this business might actually work. But now, they had two employees starting, and to her that was a sign of success. To have a couple of employees was a lot of pressure—there needed to be enough work for them, for starters! And money to pay them!—but it was also a sign of how much they'd grown the business already and how much potential there was. "They'll only be part time. Two days a week each. Erin is studying marketing, so she'll be focusing on promoting our education program and connecting with schools. Alex is setting up his own business on the side, so we're thinking of getting him to work on some of our administrative processes. And at this stage, we have Fridays to ourselves, but over time, it might be better to have Alex and Erin in together on the same days. It will all depend on how it works out, how much crossover there is."

"Even if you did one day together. Then you could have all staff meetings for planning."

Lily was impressed that Parker was clearly engaged enough to have an opinion on it, and it was a good idea—one she hadn't yet thought of. "That's a really good idea. I'll talk to Jacqui. Hopefully, they're flexible enough that they can make it work."

"And hopefully not on a Tuesday…" Parker smiled cheekily.

"Hopefully not," Lily responded, but felt unsettled by the comment. She didn't know why.

"So, is Thursday the new Tuesday?" Parker said, moving closer to Lily. "Do you want to go home with me? Or was this just a hang-out?"

She looked at Parker and wondered what on earth they were doing. Something didn't feel right. But instead of saying something, she simply nodded. "Yes. I'll take my car too."

*

THEIR AFTERNOON IN bed was amazing—as always—but Lily still felt unsettled.

"This was great," Parker said. "I've been thinking. I had a great time meeting Jacqui and Scott and spending time with Bodhi and your nieces." She looked at Lily. "Is there any chance…you and I…that we could go public?"

"Go public?" Lily suspected she knew what Parker was inferring but was hopeful she wasn't right.

"Is there any chance you'd…be my girlfriend?" She sounded anxious to ask. "And have a proper relationship, not just…this?" She gestured around the bedroom.

Lily sighed and then looked at Parker, her forehead creasing, as she shook her head. "I'm sorry…"

Parker shook her head. "Don't be. I got my hopes up, that's all. After the beach."

Lily felt awful, but she knew it wouldn't be fair to Parker, or to Megan, to try to do this. "It's just, Megan… I would hate to ruin things with you because I'm not over her."

"You don't have to be over her. I wouldn't expect you to be. She's not your ex! I'm not expecting that it's *over*. I know that if you had your way, you'd still be with Megan. I understand that I'll never replace her. I'm not asking to. All I'm asking is that you give us a chance."

Lily couldn't believe how generous Parker was being. It seemed too good to be true. To have Parker and not have to give up on Megan? Part of her wanted to jump at the chance, but the other part of her thought of Bodhi and Scott and the life they'd built together. Wouldn't saying yes to Parker be an end, not only to Lily's past, but also her present? It was nearly impossible to explain all of that. She'd sound crazy. "I just don't think…"

Parker turned away, and Lily sensed her sadness. Her heart leapt for the woman who was hurting because she couldn't commit. "I'm sorry."

Parker shook her head. "Don't. Don't be sorry." Lily knew Parker was tearing up. While Parker had a moment to herself, Lily grabbed her clothes and started to dress, ready to leave.

"Have you even told anyone about us? Or am I really your dirty little secret?" Parker asked, tears in her eyes.

"Maree knows, and Jacqui knows. Jacqui loves you." Lily smiled, her voice gentle.

"At least one sister does," Parker said, still not looking at Lily.

Lily nodded, even though Parker wasn't looking. "Yes, she thinks I'm an idiot for just doing the friends with benefits thing. But…it works."

"I can't do it anymore, actually." Parker's voice squeaked. "It's unfair." Now the tears were flowing, and Lily put her arm around her. She moved away but turned to look Lily in the eye. It had been hard not seeing Parker's face, but now that she was looking at her, it seemed even harder to be confronted with the pain she'd caused. "I love being with you, but it's not right. This is not what I want."

Lily was devastated to hear it. Parker had brought so much happiness and fun to her life. And now things would be back to her old life, with no Parker, no Tuesdays. She breathed in deeply and gave Parker a small smile and nod. "Okay, I'm not going to try to convince you…but…I can't say I'm not sad."

"The thing is, Lil, I can't compete with Megan. I understand that. I always did, but I also can't compete with your relationship with Scott."

"Scott?" Lily screwed up her face. "I don't have a relationship with Scott."

"Maybe not, but you live with him, and he doesn't even know about us."

"Because of his connection with Megan."

"You've told me the reason. It doesn't make it any easier."

"I get that. And I'm really sorry."

"Lily, please don't say sorry. It is what it is. You always told me… I got my hopes up that things were changing, but I was wrong. That's my fault, not yours."

Lily felt like the worst person on earth. She just nodded and backed away. "I like you, Parker. A lot. It's just…"

"Don't." Parker's look gave Lily a warning.

In return, Lily glanced down at the floor, not wanting to meet Parker's eye. Finally, she did. "Are we going to be okay?" She was worried that Parker seemed upset—perhaps even angry—and she was still Bodhi's teacher.

Parker gave her a thin smile. "This isn't about Bodhi if that's what you mean. I'm a professional."

Lily was instantly relieved and nodded. "Thanks." Deep down, she'd known it wouldn't be an issue. Parker was great—mature, sensible, kind. All the things she wanted in a partner when she was ready. And incredibly sexy to boot. Even when she was glaring at her, even with her eyes filled with tears, she had a certain something and not for the first time, Lily wondered if she was crazy. She drove home imagining what Megan would think of it all.

"That girl is hot," Megan would no doubt be saying, from wherever she was. "What on earth are you doing Lily?" Even Megan would think she was crazy, and Lily couldn't help but wonder if she would be right.

Chapter Twenty-Two

PARKER

"Remember I thought she had a husband and I hated that? Well it's the dead wife I can't compete with. A husband might have been easier," Parker groaned.

"I don't see how!" Nathan replied. "A dead wife is out of the picture, at least."

Parker rolled her eyes. "At least a husband would leave his socks on the bedroom floor, not wash up the dishes, and would probably stay out too late with his mates. A dead wife is just…perfect. And that will never change."

"You think she has rose-coloured glasses on?"

Parker shrugged. "Not really. She certainly hasn't gone on and on about how perfect she was or anything like that, but they were clearly very much in love. The issue is that she feels she's cheating on her." Parker had decided that Megan sounded great—Scott and Lily both clearly felt this way—and that was probably accurate. It wasn't so much rose-coloured glasses as a sense that Lily wasn't going to allow anyone to get close to her. Perhaps she didn't want to lose someone again. And then there was Scott. "I think the problem is Scott."

"How?" Now that she had mentioned Scott, she had Nathan's full interest.

"Just that Scott doesn't date. I think she feels scared to disrupt their arrangement."

Nathan frowned. "Have you found out if he's gay?"

Parker didn't know whether to tell Nathan. "I really don't care. The fact is he doesn't have a boyfriend, or a girlfriend, and so now Lily won't be my girlfriend."

"It's just, maybe I could help…if he was gay."

Parker groaned and shook her head. "With all due respect, Mr Stenlake, your *help* would no doubt be more of a hindrance when it comes to dating her housemate!"

"Maybe I've changed."

"I'll believe it when I see it. No, I just need to move on from Lily, and you need to move on from Scott. I need to get back on the horse."

"Dating?"

She nodded. She really didn't want to, but she believed the ideal way to get over someone was to get distracted. Have fun. It might not be the best recommendation for a person getting over someone, and it was never nice for the rebound girl, but ultimately it was more fun than pining alone at home. Some of Parker's greatest flings had been in rebound stage. Not great from a longevity point of view, but certainly plenty of fun. Trouble was, she only wanted fun with Lily right now—no one else.

What if Nathan felt that way about Scott? Suddenly she felt a little guilty for withholding information from Nathan. "Okay, he's gay," she confessed.

"I'm sorry?"

"He's gay. He came out as a teenager."

Nathan feigned mock horror. "Please don't tell me you've known this since I first asked!" Parker blushed, and Nathan play-whacked her. "He's gay!" He grinned. He looked thrilled.

"He's gay, and he's the father of one of our students, and you've been lecturing me about sleeping with the mother of a student, so you can't go there either." Parker grinned.

"I promise I won't try anything just yet." Nathan was scheming, and Parker didn't want to know what he had in mind.

"Come on. Back to me. We're talking about my plans for online dating, not your plan to try and seduce a student's father."

"Meh. You make it sound so awful when you put it that way."

She rolled her eyes. "*You* made it sound that way when I was seeing Lily. It would be totally hypocritical for you to do the same thing."

Nathan weighed it up. "Bodhi's not my student though." He had a point, but Parker still hoped he would avoid the Delaney-Jones family entirely. She needed to move on, and the sooner she stopped thinking about Lily and Scott, the better.

"For now, my relationship with the Delaney-Jones family is purely professional. Doting teacher, period. I'll get my fun on the side." She wished she was as committed to her plan as she sounded.

"Great. So what's the plan?"

Parker ran through a few different sites with him, finally settling on two. "Have you got time to help me create a profile?"

Nathan nodded, then added, "Haven't you got old profiles you can recycle? I'm sure we've done this before." He yawned.

What they did worked because Parker was soon getting matches. None of them appealed to her, but then, remembering why she was doing it, she took a slightly less critical look and ended up responding to a few.

"Do I want to date another teacher?" Parker asked Nathan the next day at school. "One has asked me for coffee." She rolled her eyes. Her heart wasn't in it.

"Sure." He shrugged. "Why not? Could be good. And, hey, if it works, at least you get holidays off together."

With those words, Parker found herself on a date with Anna a few evenings later. She was a grade five teacher—a cute, short woman with cropped brunette tousled curls and big brown eyes.

"Tell me about yourself," Anna said. "Your profile didn't have much info in it, but I hear the community around here is fairly small, so when I saw a new member, I thought I'd catch up with you before you became jaded with online dating." She laughed, and Parker found herself laughing too. The rapport was easy with Anna, she just didn't sense any chemistry. It wasn't that Anna wasn't adorable—she was—it just—didn't feel like someone she wanted to jump into a relationship with. She was determined to give it a go though.

"Well, I teach grade three. I used to teach older grades though. I've taught grade five before."

Anna nodded. "Which do you prefer?"

Parker shrugged. "I like the variety. As long as I'm not teaching the same grade for too long, I'm happy." She was sure she'd been asked that very question in her job interview and responded in exactly the same way.

Anna nodded. "I prefer to stick with one grade for a time due to all the prep work. I like to get familiar with the grade."

Soon they were talking teaching styles, and while the commonality was great for breaking the ice, she couldn't help wondering if they had anything else in common. Trying to change the topic from work, she asked Anna what she liked to do on weekends.

"I read a lot and go for long walks. I'm just out of a relationship, and I'd moved here because of that relationship, so I'm still finding my feet. Making friends and hopefully more," Anna admitted. Parker was relieved— she liked Anna and maybe they could be friends if the dating thing didn't work out.

Luckily, the rest of the evening got more relaxed, although Parker couldn't quite see potential romantically. At the end of the night, as Anna leapt forward and kissed her, she realised she was definitely right—the chemistry was lacking. The old Parker wouldn't have cared. The old Parker would have seen how things progressed, anyway, given Anna's apparent interest. The new Parker had no interest in seeing how things progressed although she felt bad to reject someone she'd just met, so she didn't completely. "Thanks, it was a great evening."

"I'd love to catch up again sometime soon."

"Sure, just let me know." She wasn't lying, exactly—she was happy to catch up and be Anna's friend. She just wasn't sure they had potential for romance.

"Well, then, you have to get back on the horse," Nathan said.

"Ugh, the image you paint of a horse." Parker shook her head. "I don't think I want that!"

Nathan playfully whacked her. "I'm just saying, if Annie or Anna, or whatever her name is, isn't the girl for you, we just need to move to the next one on the list. Cat something or other? She was number two. I think you said you'd been chatting to her?"

Parker was bemused that Nathan had taken so much interest in her internet dating when he'd been so discouraging of her pseudo-relationship with Lily. Perhaps that was why he was keen for her to internet date and was being so supportive. Parker scrolled through her phone. "Yes, CatInAHat. She seems nice enough." She shrugged.

He nodded. "Well, come on then, chat to her. Line up a coffee."

Chapter Twenty-Three

LILY

Lily was cutting vegetables to throw into a casserole when Scott walked past the kitchen. "Don't do a serve for me. I'm going out for dinner tonight if that's okay?" Normally, on Sunday nights they ran through the week ahead. This mid-week dinner hadn't been mentioned, so Lily was surprised but not worried. "Spur of the moment invitation. A date, I suppose," he explained and looked embarrassed. He was trying hard to be casual. Lily could tell.

She paused before responding, trying to match his casual style. "Oh, sure, not a problem. There's plenty, though, if you want a lunch serve to-morrow. Jacqui is coming over tonight." She didn't know whether to ask anything, but felt it best to let Scott divulge what he wanted when he was ready.

"That's right. John's away, isn't he?" Scott clearly recalled Lily mentioning dinner with her sister because her kids would all be busy that evening, and Jacqui's husband was away. "Look. I might take you up on the lunch serve tomorrow. Anyway, I shouldn't be too late, so I might see Jacqui when I get home."

Lily nodded, not knowing what to say or ask, though she was very curious. This was, as far as she knew, the first date Scott had been on in years—about eight years! Where did he meet someone? Was he looking? Online perhaps? Or did he just meet someone randomly? It all seemed so bizarre. And why did it need to happen now after she'd told Parker she wasn't able to date? Could this be a signal that it was possibly time?

*

THE HOUSE HAD the smell of a simmering casserole circulating by the time Jacqui arrived, breezing in and kissing her nephew. "Yum, that smells delicious!"

"Good, there's plenty. Scott isn't joining us tonight."

Jacqui nodded but didn't say anything. She went into Bodhi's room to see his new toys and then ventured out to the kitchen.

"He's on a date," Lily blurted out.

Jacqui looked confused and shook her head. "A date? Who?"

"Scott. Scott's on a date." Lily made sure Bodhi couldn't hear her—they had never broached the topic of his parents dating anyone because it had never been an issue before. She didn't really understand what Bodhi thought of dating and how he made sense of the world. Perhaps he never even thought that parents were usually romantically connected. In his world, perhaps parents were just friends who lived together. Sure, she and Scott had explained marriage to him, and how most parents were married, but how much sense did that make to an eight-year-old boy who had never really seen parents being romantically linked?

"Who is he dating?"

"I have no idea. He didn't say. I didn't ask. I was shocked."

Jacqui raised her eyebrows. "I bet. Does this mean you'll come out about your relationship with Parker?"

"We don't have a relationship."

"You call it tomato. I call it to-mah-to," Jacqui said, laughing. "Friends with benefits or relationship—same diff." She shrugged.

"No, I'm serious. Parker ended it."

Jacqui's eyes widened. "She ended it?" She looked really surprised. "I thought she was really into you."

Lily felt both awful for any pain she'd caused and hopeful for the future when she said that. "She was really into me. And that's why she ended it because I couldn't commit."

Jacqui gave her a sympathetic look. "Well maybe now you can."

A questioning look crossed her face, and Lily shrugged, shaking her head slowly. "I don't know. Maybe that ship's sailed already. Maybe I upset her too much. Maybe…it's too late to start again?"

"Oh, come on. She ended your FWB thing because she was too into it. This is like a romance movie set-up. You run to the airport before she boards that plane—that kind of thing."

"It's been a few weeks, and I haven't heard from her, and I've avoided the classroom. If she was interested, I think I'd have heard from her."

"Liliana. You basically told her that your heart belongs to Megan. That she can have you sexually, providing no one knows about it, including the man you live with. Your best friend. She could just be your dirty little secret."

Lily felt like she'd been slapped. It sounded awful the way Jacqui put it. "Well, it wasn't exactly like that. It's complicated."

"Sure. And Parker told you that she wants more. That doesn't sound to me like she's not interested. It sounds like someone who was hurting."

Lily was silent as she pondered Jacqui's words. Maybe Jacqui was right, but she didn't want to admit it to herself. Part of her reason for not wanting to date had been Scott. Another part of her reason was loyalty to Megan. She was attracted to Parker but hadn't even thought about whether she wanted a relationship with her—she'd been so closed off to the idea. If she felt ready to take the leap to have a relationship, was Parker actually the person she wanted to be with? Or had she just been a fun distraction? Lily didn't know the answer. Sure, she'd enjoyed Parker's company, but they were just friends, right? Friends that had amazing sexual chemistry, sure, but relationships were more than that. They were many things, perhaps most notably teacher and parent. Lovers. Friends. But were they relationship material? She had to think that over, but she knew that even if she wanted it, Parker might be closed off from the idea by now.

"Do you actually see us together?"

Jacqui grinned. "I do. You know…if, months ago, you'd asked me who I imagined as your next partner, I would have imagined someone like Megan, because…well, because of Megan. That's all I knew. But now I've seen you with Parker, I can absolutely see you with her. You work together nicely."

"Really?" Lily's brow creased in confusion as Jacqui nodded, her eyes glinting with happiness. Lily wasn't sure. She'd been on a roller coaster over the past couple of weeks, since Parker had exited her life in every way except as her son's teacher.

Actually, she'd been on a roller coaster of emotions ever since she'd first met Parker. No one really understood how hard it was to have pictured life going down one path and it changing so suddenly and unexpectedly. No one, that is, except perhaps Scott, whose life had changed just as dramatically as her own.

Lily sighed audibly. Jacqui looked at her sister with compassion. Lily knew Jacqui did somewhat understand the journey Lily had been through but still encouraged her to move on. Perhaps if she hadn't had Bodhi to raise, dating would have been on her mind sooner. As Bodhi was becoming more independent, the idea of having a relationship seemed more possible. Maybe it would be nice, after all. Risky, but potentially worth the risk.

"Look, if you want my two cents… I think you need to see her. I think you need to just put it out there. Tell her you're keen, but you just want to take it slow."

"That's exactly what we were doing," Lily protested, but Jacqui shook her head.

"No, you were sex buddies. That was all you ever offered her. You weren't taking steps towards a relationship, Lily. That's what I'm saying now. Small steps."

"I'll give it some thought."

"Just don't think too long. A woman like her will get snapped up quickly."

"If she likes me as much as you say she does, she won't."

Chapter Twenty-Four

PARKER

Parker gelled her hair up, had a quick look in the mirror, and then grabbed her wallet to walk out the door. It was her third date with Cat, and she was enjoying her company. Cat was certainly a lot more her type than Anna had been, and though she hadn't yet felt the chemistry she'd felt with Lily, there seemed to be potential. Jumping into her car, she was surprised to be actually looking forward to the date. Cat was very interested in Parker, and while Parker wasn't yet certain, with time that could change. After Lily, it was nice to have someone who was interested in a relationship. Cat was enthusiastic and had made it clear, without saying it explicitly, that if Parker was keen on a relationship, she would be too.

Nathan had been excited to hear that the first date had gone well, and though she hadn't filled him in on any details, he knew they were now up to date number three and was pleased for her. He'd been a little preoccupied lately himself, clearly having moved on from the idea of Scott. Turned out he'd met some new guy, but he'd been quite candid about it all. He said they'd go out for a drink, and he'd fill her in. She was just relieved Scott seemed to be off his mind. He was probably up to date number four or perhaps even five by now with this new guy. That was surprising since he usually didn't have more than a second date. It seemed that, soon enough, both Nathan and Parker could be coupled up. It had been a long time since that had happened. She hoped it wouldn't change their friendship, but they'd been best friends for so long, surely it wouldn't.

Parker arrived at the busy restaurant district. It was their first Saturday evening date. Actually, it was their first evening date, and that in itself seemed symbolic of a shift from online chatting to coffee, then lunch, and now dinner out. They'd talked so much Parker couldn't even remember who had asked who to the dinner.

Cat was already seated and grinned widely when she spotted Parker. "Hey," she said, "it's nice to see you." She rose and gave her a peck on the lips, and Parker smiled in return.

"You look lovely tonight, Cat." She did—she was wearing a fitted skirt, with tights and boots and a low-cut, long-sleeve top. She had blonde curls to her shoulders and big blue eyes, which she'd used some kind of make-up on to make her eyes stand out.

"Thank you." She grinned. "And you look hot." Parker blushed. She was wearing her stock, standard-fitted black jeans, boots, and tonight had on a red button-up shirt. "I love those jeans on you."

Parker smiled. "Tell me how things have been."

"Really good." Cat grinned. She was always so positive. "I'm loving life at the moment. I'm planning a trip to America soon, and other than that, just having fun. Having friends over. You?"

"Just teaching. Busy time of year. We're doing some standardised testing before reporting and parent-teacher interviews. When are you planning to go to the US?"

"In October, for three weeks. Shopping in New York, laying on the beach in Miami, Florida. I'm going with my best friend, and we're debating going to Hawaii too."

"That's amazing. I haven't gone on a big trip in years. I'm overdue. I love travelling, but of course I can only travel during school holidays."

"I deliberately avoid school holidays. Can't stand a plane full of kids."

Parker smiled but didn't know how to respond. For the first time, she wondered if they would be able to work long-term if that was Cat's attitude to travel and young kids. She decided to crack a joke. "If you end up dating a teacher or ever having kids, it'll be your only option down the track."

"I'm hoping I'll get to date a teacher." She winked. "But I don't want kids. Ever."

"Ah, okay." That wasn't exactly a deal-breaker—Parker would have enjoyed having Bodhi in her life, and she loved kids but wasn't exactly sure she needed to be a parent herself. She'd never given it much thought. What did disappoint her about Cat saying it, was how definite she was. She wasn't willing to discuss it with whomever ended up being her partner. It made Parker wonder how black and white Cat was in other areas of her life.

"Do you want kids?" Cat asked, frowning.

Parker shrugged. "Not necessarily. I don't know. I guess it would depend…" She paused. "I guess it would depend on who I ended up with, and what she wanted."

Cat nodded. "Well if you end up with me, it's *off* the agenda." She smiled but made it clear—the case was closed. Parker couldn't help but wonder if her dimples, big blue eyes, and blonde curls got her a long way with women in the past. It seemed Cat was used to getting her own way with no negotiation. That wasn't exactly how Parker liked things to work— she was more about conversation and making a plan that worked for everyone.

"I'll keep that in mind," she said, bemused. She knew she should admire Cat's determination—it was something she'd always been attracted to in women—but she needed to know more about her and what she might not be willing to negotiate on.

"Let's order dinner," Cat said. "They make the most amazing arancini here, if you like that."

"That's risotto balls, right?"

Cat nodded. "They're amazing. Do you like mushrooms? The mushroom ones are to…die…for!"

Parker did like mushrooms, so they ordered a serve of them with sweet potato fries and aioli to share for starters. By the time the main meals arrived, they were fairly full, but then Parker saw her cannelloni and mustered up an appetite again.

*

DINNER WAS PLEASANT. The banter between them was light, and at the end of the date, they went for a walk by the lake and ended the evening kissing. From the way Cat was kissing her, Parker was certain she could have taken her home, but it didn't feel right. She wanted to get to know her more before working out if there was a potential future between them.

"It was a lovely evening. Let's catch up soon."

"Can we catch up very soon? I'd love to get to know you more." Cat raised her eyebrows, and her intention lingered in the air.

"Sure," Parker said, stepping backwards. "Sure."

Cat had a small smile. "Well, I hope to hear from you soon, Parker." It was obvious that she was disappointed by Parker's response. Parker smiled, and suggested she walk Cat to her car. On the way, they chatted about Cat's work in travel.

Arriving at the car, Cat moved forward for another kiss, but this time it was merely a peck on the lips. She lingered momentarily, the invitation clear, but Parker didn't take it. She just pecked Cat twice more on the lips and squeezed her hand. "Catch up soon." She smiled, and Cat nodded, jumped into her car, and drove away.

The old Parker would have been in the car with her. What had changed?

Chapter Twenty-Five

LILY

Bodhi had a friend, Chris, staying over, and Lily had set them up in the TV room with a movie and big bowls of popcorn. She sat down in the lounge room. Away from the noise, with a comforting bowl of spaghetti bolognaise, she opened her book to the page she was up to. She couldn't keep her mind on what she was reading.

Ever since Jacqui had been over during the week, Lily had thought about talking to Parker about the situation. She'd seen her once at the school since then, but it wasn't the right time. Out of the blue, Scott asked if she'd mind taking control of the sleepover, as he was thinking of going on another date. Lily was surprised—it must be their second date, or perhaps even their third. Conversations about it were all very awkward, but tomorrow she vowed to talk to him about it all. Who was he? How promising did it seem? And was he keen to introduce the guy to them, or was it too soon? She couldn't help being anxious about how everything would all play out, but she was also a little envious that he'd been brave and gone for it, when she still hadn't felt ready herself. Was it really loyalty to Megan, who had given her a green light to date? Or was it simply fear? Fear of disrupting what she had with Scott and Bodhi and perhaps fear of losing someone special to her again. Falling for someone made you vulnerable, and she knew she never again wanted to feel the pain she'd felt when she'd lost Megan.

But, right now, she was waiting. Waiting for Scott to come home, waiting for Bodhi's sleepover to end, and wondering what Parker was doing. None of that made her feel exactly joyful either. Maybe she needed to follow Scott's lead and plunge in. Tomorrow she would know her path forward.

*

LILY WAS IN the kitchen scrambling eggs and frying bacon when Scott padded out to the kitchen, rubbing his eyes. "Late night?" she asked him, grinning.

"Yeah, fairly late. That smells great. Is that for the boys?"

She nodded. "I am making it for the boys, but there's plenty for the two of us too. Why don't we set the boys up, and then we can go eat on the deck and have a chat?"

Out on the deck, Scott placed large glasses of juice beside their breakfast plates, and they settled opposite each other at the outdoor table. "This is great. Thank you!" he said enthusiastically.

"How was your night out?"

"Really good." He paused for a minute and finally spoke again, "Do you remember Parker's friend, Nathan? It's him."

"Nathan?" Lily's eyes widened. She was very surprised and instantly wondered what this might mean for her and Parker.

"Remember I met him at the beach? Remember Parker and Nathan came?"

Of course she remembered Parker and Nathan came.

"Well, we spent a bit of time talking, and at one point I gave him my email address because he had some resources for Bodhi's maths. We got chatting on email, and then we caught up for a coffee." He blushed. "I should have told you sooner, but I didn't know how it would all turn out. And I know you're probably horrified that I'm dating someone at Bodhi's school." Lily nearly choked on her mouthful of bacon. "But he said it's okay. Apparently, Parker was dating a parent at the school for a while there."

"Oh, yeah?"

"Yes, but it fizzled out. She's now got a new girlfriend, who isn't a parent at the school, but Nathan thinks we're okay because of that. We might tell the school if it gets serious."

Now Lily did choke on the bite of toast and egg she'd taken. She took a moment to recover. Swallowing a large sip of juice, she finally recovered enough to talk.

"She has a girlfriend? Parker? Parker has a girlfriend?"

Scott frowned, giving Lily a strange look. "Well, yeah. You did know she was gay, didn't you? I'm sure we discussed it. Plus, it's pretty obvious. Even my gaydar was going off, and you know how crap that is. I didn't even realise Nathan was gay when I met him although I must say I hoped he was."

"I knew she was gay; I just didn't realise she had a girlfriend." Lily felt like crying. It had only been a few weeks!

"Apparently a new girlfriend, but it sounds promising. Nathan said he was happy because they haven't dated people at the same time in a while. Anyway, I wanted to be open with you, and I promise I won't introduce him as my boyfriend to Bodhi or anything like that. We can chat as we go."

Lily was silent. She couldn't believe that Scott had finally started a relationship, and she felt free and ready to date Parker and now Parker had a girlfriend! And…on top of all of that…her housemate was dating Parker's best friend!

"Are you okay?" He looked at her in concern.

She nodded. "What made you start dating?"

Scott frowned in response but didn't answer, so Lily continued.

"I mean, was it because of Megan and Bodhi and everything here that you weren't dating?"

Scott was pensive and then shook his head. "No, not really. Of course, when we first lost Megan, I grieved too much to want to date, so yes, maybe in a way. And then I was so busy being a dad, I just didn't have time for guys. But then, over the past few years, I've thought it could be nice, but I just don't really meet anyone. My gaydar is crap. You know that. Maybe I do meet eligible guys and don't even realise it. But…well, Nathan really took the lead. I was attracted to him when I met him, but I wouldn't have sought him out. I'm just not like that. I haven't been dating, just because I am too shy to make the first move, and I hate the idea of internet dating. What about you? Is it Megan? I guess so… It would be much harder for you." He gave her a sad smile.

She nodded, slowly, and couldn't believe they'd never talked about all of this. She'd made too many assumptions over the past few years. She gave him a sad smile in return and looked in his eyes. "It was Megan, at first. And Bodhi, too. Just parenting. But sometimes I think I'm just scared I'll lose someone and get hurt again. I'm also scared about what happens here." She shrugged and felt awkward but wanted to be as open as she could. They'd wasted far too long not talking to lose this opportunity.

"Happens here?" He clarified by gesturing between them. Now she had tears in her eyes as she nodded. "What do you mean?"

"Well, what if you and Nathan end up together, and he doesn't want to live with Bodhi and me? What if I met someone who wanted a different life? Do we share custody? I don't think either of us want to live away from Bodhi half our lives. I know I don't."

"Hey, you're ahead of yourself now. We don't know what the future will bring, so why pre-empt that?"

"You're right, but isn't it best to plan?"

He shrugged. "I don't know. But it's best to live life."

She nodded. Perhaps he was right, but the whole idea seemed so scary. So much could go wrong, couldn't it?

"In my view," he added, "we'd eventually all live together. Maybe it's too simplistic. I haven't thought out the logistics. I've only had a few dates with Nath, and you're not dating anyone yet." Lily was half tempted to tell him that she was the one Parker had dated. After all, Nathan knew. She was appreciative he hadn't told Scott already. But, what was the point, if Parker already had a girlfriend?

"You're right. I can't believe we've never had this conversation before."

Scott gave Lily a look. "Do you remember, at the end, how much

Megan was pushing us to talk about it? She was constantly on our backs, wanting all of the logistics ironed out."

"She'd be up there now saying, 'What! It took you six years! You idiots! I told you so!'"

"I think we didn't have the conversation then because it was too hard. Too sad. And maybe since then because we'd fought so hard not to have it, it seemed too difficult to bring it up later. Maybe even too painful." Scott was pensive, and Lily agreed with him.

"Well, now that we've started talking, can you please keep me posted on you and Nathan? Any time you want to talk, or if you're starting to think about moving in together, let's talk. Just be open with me. And I'd love for him to come for dinner sometime…as your friend. We can ease Bodhi into it."

Scott nodded. "Honest, open communication is the way," he said, making the pit in Lily's stomach feel even more noticeable.

As she went to get ready for the day ahead, she felt guilty for not being open with Scott about her relationship with Parker, but then reminded herself that there was no Lily and Parker anymore. There never really had been.

*

BODHI WAS PARTICULARLY energetic on Tuesday morning, and Lily was frustrated. "I hope you calm down for your teacher," she said in the car. As she mentioned Parker, though, she felt a pang of sadness about what wouldn't be.

Walking to the door of the classroom, she caught Parker's eye, and gave her a wry smile as she placed Bodhi's bag on his hook and kissed him goodbye. Parker followed her out.

"Hey Lily, how are you? I've barely seen you lately."

"I've been trying to ease Bodhi into a little more independence, dropping him at the gate, but today he was just too hyper, so I wanted to make sure he got in here okay."

"Oh," Parker nodded, and strangely, Lily hoped the strange reaction was disappointment. It was crazy to hope because Parker already had a new girlfriend. Lily had told Jacqui that Parker wouldn't move on with someone if she had genuine feelings for Lily. The reality told Lily enough. After glancing around, Parker lowered her voice and looked at Lily. "I miss you. I miss catching up with you."

Lily couldn't believe it—what was she doing? Stringing two women along at the same time? She rolled her eyes, and Parker must have seen it because then she added a little self-consciously, "I know you don't want anything, and I'm trying not to be a nuisance. I know I'm Bodhi's teacher first and foremost." She looked around again before continuing. Lily frowned waiting to hear what was next. "But if you ever want friendship or whatever, please let me know."

Whatever? What did that mean? Lily was curious but didn't want to talk about her new girlfriend. Besides, the school bell would ring soon. Should she ask her to elaborate or just leave it?

"Hey." A voice interrupted her thoughts. "How are you?"

Lily looked up and saw Nathan coming towards them. That solved that—she had no opportunity now to ask Parker for an explanation on anything. Parker looked disappointed, and Nathan looked happy to spot her. Now it was Parker's chance to roll her eyes, and she gave Lily a bemused smile. Lily wondered whether Parker knew about Nathan's new love interest, or whether she gave her that look because of the interruption. Either way, Parker seemed frustrated but not angry. The affection between her and her best friend was evident, and the glint in her eyes showed Lily she was used to Nathan's interruptions. "I'm going well," Lily said as Nathan neared her.

"Great." They really didn't have much to talk about, but Nathan had clearly felt the need to say hello. Maybe he was wondering what she knew, or maybe he was trying to get in her good books, as the housemate of his newest partner. Wanting to be polite and keep the conversation flowing, she decided to use small talk to break the ice. "I was just saying to Ms Parker that Bodhi is very hyperactive today. I hope the rest of the grade is more subdued, otherwise you'll have a challenging Tuesday on your hands!"

Nathan gave her a look. "It's raining, it's mid-week. There's probably a full moon or something tonight. The kids are bound to be feral."

Lily gave him an amused look, then waved her mobile phone. "Well, I better get on the road, head to work. I probably have a ton of emails and appointments by now. I hope your day is good." Parker and Nathan said goodbye and turned and walked towards the classrooms. Lily let out a sigh as she reached her car. What on earth was Parker playing at?

Chapter Twenty-Six

PARKER

If she'd had an alibi, she might have killed Nathan for intruding on her conversation with Lily. She'd taken the very brief moment alone with her to basically put it all out there—yet again—and just as she thought she might be getting somewhere, Nathan had intruded. She wondered if that was because he was now dating Lily's housemate. She'd only found out the night before—it had been top secret. She wondered if Lily knew about it or whether Scott was playing around with Nathan just as secretively as Lily had with Parker. The whole thing seemed so crazy, and so complex. Not for the first time, Parker wished she'd had an opportunity to meet Megan who was apparently so amazing she had such a hold on both Lily and Scott.

It was actually Scott and Nathan's burgeoning relationship that had inspired her to raise the matter again with Lily. Sure, Parker had said that if she couldn't be more to Lily than she was, then she didn't want to be her partner in any way. But, spending time away from her, and perhaps more so, dating other women, had really made her realise the special connection she had with Lily. Maybe Lily would change her mind if Scott was coupled up, but even if not, Parker wanted Lily in her life in some capacity, and not just as teacher and parent.

She didn't have time to focus on it, though, because the school bell rang, and suddenly she was dealing with twenty-two energetic eight- and nine-year-olds. Luckily they managed to get her mind off things—she didn't like living in the doldrums for long although she would remain hopeful until they could finish their conversation.

*

WHEN SHE FINALLY caught up with Nathan in the staff room, she asked him for more about him and Scott.

"I'm besotted," he said in such a way that Parker couldn't tell if he was seriously sharing his feelings or having a joke with her. Nathan struggled to really open up, especially about relationships. She sighed and then asked him if he saw a future with Scott. He thought for a moment as if he hadn't given the idea any consideration before the question. "I think so. I really do like him."

She was surprised, not because Scott didn't seem like a great guy but because Nathan didn't tend to plunge in. "Can you see yourself as Bodhi's stepdad?"

Nathan looked amused. "I suppose a relationship with Scott would mean that would be on the cards. I'd have to sign up for it. But he has two committed parents in Lily and Scott, so I'd just be another parental figure there."

"Do you know whether you'd live with Lily or…"

Nathan put his hands in the air and gestured frantically. "Hang on a second. We've been together, what, a month? Six weeks? None of this planning to live together. We aren't lesbians," he scoffed with a note of laughter in his voice.

Parker couldn't believe he was standing here saying on the one hand he was besotted and wanted a future with the guy, but on the other hand they hadn't discussed the logistics of making that work. Surely that had to be discussed, given the unique circumstances Scott lived in. "I'd be talking about that soon enough. What if he wants you to live with Lily and Bodhi if you move in together?"

"What if?"

"And what if Lily has a girlfriend? Do you really want a group house? You need to think these things through."

"You should date Lily. Then the four of us could live together with Bodhi." He had a cheeky grin on his face, and it made Parker blush.

"Believe me, if I could make it happen, I would."

"What about CatInTheHat? Aren't you still seeing her?"

It must have been the day for interruptions because, next thing, Kelly appeared. "Hey, grade three folk! How are things?"

They got talking about school and soon the whole discussion of Nathan and Scott, and Parker, Lily, and CatInTheHat was long forgotten.

*

RETURNING HOME TO her empty house was normally a joy at the end of a long day, but now Parker felt lonely, especially because it was a Tuesday evening. She'd gotten to a point of really looking forward to Tuesday evenings, and now, yet another lonely Tuesday night loomed ahead of her. What she would have done to have Lily breeze in and embrace her. What she would have done to wonder how long she would have the pleasure of her company—it had changed each week, from an hour on busy Tuesdays through to many hours on amazing Tuesdays. Seeing Lily that morning had been a bright spot in the long day that followed, but they never did have the conversation she'd intended to have. She'd tried hard not to dwell on it and get busy, but it was hard.

Deciding to at least make use of her time, she made a big lasagna, music playing on the stereo in the background. As she bopped away to the music while she prepped the lasanga, she tried to focus on anything but Lily, and eventually her mind wandered to Cat. Could she see herself with Cat? Would she be this excited to see Cat?

There was nothing wrong with Cat. She seemed to be a great girl—very confident and self-assured. There was some chemistry there. Nothing like the connection she had with Lily, but Lily was no longer an option. Or was she? Parker really wanted to understand what Lily's main reason was for them not dating—Scott, Bodhi, or Megan? It was complex.

The lasagna was sizzling in her oven. At least something in her life sizzled. Her romantic life certainly did not.

Chapter Twenty-Seven

LILY

Walking into the house after work on Friday, Lily breathed in the aroma of curries bubbling away. "Smells great."

"Thank you!" Scott exclaimed. "Our son is at Chris's house for the night, and Nathan is due here in an hour."

"Great!" Lily was looking forward to their evening and having the opportunity to get to know Nathan a little more. When the doorbell rang, she answered it because by then Scott was getting ready in his bedroom.

"Hey, Nathan, come on in." She got him a drink and made small talk with him until Scott came downstairs and joined them. The men greeted each other with a kiss on the lips and an embrace, and Lily's heart lurched in envy. Seeing how comfortable they were reminded her of what she had lost when Megan had passed away. Being with Parker had been a wonderful whirlwind of fun and sexy times, but when she was really honest with herself, she knew it was more than just fun. There was an emotional connection too. It was a connection she missed, and not for the first time, she wished she hadn't pushed her away. Seeing Scott and Nathan together, she could barely remember what she'd been worried about.

*

OVER DINNER, THE trio chatted easily, and Lily was relieved that they got along so well. They'd planned a dinner for when Bodhi was out of the house so they could focus on conversation. Over time, Bodhi would get comfortable with Nathan—he already knew him through school, of course, but suddenly having a teacher in your house would be a surprise to a child. Ever since they'd had their first heart-to-heart chat a few weeks ago, they'd chatted more openly and seemed to be on the same page. Lily couldn't believe it had taken them this long to talk so easily. At least that was one good thing to come out of it all.

Over dessert and a few wines in, Nathan raised the Parker issue with Lily. "Parker said you didn't want a relationship because you were scared of what would happen between you and Scott. Because Scott was single. But now he's not." He gazed adoringly at his boyfriend, and Lily casually looked away for a second to give them a private moment of adoration. "So, what does that mean for you and Parker now?"

"Lily and Parker? What do you mean?" Scott asked, confused.

"You didn't know?" Nathan seemed surprised, and Scott shook his head, frowning. Lily felt awful for not talking with Scott about it. They'd talked openly recently about everything, but she had deliberately held this back.

"Sorry, Scott. I love Megan, you know that."

"That's not in question," he said. "It never has been and never would be."

"I love Megan so much, but I met Parker, and…" She shook her head, knowing her discomfort was clearly evident.

"It's okay. It has been six years, Lily."

She agreed, but tears sprang to her eyes anyway. "So, Parker, and I… We dated a couple of times." She didn't want to meet Nathan's eye, but she spotted him smiling a little at her calling it dating. "She ended it because…" She trailed off and shrugged. "I'm not really sure. I just didn't feel right, and I was scared. Scared about so much. And she couldn't be with me if I couldn't be open about it." Now she turned her attention to Nathan and frowned. "But Scott said she's got a new girlfriend anyway."

Nathan nodded. "Yes, I think so, but I'm not sure how serious it is."

"Isn't she your best friend?"

Nathan nodded, and Lily continued, "Then how can you not know?"

"We haven't had much time to talk this week. We started talking about it and got interrupted, and I forgot to ask again." He shrugged.

"Well, *we* were talking early in the week when you interrupted *us*," she said, grinning.

"Oh, shit, I'm sorry."

"What's this?" Scott asked. "What were you talking about?"

"Parker said to me at school drop-off that, if things were ever different for me, to let her know, and then Nathan came bounding down the hall, screaming, 'Helllooo, everyone!'" The trio laughed as they all pictured the moment.

"So that's why you're still enjoying school drop-off?" He had a bemused look as he turned to Nathan. "I've been trying to get her to stop going into the school because, at eight, Bodhi needs to be more independent, and she can just drop him at the gate. But she's been flirting with a teacher!"

"Hey, you can't talk. No, I have been dropping him to the gate, mostly. I agree with you although, yes, there is some eye candy at the school."

"Ain't that the truth?" Scott said.

"Anyway, I've been dropping him at the gate lately, but on Tuesday, he was acting crazy in the car, and I couldn't settle him, so I walked in. Seeing Parker was a bonus. Or maybe not—my mind has been spinning since."

"Well, let's get you back together," Nathan said.

"Great idea," Scott said. "I've been thinking it was time you dated someone, and Parker could be perfect. One big happy family."

Lily gave him a strange look. "It's a bit risky if we're all double-dating. What if one of the relationships doesn't work out?"

"We're all adults," Nathan said. "Maybe we can be mature about it if it doesn't work out. And if it did work out, we could all move in together!"

"Now we know the wine's gone to his head," Scott said, giving Lily an apologetic look. "We haven't talked about this."

"No, we haven't, but Parker thinks we should."

"So does Megan," Lily said dryly.

"Megan? That's your wife who passed away? Six years ago? And she has an opinion on this?" Nathan gestured between him, Scott, and Lily, and that cracked up everyone laughing.

*

AS LILY FINALLY crawled into bed, she grinned about the evening they'd shared. It had felt heart-warming, happy, and fun. Nathan was awesome—she could see why Parker loved him so much. And Scott, for that matter. The night reminded her of evenings back when she was much younger, and Megan, Scott, and Lily had sat around talking without a care in the world: Evenings they'd had before they'd become parents and were more concerned about getting as much sleep as possible; evenings they'd had before Megan had gotten sick. It had felt like a long time since she'd been so care-free and light.

They were on to their second, or maybe third, bottle of wine when the plan was hatched. Nathan was going to organise a catch-up with Parker on Tuesday evening, and Scott and Lily were going to gatecrash it. Tuesday night was selected because that was their old night together. It seemed to make sense, especially a few glasses in, but that didn't mean it wasn't risky. They'd lock in the final plans in the morning, as Nathan was staying over, but Lily was a little worried. What if Parker was actually interested in this woman she'd apparently met online? And why was she even online dating if she really did have feelings for Lily? For now, her pillow called her name, and with the happiness of the evening on her mind, and the wine relaxing her, she drifted off into a deep, content sleep. A hopeful sleep.

Chapter Twenty-Eight

PARKER

Sipping a coffee at work on Monday, Nathan interrupted her thoughts.

"Do you have plans tomorrow night?"

"No, why? What you got in mind?"

"Pizza and beers at your place?"

She was pleasantly surprised. She hadn't spent much time outside of work with him lately, so was looking forward to the idea of sitting and chatting about everything and nothing with him. "How was your weekend?" she asked him, after making the plan for Tuesday night.

"Great. I caught up with Scott. We had dinner together. I also got some organising done around home—my garage was such a mess! What about yours?"

"That's great. I had a fairly quiet weekend."

"Are you still seeing Cat?"

"No. We did catch up on Saturday, for lunch. She was super keen, I knew that the last time. I just don't… I don't know… I feel stupid walking away—she's a great girl, and she's gorgeous, it's just…"

"She's not Lily?" He sounded pleased.

"I know. It's stupid. Lily doesn't want anything. I've made it really clear to her that I'm here if she does, but I'm assuming it won't happen." She paused and then, feeling self-conscious about what Nathan would be thinking, added, "I'll definitely not wait around forever. I promise I'll keep online dating." She paused, then added, "But maybe over time, with Lily seeing you and Scott together, she might be more comfortable. Or maybe Scott was just an excuse, and she just didn't want a relationship…with me, anyway."

"Who knows? Anyway, ten minutes til class is back, so I might run away to get organised. I'll catch you later but looking forward to tomorrow night."

"Catch you."

*

PARKER HAD NOT long got home on Tuesday evening when Nathan rang the doorbell. "I'm starving, let's order pizzas early," he said.

"What do you want? BBQ meat lovers, chicken and bacon, cheese, or Mexican?" she asked, scrolling through the menu on her computer.

"Let's get a chicken and bacon and a Mexican?"

"We hardly need two pizzas between us!" Parker protested. Sometimes Nathan's eyes were bigger than his belly.

"Let's get two anyway. Then we can share leftovers for lunch tomorrow and make Kelly jealous. And get garlic bread, too, please. And salad."

Parker shook her head but indulged him with the large order. Twenty or thirty minutes later, she was surprised when the doorbell rang again. "Wow, that was fast." She opened the door and was confused to see Scott standing there. "Scott? Oh, I was expecting a pizza."

"I'm not a pizza," he said, smiling. "I heard Nathan might be here, and I thought it could be fun to crash your evening."

"Oh, right." Parker couldn't help but feel annoyed—she'd been keen to spend time chatting to Nathan, but that was now off the cards. Still, trying to be optimistic about it, it would be good for her to get to know Scott a bit more. "Come on in." Turning to Nathan, she said, "Luckily, we ordered the extra pizza. Scott's here."

Nathan didn't look as surprised as she felt, and she couldn't help wondering if he'd invited him. If that was the case, she was even more disappointed, as they were overdue for a catch-up. It would make sense, given his insistence they order two pizzas. She secretly rolled her eyes as they greeted each other but then settled in to chat to the two guys. Within about five minutes, the doorbell rang again. She sighed but knew this time it would be the pizzas. Opening the door, she was shocked to see Lily standing there, grinning, and holding a bunch of flowers. "Hi?" Parker said.

"Hi," Lily said in response.

"Nathan and Scott are here." She pointed into the house.

"Are they?" Lily's grin told Parker all she needed to know—this had been a plan they were all in.

"It's Tuesday night. Our night." Lily shrugged and tried to hide a smile. "So I thought I'd come and say g'day."

"G'day." Parker couldn't wipe the grin off her face although her mind was racing, wondering what it all meant. It wasn't the time to wonder though. She just wanted to live in the moment and enjoy Lily's company. "Come in." Addressing the room, she said, "And it turns out Lily's here too."

"What a surprise!" Nathan exclaimed.

Parker nodded. "A surprise to me. Luckily you insisted on your mammoth pizza order though there goes my lunch for tomorrow now."

The fourth doorbell for the evening brought no more surprises—it was the pizzas. They spent time putting pizza, salad, and garlic bread on plates, grabbing drinks, and then getting comfortable, with Nathan and Scott sitting on one sofa, and Parker and Lily on the other.

"So, tonight is just a social catch-up?" Parker said before biting into her pizza.

Lily nodded. "We had a catch-up on the weekend, and we had so much fun, we didn't want you to miss out. We figured we'd bring the fun to you."

"I didn't know you'd all caught up. Nathan had mentioned he and Scott had dinner on the weekend," Parker said.

"Dinner and a *sleepover*!" Lily emphasised. "Bodhi went to a friend's house."

"Where is Bodhi tonight?"

"Aunt Jacqui's." Apparently, this was all well-planned. "We haven't yet told Bodhi about the change in Dad's relationship status, but we will. We just want the time to be right."

Parker hoped there might be potential to share with Bodhi a change in both Mum *and* Dad's relationship statuses. Did she dare hope that this was what the surprise visit was about? It was a Tuesday, after all.

"Wow, that's great," she said when she finally spoke.

Nathan nodded and looked at Scott with a twinkle in his eye. Scott grinned back at him.

"Aww, you guys are so cute," Parker said. She hadn't seen Nathan so comfortable with a guy in a long time. Lily smiled at the two guys and then smiled at Parker. She naturally smiled back and couldn't help feeling a pang of envy at Nathan and Scott for seemingly having it all worked out.

As they continued to eat the pizzas, they discussed what they'd all been up to, how work was going, and Lily shared how her new staff were settling in. "They need a bit of training, but they're great so far. Very en-thusiastic."

"That's fantastic."

"It's a real help because we have a few schools hiring us for our par-enting programs. I can't believe it; it all seems to be going well."

"Do you have one focusing on one aspect or the other?" Parker asked, genuinely interested.

"Yes, Erin is mostly working on the magazine and Alex mostly on the events, as it's a new initiative and that's his thing. But they both pitch in wherever. We all do. It's a joint effort." Lily shrugged and smiled, looking a little bashful.

Parker felt nothing but pride and admiration toward Lily. She was impressed with her energy and drive. She shook her head in marvel, grin-ning, and Lily got even more embarrassed.

Thankfully Scott interrupted, as it had started to feel like they were alone in their own world until then. "You should ask your school to invite Lily and Jacqui to present."

Nathan nodded. "We can do that, can't we, Parker?"

Parker shrugged. "You've been there long than me. But I don't see why not."

"All right, I'll talk to Anthea on Monday." Anthea, the school principal, was quite inspiring, and Parker had taken a liking to her already.

"All right, let's liven this evening up a bit," Parker said. "I wasn't really expecting more than Nathan tonight, but I reckon I've got enough ice cream in that freezer of mine to serve you up a bowl each?" Everyone nodded enthusiastically.

Nathan rolled his eyes. "Please. Parker is the queen of dessert. I'm sure she has about four different tubs of ice cream in there. A small army could turn up unexpectedly, and she may not have enough food for them, but dessert she'd have."

"You never know when you'll get the craving." She rummaged through the freezer. "Not four! Three." She had vanilla, chocolate chip cookie dough, and English toffee ice creams, so everyone piled their bowls high with their choices.

"Bodhi will love visiting here if you're really the ice cream woman. And why did you never offer me ice cream whenever I've visited before? It's like a secret stash I never knew about."

Parker went to reply, but Nathan started speaking first. "I don't really think you were here for ice cream," he quipped. "I think Parker had other things on her mind, if you get my drift…" He had a comical look on his face.

Scott said, "I think we all get your drift."

Parker blushed, more worried about how Lily would feel about the attention on them, especially in Scott's presence, but when she finally looked at her, Lily was grinning too. Blushing a little, but looking more happy and flushed than being completely mortified.

"True, we had some fun times—didn't we, Parker?" She gave Parker a cheeky grin, and then Scott shook his head.

"And all behind my back," he chastised lightly. "And here I was, thinking *we* were best friends."

"We are best friends." She put her arm around him, grinning. "And how lucky are we? Two best friends to have found an amazing best friend set here?" She glanced at Parker and Nathan. "You've just nabbed yours, and I still have a bit of work to do to get mine."

Parker pulled her head backwards in surprise. She hadn't expected Lily to be so brazen in front of the two guys. Come to think of it, maybe that was *why* she was being brazen—the cheeky atmosphere was giving her confidence. But she caught Lily's eye and gave her a knowing smile. Lily gave her a dazzling smile back that nearly melted Parker's heart.

Catching it, Scott said to Nathan, "You right to drive me home? Let's eat these ice creams and go. I think the girls have some chatting to do."

Nathan winked at him. "Chatting? I'm not so sure about that."

Scott shook his head, grinning. "You're crazy," he said, laughing. "Anyway, will you take me home? I took a cab."

Nathan raised his eyebrows at Scott. "Absolutely. I'll take you home." The inuendo was clear.

Parker savoured her ice cream, while the guys rushed eating their bowls. "Would you like us to take the pizza boxes out to the bin?" Scott asked, as he tidied up a few of the glasses.

She was grateful, but told him there was no need; she'd clean it up later. She didn't want to delay their departure. Both Nathan and Scott gave the two women pecks on the cheek and walked out the door holding hands.

"They're cute," Parker said, gazing after them before she shut the door. She turned to Lily. "How do you feel about Scott dating now?"

Lily shrugged, and Parker joined her on the couch. "I'm surprised. I was surprised he was dating and definitely surprised it was Nathan."

"Nathan told me he had a crush on him after the beach."

"Did he? I didn't even realise."

"Yeah, he was asking me if he was gay, and I didn't tell him for a while. Nathan usually isn't a relationship guy, so I wanted him to run a mile away from Scott, and *not* go there! But he seems really invested." She smiled.

"Scott does too. It's nice."

"And how does it make you feel?"

Lily pondered for a minute. "I'm happy. I can overthink the future: What if they live together? What if Nathan doesn't want to live with me?" Parker nodded and Lily continued, "But ultimately I think let's just let them enjoy getting to know each other. Who knows what the future could hold for any of us?"

"Exactly. And what about your future?"

"Scott told me you had a girlfriend."

Damn Nathan!

"Not a girlfriend." Parker shook her head. "I met a girl online. We've been on a few dates now."

"And?"

"And, before tonight, I was already going to tell her I didn't think it was right. She isn't the girl for me."

"And why is that?" Lily raised an eyebrow.

"Because I'd already met the girl for me. And because…just because."

"Okay. Well, then you sort that out, and let me know when it's done." Lily paused for a moment and then added, "A few dates? How serious?"

"Just dates—in public. We kissed." Parker wanted to be honest. Lily looked relieved. "Are you happy for a relationship, Lily? Now that Scott's dating? Will you be my girlfriend, or my friend with amazing benefits?"

Lily gave her a smile. "I want to be your girlfriend. But if not, I'll be just your friend. No benefits. It's too hard for us both. The feelings are too strong."

"Well, in that case, you better be my girlfriend." Parker couldn't have been happier.

"Great. After you've ended things with your girlfriend."

"Cat. And she's not my girlfriend, but thank you. I understand and fully respect that."

A worried look crossed Lily's face. "What if Scott and Nathan break up? Or you and me? It could be messy, a set of best friends dating another set of best friends? What do you think?"

"I think you worry too much," Parker said kindly. She understood Lily had a lot more at risk than she did, but she knew you couldn't guarantee a future. Lily did too. She would know that better than anyone.

Lily smiled sadly. "I know I do. I'm a planner. And an overthinker. But I also know you can't plan." There—Lily had said out loud what Parker had been thinking. "Perhaps better than most. I know that. I also know I need to stop thinking and start living."

"That sounds great. And I want to be part of your life, but like I've said before, I don't want to replace Megan. I'd love to hear all about her. And as a family, with Bodhi, we can honour her."

Lily looked gratefully at Parker. "Thank you. Now, I better get home before I kiss you!"

"Would that be such a bad thing?" Parker asked, raising her eyebrows.

"I don't know. I just think… Scott said you had a girlfriend…"

Parker cringed. She really was cranky with Nathan for that! "Like I said…she's not my girlfriend, and she's under no illusions of that. We went out a few times. She asked me home the other night. Maybe not directly, but she implied it. I didn't go. We went for lunch on Saturday, but I made an excuse to leave. I haven't heard from her since, but I haven't contacted her either." Parker knew she sounded like she was pleading with Lily, and she wasn't trying to. "But, I agree. Tonight, you should go home, and let's start fresh. I'll take you on a date. Saturday?"

Lily smiled. "Saturday works, I think. I'll double-check with Scott. Where will you take me?"

"I don't know. Somewhere fancy. I want to see you all dressed up. And tell Scott you won't be home that night."

Chapter Twenty-Nine

LILY

Lily was putting the finishing touches on her make-up and looked at herself in the mirror. She had a fitted, chocolate-brown dress on, with a matching cardigan. The look was sexy, but not over the top. When she walked past the kitchen, she saw Scott, Nathan, and Bodhi about to sit down to dinner. They'd explained to him earlier in the week that Nathan and Parker had become friends with Mum and Dad. He'd said he already known that—they'd gone to the beach together, after all. They hadn't yet had the proper relationship chat with him. Lily really wanted to see how things went with Parker first, but she expected they'd soon enough be talking about that. It was hard to know how to tackle it though. What did a relationship mean to an eight-year-old? How could you make a new romance sound age appropriate, but also different from a friendship? That was something they'd have to work out between the four of them or at least between her and Scott.

"Have a nice night, Mum!" Bodhi said. "You should have had Ms Parker over here tonight. We could have all played board games."

"That would have been nice, wouldn't it? But Ms Parker and I wanted to try a new restaurant. They do seven or eight different courses. They'll have to roll me out of the restaurant at the end." When Parker had suggested a degustation, Lily was thrilled—she'd always wanted to try one. It did indeed sound fancy.

"I couldn't eat eight courses," Bodhi said, laughing. "And I eat a lot!"

"They're mini courses, I think, but I'll take some photos for you and show you tomorrow."

"Okay." He grinned and then bit into his chicken schnitzel.

"Have fun," Nathan said, and then he raced around to the other side of the table to give her a peck on the cheek. He seemed like a great guy, and she thought his enthusiasm for their growing friendship was genuine. He always greeted her with a kiss and seemed pleased to spend any time with her, which was so important, given she lived and co-parented with his partner. She only hoped the positivity between them continued.

"Yes, have a lovely time," Scott said, waving from the table. They'd never had a particularly affectionate relationship although he had started to peck Lily on the cheek whenever Nathan did, clearly following his lead, either consciously or subconsciously.

"You guys have fun too. Buy Park Place, Bodhi." She winked at him and walked out the door.

*

"WOW," PARKER SAID when she opened the door. "You look amazing." Parker grabbed her into a bear hug and then kissed her.

"Mmm," Lily said, breaking away from the kiss. "I've missed that."

"Me too," Parker said before kissing her once more, moaning into her mouth.

"Careful, or we won't want to go to dinner," Lily said, laughing and taking a step back. "Wow, you look incredible."

Parker had a white shirt on with fitted black pants. The white shirt offset her olive skin perfectly, and her bright blue eyes were dazzling. Lily felt like melting back into her arms. "Let's go," she said quickly, placing her overnight bag by the kitchen bench. She readjusted her handbag as a signal she was ready. Parker nodded and placed her wallet into her back pocket. Picking up her keys, she escorted Lily out the door where they waited for a taxi.

*

"GOOD EVENING," THE waitress said as she greeted them at the door. "Reservation?"

Parker nodded. "We have a booking for Parker."

"Sure, this way please." She seated them at a table in a corner of the room with shimmering candles reflecting on the crisp, white tablecloths. "You're having the nine-course degustation?" she asked.

"Yes, with the matched wines, please," Parker said. The waitress nodded and then swiftly disappeared, before returning with new cutlery, which she set rapidly on the table. Lily gave Parker a bemused smile, shaking her head at the waitress's speed. When they were finally alone, Lily took the opportunity to speak.

"Nine courses? I thought it was seven!" Lily said. She wasn't sure how she'd fit it all in.

Parker gave her a killer smile. "It'll be fine. Trust me." Soon, the first course arrived—a mousse made of sweet potato, with various flavourings and topped with goat cheese that tasted much more incredible than it should have from how it sounded.

The chef had designed a menu with the most intricate attention to detail. Both Parker and Lily loved every single course—each one seemed better than the last. There was a sorbet, various meats—from chicken, to duck, to lamb, and kangaroo, all cooked in the most amazing ways. Small, tender portions, accompanied with vegetable mousses, sauces, garnishes, or little sides, so each mouthful exploded with flavour.

"Wow," Lily said, shaking her head after eating a bite of duck with an onion sauce, feta cheese, and an orange sauce over the top. "That's remarkable."

"I don't know how they come up with the combinations," Parker said. "But they seem to all work amazingly."

"They certainly do. And each course looks like a piece of art. I almost don't want to eat it!"

"Is that why you've been photographing each course?" She'd seemed surprised when Lily had whipped out her phone to photograph the courses, but Lily had never seen food look so beautiful and wanted to show her parents and Jacqui. Plus, she'd promised Bodhi she would show him photos.

"I told Bodhi I would," she said, blushing and laughing.

"Oh, really? That's great. How was he?"

"He wanted to know why you weren't keen to just come over and play games with his dad and Nathan."

"Aww, that's sweet," Parker said. "I will have to come over soon."

Lily nodded. "I think he'd love that. He seemed pretty chuffed to have Nathan over tonight. They were eating chicken schnitzels and playing board games. He won't want an early night, and I'm sure Scott and Nathan would love him to have an early night." They laughed in response, just imagining the difficulty the guys would face getting an excited eight-year-old off to bed.

"Chicken schnitzels, hey? That's one of my favourite foods, but after tonight," Parker said, gesturing to her lamb course. "I don't know if I could eat some massive fried thing again. I think I'm ruined now. Gourmet morsels of delicacies for me from here on out."

"I hope you have a personal chef, then. My speciality is cheese on toast."

"Mine is baked beans on toast. No, I lie, I do make a mean bacon and eggs breakfast."

Lily nodded. "I lie too. I'm a fairly good cook, but nothing like this."

"Yeah, my mum and dad really encouraged us to cook. As teenagers, the three of us would have to cook once a week. Then Mum and Dad cooked one night each, and there was a night for a dinner out or takeaway night, and a night for 'Find whatever you can.' Toast and baked beans, noodles, bacon and eggs." She shrugged. "I used to make spaghetti bolognaise almost every week, but sometimes I'd mix it up—tacos, burritos, or lasanga. Always mince! Briony and Nick tried a new recipe each week, but I didn't like following recipes. I still don't. I tend to cook about ten different dishes, and that's it. Oh well, at least I can cook."

Lily nodded. "I'm like your siblings. I follow recipes. I enjoy looking at cookbooks and picking out something."

"You'll need to cook for me some time," Parker said, grinning.

Lily liked her confidence—Parker didn't seem to be the type of person who'd struggle to ask for what she needed in a relationship, and Lily liked that. It was always something she'd admired in Megan too. Perhaps they weren't as different as she'd initially thought. Still, thinking of Megan gave her a pang of guilt. Sometimes she wondered what she was doing pursuing a relationship, but she reassured herself by knowing that Megan would have wanted it.

The meal was amazing. Lily enjoyed their discussion and getting to know Parker a little more. Sometimes she thought she knew so much about her already, but other times she was reminded that there was so much more to know. And she was looking forward to finding out all about her.

By the end of the meal they felt incredibly satisfied—not over full, but certainly a little on the tipsy side.

"Let's go for a stroll," Parker said, and they walked by the lake, the moonlight, and nearby lights, shimmering on the waterfront. It was a beautiful evening, and as they strolled in contented silence, they held hands and smiled at each other from time to time.

Returning to Parker's house, they retreated to the bedroom immediately, and enjoyed the same benefits they had enjoyed many times before, but this time, as girlfriends, not only as friends.

*

PARKER ROLLED OVER in bed and kissed Lily. "Good morning. Bacon and eggs?"

Lily cuddled Parker. "Not so fast. We had a huge meal last night; you can't be hungry just yet. Stay and cuddle."

"One thing you'll learn about me is that I'm always hungry. But cuddles trump hunger, so let's stay in bed a little longer."

"Or a lot longer," Lily said, and she began stroking Parker's body.

*

AFTER THE BREAKFAST dishes were washed and the women were showered, Lily was feeling a little anxious about getting back to Bodhi. "It's crazy. I know he's fine with the guys. I just don't spend loads of time without him."

"Well, you should go home. I'm okay if you want to."

Lily felt torn. She was enjoying their time together but more than anything, she wanted to be surrounded by her family and Parker, together. "Come over."

"What?" Parker said, laughing.

"Come over. We can take Bodhi out grocery shopping to get organised for the week ahead. I'll do a cook up. I'll double-check with Scott if you're keen."

Parker grinned. "I want to be wherever you are."

An hour later, they arrived home to Lily's house. Bodhi was thrilled to see his teacher in his house and was full of stories about his evening and morning with his dad and Nathan. He had won his board game. The atmosphere was buzzing, but all Lily wanted to do was reach out and put her arm around Parker while they were talking, and from the gazes she got from her, the feeling was mutual. It just felt so natural to want to be together.

After chatting for some time, Lily suggested they go grocery shopping for the week, and Bodhi jumped at the chance to shop with Parker. They went to a grocery store a little farther away from home because there would be less chance of running into school families. Parker took the opportunity to spoil him, buying him chocolate milk and a packet of lollies. Bodhi was thrilled, and his mother grinned, but shook her head and rolled her eyes comically. This made Bodhi and Parker buddy up and have a giggle together, so Lily kept up the act of disapproval. She loved seeing Bodhi and Parker having a laugh together, even when it was at her expense. She felt content. Her heart was warm, and she enjoyed being a couple, spending time with her son. She'd always imagined grocery shopping or hanging out with the kids with Megan by her side, but right now, she was very happy to have Parker there with her.

Chapter Thirty

PARKER

Parker sat back in her chair and looked around the table. Bodhi had gone to bed about half an hour earlier, and it was time she went home and got organised for the week ahead. She'd spent the afternoon helping Lily cook up some meals for lunches and dinners and prepare dinner for the evening. She'd even packed Bodhi's lunch for school. She'd chatted a lot with Scott and Nathan, and finally got roped into a board game with Bodhi. It was a great afternoon. Low key, relaxed, and chilled out, but definitely domestic. The kind of domestic weekend she'd never imagined, but she felt more content than she would have ever anticipated. Every so often she'd stolen a look with Lily, but not being able to reach out and touch her in front of Bodhi had felt torturous. They needed to discuss that, and Parker decided to raise it around the table.

"I don't want anyone to feel pressured, so please feel free to say 'Shut up, Parker,' but…"

"Shut up, Parker," Nathan and Lily both said in unison and then cracked up laughing.

"Snap!" Nathan said, and that started Scott laughing too.

Parker rolled her eyes. "If you're finished…" She glared but was enjoying the light-hearted spirit in the room. "If you're finished, I'll talk. I'm just wondering what the plan is from here. We have two couples and some people who should probably know about us."

"People?" Lily asked, her brow creasing in confusion. "Or just Bodhi?"

"Bodhi, and Mrs Jackman, the school principal."

"Oh." Lily shot a worried look first to Scott, and then to Nathan and Parker.

Parker nodded. "I think we should tell Anthea. Today, we went to the shops fifteen minutes away, but we won't always want to, and we wouldn't want to feel like we're deceiving anyone."

"You tell her, then," Nathan said. "But I don't know if I have to."

"Hey, you're dating a school parent too."

He shrugged. "Not a parent of a kid in my class."

"While we're doing the disclosures, I'd just do it. I don't know if you need to, but it can't hurt," Parker said.

"What if she asks how we got together? Well Ms Parker was just friends with benefits with a school mum, but then Mr Stenlake and Scott met, and…" Nathan quipped, smiling.

"It's going to be so awkward," Parker agreed, "but I think we stick to the facts. I knew Lily before school, and we reconnected and the four of us caught up, and…"

Lily nodded. "That sounds reasonable. But maybe you should lock her in for my parenting program before you tell her!"

Everyone laughed.

"What?" Lily asked. She must have been serious in her request, but Parker knew she had to tell her boss sooner rather than later and told her so. Lily agreed.

"So, that awkward conversation over, how do you tell an eight-year-old?" Lily asked and then looked over toward Scott for his thoughts.

He shrugged. "That's another awkward conversation."

Eight-year-olds were Parker's expertise, so she chimed in. "Well, it doesn't have to be, does it? Does he understand the story about you and Megan?"

Lily nodded.

"So, he doesn't think you and Scott are a couple or anything?"

Lily shook her head.

"And does he know you're gay?" She looked at Scott.

He nodded and then added, "But what that means to him, exactly, I don't know."

"But he understands some boys like boys, and some girls like girls?"

They both nodded, so she shrugged. "Well I think you just explain that it's been a long time since Mama Megan passed away, and you love her very much, and she had wanted you, one day, to meet someone. And…" Parker now blushed a little, before adding, "Then you say how much you adore me, how charming and wonderful I am, how you couldn't resist me, and…don't forget to say how incredible I am…. And all of that."

Lily grabbed Parker's hand. "Perfect. I'll say it exactly like that."

"And you say that Daddy met Nathan at the beach that day, and they became friends, and realised they liked each other. Does that sound like it would all make sense to Bodhi?"

"I think so. What do you think?" Lily looked to Scott for feedback.

"I think it sounds great," he said. "Unless you have another strategy, being another teacher of eight-year-olds." He glanced at Nathan for advice.

"No, Parker has a good plan there. The question is do you do it together, or apart? And with or without Parker and me?"

"Without," everyone said and laughed amongst themselves.

"Great. We're all in agreement. You two talk to the principal, and Scott and I'll talk to Bodhi. I guess the goal here is to get Bodhi comfortable seeing us together, and maybe having sleepovers," Lily said.

"I had to sneak out at about five this morning and sleep in the spare room." Nathan said.

"Yes, so eventually we want to do away with that. But I will warn you, it might take some time. That's the challenge of dating parents," Lily admitted. "The kids come first."

"But, we can take turns and go to your places," Scott said. "Like last night, Lil went to Parker's. I could go to your house one weekend." He looked towards Nathan.

"Yes, a good measure while Bodhi gets comfortable with it all. Ideally, we don't want to spend loads of time away from him, but it could be a good idea initially," Lily agreed.

"I had another idea," Parker said. "I was going to suggest taking Bodhi camping next weekend. The five of us."

"Oh, that's a great idea. Maybe I could bring along Tyson too," Nathan said, looking at Scott.

"Tyson?" asked Lily, her brow creasing in confusion.

"Tyson is my ten-year-old nephew," he explained to Lily. "I've been thinking he could be good company for Bodhi, and he loves camping."

"Great. Bodhi will love the company and he'd love to go camping. Maybe we can tell him when we share the whole thing," Lily said, glancing at Scott as she spoke. Scott nodded at her suggestion.

*

ON MONDAY, PARKER woke feeling a sense of dread. Anthea Jackman was probably about fifteen years older than Parker and quite sage in how she gave out advice. She was always friendly whenever she saw Parker and would seek her out in a crowd to check in with her. She certainly wasn't scary, but Parker still felt uncomfortable whenever she had to see a school principal, and today's topic was certainly doing nothing to calm her nerves.

She didn't know what it was about visiting a principal's office, but she still felt like the naughty school girl she once was whenever she made her way there. Most people assumed teachers were good school kids, and that was probably correct for most teachers, but Parker was certainly not the good school kid. In primary school she was fairly well behaved, but only because she was shy and kept to herself. She wasn't loud, she certainly wasn't disruptive, and she followed the rules, but it was merely not to draw attention to herself. Little Louise Parker did not want to be well known, and certainly didn't want a teacher talking to her unnecessarily.

By the time she'd gotten to high school, Parker felt more self-confident, and found a tribe of friends. Much to her parents' dismay, the tribe she associated with were more disruptive, and sometimes even liked to skip classes. Parker claimed she just went along with it—she was never one to say no to someone's request, and that was part of her problem as a young teenager. By the end of high school, she'd developed a bit of a reputation as someone you didn't mess with. She was never quite sure how—she wouldn't hurt a mouse!—but it must have been her appearance. It meant that even the teachers judged her, despite the fact she'd never done anything particularly bad.

Parker was never quite sure how she ended up a teacher. She started studying an arts degree, but after doing a childhood development unit, opted to move into education. She had no idea what career she would end up in, but she felt at home in education and surprised herself by how much she enjoyed it. She approached the whole thing intellectually, considering childhood development and what was in a child's best interests. She surprised herself by doing remarkably well. Meeting Nathan was the cherry on top. She suddenly had a best friend, an interesting education, and felt like she had a clear path ahead.

She'd never really outgrown her fear of principals, although she'd worked with, and impressed, her fair share of them as an adult. Going to the principal's office to discuss such a personal matter as her relationship was daunting. The fact that it was still early days in her relationship with Lily made her worried it was overkill, but she really wanted to be honest with Anthea, mainly so she could feel free to enjoy Lily's company. It might be early days, but she'd never felt so sure before. She was doing this to feel comfortable with Lily by her side. Having Nathan by her side in the meeting certainly helped. He'd talked with Anthea's assistant and organised an appointment with her for after school. Parker had rehearsed their opening line about fifteen times by the end of the day and still didn't know how to start the conversation.

*

"NATHAN, PARKER, HOW are you both doing?" Anthea said, smiling as they sat in the plush leather seats across from her. She shuffled some papers, piling them on top of a large pile, then pulled a notebook and pen in front of her.

"Going well, thanks," Parker said nervously. "I'm really loving my class."

"That's wonderful," Anthea beamed genuinely. "I'm really pleased to hear your transition here has been smooth so far. It's nice that you and Nathan have such a good friendship, too, and Kelly said the three of you really get along, which is lovely."

"Yes," Parker said, wondering what on earth to say.

"So what's on your mind? Linda didn't give me an agenda for today."

Parker shook her head. "Err…it's a personal matter."

Anthea frowned and looked between Nathan and Parker. Parker glanced at Nathan for moral support, then realised he wasn't going to speak up, so she did. "Look, I don't know how to say this, so I'm just going to say it." Seeing Anthea react to Parker's prelude made her even more anxious. Anthea looked concerned. "Nathan and I have…errr…developed relationships."

Anthea sat back in her sat and looked even more confused. "Oh. I thought you were both…gay."

Parker and Nathan laughed. "Sorry, not with one another," Parker clarified.

"Oh! You mean you've both entered relationships, but not with each other? Oh, thank goodness. I was so confused." Anthea laughed, perhaps a little self-conscious, and that set Nathan off laughing once again.

"I would never, ever…" He shook his head, and Parker glared at him.

"Thanks a lot," she muttered, but returning her gaze to Anthea, she tried to be as professional as possible. Well, as professional as possible while telling her boss she was now dating a school mum. "We've both started relationships with parents at the school. It's all very new."

"Oh," Anthea said, her eyebrows raising in surprise. "Both of you?"

Parker nodded. "The woman I've started to see is actually a parent in my class." She cringed. "Nathan is dating a father in my class."

"Wow. So your class is where all the action is," Anthea said and giggled.

Parker swallowed, more because she didn't know what to say or do, and was feeling anxious, trying to read Anthea's reaction. She didn't seem furious, but she did seem very surprised. "Well, nothing has happened in class," she finally said and then nearly kicked herself for saying it.

Anthea laughed again, and now spoke in a slightly high-pitched voice. "Oh, I would hope not. I just mean… Oh, never mind… Which parents are they?"

"They're Bodhi Delaney-Jones's parents," Nathan said.

"Oh, you're dating his mother *and* father? Lovely," Anthea said, and now it was impossible to read her reaction.

"When you say it like that… I mean… They've never been a couple," Parker said, stumbling over her words, and worrying she was oversharing. "I don't know if you know the story, but…" She shrugged. "I don't know. It's not like a 'Mum and Dad'. Just so you know."

Anthea's eyes glinted, and she tried to hide a smile, perhaps of embarrassment, but her grin was evident. "Yes, I don't know the story, but I did know they were not together. They live together, though, don't they?"

"They do," Nathan said.

"We really just wanted to let you know. I'm not sure if there's a process for this," Parker interrupted, wanting to stop focusing on the details.

"I can't say I've ever had a situation like this, not in my twenty years of school leadership." Anthea's brow creased in thought. "But I have had parents teach their own children before. Almost always when the teacher has taken over from someone who left the school. I don't think it would ever be intentional. It's deemed as appropriate, providing the report cards are moderated by someone else. Perhaps Kelly could provide support in this way. It's probably better than moving Bodhi to Kelly's class during the school year."

Parker was relieved. She didn't want him to have to face upheaval because of his parents' relationships. She nodded. "I think that would be best for Bodhi. Please, rest assured that I will be incredibly professional and not treat Bodhi differently in any way."

Anthea nodded and considered it further. "I will seek advice from one of my colleagues at another school, just to be confident I'm making the right decision here. I really like you, Parker, and I've been really impressed with you since you started at the school. It's important that I get an impartial view from someone who doesn't know you."

Parker was flattered by her kind words and also completely understood why Anthea needed a second opinion. "Of course, that sounds good."

"I'm less concerned about the situation with Nathan, but I really appreciate you both coming forward. It's not that I don't trust you, Parker, it's just..."

"I understand." She nodded. "I'd absolutely do the same in your position."

*

ONCE THEY SAID farewell and left the office, Parker finally breathed a sigh of relief. She turned to Nathan and said, "That was the hardest thing I've ever had to do. Let's go for something sugary. I need to debrief."

He rolled his eyes. "Oh, c'mon, she was a pussy cat. It was easy."

"Please! My face is burning; my armpits are sweating. Easy? I felt like I'd cheated in the history exam!"

He shook his head in amusement.

"Oh, it's okay for you. You hardly spoke!" Parker said and gently whacked him.

They made their way to the local coffee shop, where they ordered shakes and donuts, and talked about how mortified she was feeling, and how calm he was. "Ultimately, it was a good reaction. Anthea's good," he said.

She nodded. "It was a good reaction, but it doesn't change how awkward that felt. I really hope they're worth it," she joked.

"You know they are. We've both hit relationship gold here," he said seriously for a moment.

It threw Parker off-kilter a bit; she wasn't really used to Nathan being so serious. She smiled at him and nodded. "We're so lucky. Who ever thought we'd end up dating best friends?"

"I certainly didn't," he said, his eyes twinkling.

"I didn't foresee you ever in a relationship. But it's really all on, isn't it?

He nodded. "Funny how it hits you. He's amazing. Sexy, fun, smart…"

"I'm so happy for you both. I can't believe I thought he was Lily's husband."

They both laughed, and she continued, "Have you said the *L* word yet?"

Nathan smiled. "He said it first. On the weekend actually."

"I am too scared to. Because of Megan. So, I'm leaving it to her."

He looked at Parker, a little confused. "Why because of Megan?"

She shrugged. "I don't know. I guess I just think it would be a big step for her. There's no rush. I know how I feel. That won't change. I want her to set the pace." She glanced down at the table, and then back up at her best friend. "Do you believe in love at first sight? I feel like I knew even back then!"

Nathan rolled his eyes and gave her a cheeky grin. "The way you carried on about the amazing night you had, I'd say you're right. Ugh, it was intense!"

"Exactly. And I think I got there in the feelings stake much earlier than Lily. Lily still might not be feeling it, you know. I'm not going to push it. I'll leave it to her to work out how she feels. It'll happen in good time, I'm sure, and if not, better I don't make a fool of myself. I've never dated someone who was still in love with their previous partner before, and she always will be. It won't change. It can't."

"That must be hard. The way Scott talks about her… She sounds like an amazing woman."

"It's so hard to compete with that." For all her confidence and bravado with women, in love, Parker lacked confidence.

"You're amazing, too, Parker," he said, reaching out to squeeze her hand. "Don't ever forget it. And if Lily's worth your time, she'll see it too. Assuming she hasn't already. I suspect she has."

"Thanks," she said, feeling relieved.

*

WHEN SHE GOT home, Parker rang Lily and filled her in on the conversation with Anthea. Lily was amused by Parker's exaggerated tales about the sweat pooling at her feet, her hair sticking to her forehead, and literally shaking in her boots. As she climbed into bed, Parker felt pleased she'd approached the matter tactfully, and as maturely as possible. She hoped Lily and Scott's conversation with Bodhi was also going well.

Chapter Thirty-One

LILY

After dinner, Scott, Lily, and Bodhi went into the lounge room with large bowls of ice cream.

"How's school, honey?" Lily asked.

"Good." Bodhi shrugged. "Molly was sitting beside me, but Ms Parker moved her because she kept talking. She's now sitting with Kayleigh, and Aidan is next to me."

"Ah, okay," Lily said. "Do you like sitting next to Aidan?"

"Yeah, but Ms Parker moved Molly because she was talking, and Aidan talks just as much, but I like what he says better anyway."

"Daddy and I are really pleased you like school," she said, and glanced at Scott, wondering what the best way to start the conversation might be. "We really like Ms Parker and Mr Stenlake."

"It was fun having them over," Bodhi said, grinning. "Mr Stenlake really isn't good at board games. I thought a teacher would be."

"I'll tell him you said that."

"No, don't!" Bodhi giggled. "I might get in trouble for being rude or hurt his feelings!"

Lily grinned. Bodhi was such a thoughtful child.

"Bodhi, would you like to go away with Mr Stenlake and Ms Parker? We were thinking of going camping next weekend," Lily asked, glancing at Scott for feedback.

"Camping? Yeah, I'd love to go camping. Yay."

"And a ten-year-old boy called Tyson might come," Scott said. "That will be fun. He's Mr Stenlake's nephew."

"Cool." Bodhi scraped his ice cream bowl. This wasn't getting them anywhere in terms of Bodhi's understanding, so Lily took a deep breath, and just decided to launch into it.

"Baby, you know how Mummy Megan and I were in love?"

Bodhi nodded.

"I haven't dated anyone since Mummy Megan. And Daddy hasn't dated anyone either. But we both really like Mr Stenlake and Ms Parker, and we are going to go on some dates with them. Daddy and Mr Stenlake will go on dates, and me and Ms Parker," she clarified to be sure Bodhi understood.

"Really? Wow."

"You can call Mr Stenlake Nathan when we are outside school," Scott said. "But Ms Parker's name is Parker, so you can just call her Parker at home."

Bodhi nodded. "What do I call her when we're camping?"

Lily smiled. "Dad means call her Parker outside of school, so at camping you can call her Parker. But sometimes you might still call her Ms Parker. She's still your teacher."

"Is she my stepmum?" he asked, frowning in confusion.

Lily shook her head. "No, she's not your stepmum. Maybe one day, but we'll let you know if that happens. And same with Nathan. He's not your stepdad, but maybe someday."

"Okay," Bodhi said. He smiled and then blushed a little. "I sometimes wish I still had two mums. I would like to have a stepmum one day."

Lily was relieved.

"And what about two dads?" Scott asked.

Bodhi shrugged. "Yeah, I think so. I've only ever had one dad, so I haven't really thought about it, but I used to have two mums."

Lily wiped a tear out of her eye. "Honey, Mummy Megan will always be your mum. You've still got two mums," she smiled. "Maybe one day you could have a third mum."

He nodded. "I love you, Mum," he said, and hugged her. "And Dad, I love you." He reached over and gave Scott a hug. Lily and Scott caught each other's eyes, and both gave a smile that was a mixture of happiness, relief, and sadness.

"It's almost bedtime," Scott said. "But I reckon we stay up a little later tonight and watch a half hour TV show?"

Lily nodded in relief. It was a great idea so that Bodhi wasn't going to sleep immediately after the serious conversation. Scott always seemed to suggest activities like this at just the right time. The rest of the evening went well—Scott put some silly sitcom on, and everyone laughed along.

Lily wasn't exactly concentrating but laughed along with them. It wasn't that she was faking, it was that their laughter was infectious, and she was thrilled to see Bodhi so carefree, despite making the biggest announcement of his life to date. She knew that this could absolutely change his life—if the two promising relationships continued down the path they were going, they could become a family of five, not a family of three. What would that mean for Bodhi? She hoped it would all be positive—more people to love him surely couldn't be a bad thing—but she also knew change could be overwhelming for a child. Bodhi had experienced a lot of change in his life already. Lily couldn't help but worry, but also knew they had to take it day by day.

Bodhi was a good kid. They'd work it out.

*

BODHI COULDN'T HAVE been more excited about the weekend camping trip. "Maybe we've deprived him," Lily said to Scott, smiling, as they packed for the weekend away.

Scott shrugged. "Neither of us are really the camping types, are we?"

"We did do that camping trip with him once."

Scott had an amused smile as he said, "Lil, we stayed in a two-bedroom cabin. With a kitchenette."

Lily laughed and said, "It felt like camping."

"Well, I'm afraid Nathan and Parker seem like the real-deal camping types to me. I suspect there's a tent involved."

Lily pretended to fan herself in response. "Oh, God, help me," she said, and then added, more seriously, "I did ask, and Parker said they got us an en-suite site."

The amused look was back. "An en-suite site? What's that?"

"Apparently tents don't have bathrooms," Lily said, putting on a look of mock horror. "But they got us one with a loo and shower just for us. We don't have to go to the shower block with all the campers."

"Oh, that's a relief, isn't it?"

Lily nodded. "Absolutely. I'm not ready for a toilet block just yet."

*

LILY FEIGNED SHOCK and horror when they pulled up to the campsite, but the truth was she was looking forward to their weekend away. While she and Scott had never thought to take Bodhi camping—and never actually had experiences camping themselves—she was looking forward to experiencing it and letting Bodhi experience something new. Apparently, something new meant the car was jam-packed. With Tyson joining them, they'd taken two cars—Parker's and Nathan's. Apparently, their four-wheel drives were much better equipped to the camping lifestyle than Scott and Lily's sedans. Tyson and Bodhi had joined Parker and Lily in Parker's car, and Scott and Nathan carried most of the camping equipment.

Bodhi was a fairly shy kid, but Tyson was one of those kids that didn't leave room for shyness. He got familiar with Bodhi immediately, and they talked the entire two-hour car trip to the coast. Lily loved hearing them. It was sweet to see Bodhi having fun with a kid he'd just met, and someone who might become a 'cousin' to him. Their constant chatter also gave Lily and Parker an opportunity to chat. Parker had known Tyson since he was a baby. He was a big part of Nathan's life since birth, and so, by default, also a big part of Parker's life. They'd camped with Tyson as a trio, and they'd camped with Nathan's sister, her husband, and Tyson a number of times. Parker was just as delighted to see Bodhi and Tyson connecting.

"What do we do?" Lily asked, and Parker had explained that most of the fun of camping really was not planning anything at all. "Sitting in a camp chair, chatting. Getting so bored you play games, or watch birds, or go for a paddle in the water. It's really about unstructured days. Reading a book, going on a walk, and just relaxing."

"So that's the objective? To relax?" Lily had asked, and Parker had laughed in response. Again, she'd tried to explain there was no real objective, but that relaxation was important. "It might not be the objective, but by the end of a weekend of camping, you should feel relaxed. Just enjoy yourself. Do what you feel like doing, but don't feel like you have to plan anything."

Lily sighed. As a single mum, albeit one who co-parented with her housemate, or perhaps because of that, her entire life revolved around plans. Who was picking Bodhi up, who was cooking dinner, what groceries needed to be bought for the week ahead, how to juggle a busy work week with school and sporting events? Even weekends tended to be planned, from parties and play dates to sports. Lily even planned relaxation time for her weekends. She could barely remember life before she became a parent, but she was quite certain she hadn't planned every minute of her life before Bodhi came along. Whatever did she do with her time? She couldn't remember. Not for the first time, Lily wondered who she even was anymore. She felt like her whole life revolved around plans. Maybe—just maybe— being with Parker would have a really positive outcome on her.

"Do you usually plan your weekends?" Lily asked out of the blue.

Parker seemed surprised but thought for a moment. "Well it's hard to say. If I have something on, of course I plan it."

"Do you make a plan to relax?"

Parker chuckled in response and said, "I don't think so. Don't you just relax? I mean, I plan to relax this weekend, but that's nothing more than knowing we're going camping. Why?"

Lily smiled. "I was just thinking that the concept of relaxing all weekend is unusual to me. To have no plans. I plan everything. I even plan structured time to relax. Like after soccer on Sunday, we'll meal plan, grocery shop in the afternoon, and then relax prior to cooking dinner, then packing the school lunch."

"I assume you have to plan when you're a mum, though. You're not just organising yourself. But Bodhi is eight. Soon enough he'll be eighteen," Parker said.

"Oh, God!" Lily couldn't imagine a time when Bodhi was an adult. She wasn't sure she wanted to.

"No, but I mean, of course your life revolves around him, but you also have to know what makes Lily tick. What Lily likes."

Lily nodded. "Yes. I think this year has been my year of that. Just dating you is so different from how I lived my life before. I've devoted myself to Scott and Bodhi." She lowered her voice and, noticing Bodhi was laughing with Tyson, added, "And Megan."

Parker didn't respond, and Lily worried she'd upset her, but she was just being pensive. Suddenly she spoke up, "Maybe I can help you discover Lily a little bit. Help you find out what makes you really happy."

Lily smiled in response. "I'd love that. I haven't been unhappy, but with you, I think I can be even happier."

Parker reached over and grabbed Lily's hand. Lily wondered if Bodhi noticed and, if he did, whether he cared, but the chatter continued, the world didn't implode, and Lily's heart melted in happiness.

Chapter Thirty-Two

PARKER

The thing about camping is that no matter how practiced you were, or how well you'd planned things out, putting the tent up was always the most awful, or most funny, part of the entire camping trip. Over her years of camping, Parker had seen tent erecting lead to divorce for many couples who blamed one another for not doing it right, or not doing it as well as they did.

Parker was a pretty seasoned camper, and she and Nathan had spent a lot of time putting various tents up over the years. They almost always volunteered to help their camping neighbours. They were well practiced. This time, Nathan had brought his brand new, large family tent, which he'd initially purchased for large group camping trips, but was now coming in handy for the actual purpose—family camping. They'd never imagined when they'd bought this one that they could become pseudo-step-parents within the year.

"This looks complicated." Parker grimaced as they stood in front of sheets of coloured canvas.

Nathan shrugged. "We'll make it work."

She blew her cheeks out in response, showing Nathan she was already exasperated. She may have loved camping, but she never loved the set-up stage.

"Going okay?" Scott said, looking concerned. "I feel like, as a man, I should know what I'm doing, but that looks like the size of a mini circus tent, and there doesn't seem to be an instruction sheet, not even a build-it-yourself-furniture type of instruction sheet."

"Listen to him," Parker scoffed good-naturedly, "'as a man'. Let this *lady* show you how it's done." She winked at him, and he laughed in response.

Lily looked up, amused. "Don't listen to him. He can't even build IKEA stuff. John and Dad usually come over when we need to build something."

"Hey, I built that bookshelf."

"The one we got rid of recently because it always wobbled?" Lily tried to hide her smile.

"Hey! You're no better!" he said defensively.

"You're right." She nodded. "Im pretty crap at that stuff too. So you're on your own with the tent, I'm afraid."

"Lucky you scored yourself some pretty practical people in us, then," Parker said, laughing. She then looked at Nathan. "And listen to these two, squabbling. We're the ones putting the tent up. The rule of erecting any tent is that you end up squabbling, but you're doing a good enough job for the two of us. Maybe we won't squabble today, Nath."

"Perhaps not. Though you are putting the stake too close to mine. Step back."

She rolled her eyes but was amused. This was going to be a good weekend. She could feel it in her bones.

*

THE TENT WAS massive—four rooms. They set up a room for each of the couples, a room for the boys, and a sitting room where they put some camp chairs and stored bags. There was also an annexe where they placed some more camp chairs and a mini camp kitchen. By the time they finally sat down, they all laughed at how long the set-up had taken, and it seemed crazy, especially for a two-night getaway.

"It's pretty relaxing though," Lily said. "So worthwhile."

"Yeah, but you didn't set that beast of a tent up." Parker groaned but smiled as she spoke. "I reckon I deserve the night off camp cooking tonight. What do you say, Nath?"

Nathan nodded. "Yep, it's Lily and Scott's night tonight. So, what's for dinner?"

Lily said, "We were aiming for golden, battered fish, accompanied with potato chips, maybe a salad for the health conscious among you."

"You're making fish and chips?" Nathan asked, looking surprised. Lily shook her head and explained they'd planned to get fish and chips from the shop across the road. Parker was thrilled—nothing better than Friday night fish and chips.

"We can cook tomorrow night if you want us to," Lily said, "but tonight is relaxation night for all of us."

"I thought we'd do a barbeque tomorrow night," Scott said. "What do you think?"

Everyone nodded their consent, and after taking fish and chip orders, Scott and Lily got ready to order the takeaway. "Want to come with your mum and dad, Bodhi?" Scott asked.

Bodhi glanced at Tyson, and then shook his head. "Nah, I'll stay here with Tyson."

As Lily and Scott walked away, Parker thought two things—first, it still seemed so surprising to hear Lily and Scott collectively be called Mum and Dad as a unit, even though they were absolutely never a couple. Second, she thought how amazing Lily's ass looked in those jeans!

*

HEARING LILY'S GENTLE laughter as she and Scott made their way back to the campsite, laden down with bags and drinks, warmed Parker's heart. She'd had a nice time chatting with Nathan, Bodhi, and Tyson while they were gone and hadn't even realised how much she looked forward to seeing Lily again—she'd only been gone about forty minutes, for crying out loud! Parker had it bad. Luckily, it finally seemed that her feelings were reciprocated. Her heart full, she stood and greeted Lily by the table.

"You seem eager for dinner," Lily said, laughing. She had no clue that her eagerness to stand by Lily's side was not about the food—which smelt amazing—but was about being around her.

Parker smiled. "Are you feeding an army?"

Lily shrugged. "We weren't sure. We thought having a little extra was better than hungry tummies. Besides you and Nathan did all that work with the set-up, so we thought you might have worked up an appetite."

Parker winked at Lily. "It wasn't that much work. We griped, but it was nothing. I'm a fairly busy person, always finding work around the house or wherever I am. Give me a hammer or drill, and I'm happy."

"Really? Something about that turns me on," Lily said, shaking her head.

Parker reacted instantly, feeling a flutter in her pants. She stole a peck on Lily's lips and whispered, "Well, maybe we'll work up an appetite after dinner, not before." She grinned her cheeky grin and Lily blushed and shook her head.

"The walls are pretty thin," she said, pointing her head toward the tent. "I'm surprised Bodhi hasn't even questioned the bedroom configurations, but I'm not sure I'm ready for…that. I'd be too worried."

Parker completely understood, and she had to keep reminding herself she was Bodhi's teacher. It must be strange for him—to have gone from just having his mother and father around for most of his life to suddenly seeing them both in relationships, and with his teacher and another teacher at that. Though, glancing at Bodhi playing a card game with Tyson and laughing, she figured he'd barely even noticed what his parents were up to.

"Are we getting fed tonight, or what?" Nathan called out, snapping them out of their daze.

Scott joined Parker and Lily and dished fish and chips onto plates. "There's plenty more," Scott said, dumping parcels of fish and chips onto a table, "but eat up. If you're still hungry, please, don't be shy."

"We really did buy enough for an army," Lily said. "A small army, but an army nevertheless!"

"Good, I'm starving," Bodhi exclaimed.

"Me too! I really hope there's heaps," Tyson said, grabbing his plate. It was loaded high with fish, chips, and potato cakes, but he screwed up his face and said, "I'll definitely be having seconds."

Everyone laughed—the mood was light and fun, and stories were shared between mouthfuls of food. It was a lovely evening, and once everyone was busy eating and chatting, Parker sat back, surveying the scene. Her belly was full, but mostly, her heart was full. Seeing her best friend happy with a new guy while also chatting easily with the woman she had well and truly fallen for made her happier than she'd been in years.

*

"I WASN'T SURE if we'd be sleeping on the ground. I'm pleased you brought air mattresses," Lily confessed, laughing as they climbed into bed.

Parker grinned at her. She usually did camp with air mattresses—life was too short to sleep on the ground!—and between her and Nathan, they'd packed enough for everyone, with double mattresses for the two couples. Bodhi and Tyson were tucked up in their 'tent room' and absolutely thrilled to have their own room.

Nathan and Scott were still outside talking by the fire, and Lily and Parker had opted to go to bed. They climbed into the sleeping bags placed on top of the air mattress, laughing as they had to manoeuvre their bodies this way and that to get comfortable. Once they did, Parker wriggled close to Lily and started to kiss her. Breaking away and glancing down at the green sleeping bag she was encased in, Lily laughed and said, "These things are the modern day chastity belt, aren't they?"

Parker laughed in response and spoke quietly. "Well, I could have joined the two, but it's warmer to have your own, and you said before you wouldn't be in the mood with all our flatmates just a flimsy wall away."

"You're probably right, although Bodhi sleeps soundly, and I'm sure he'd sleep through, being completely worn out already. But I disagree with you about the warmth. Surely the body heat we'd generate by being close would be warmer than being alone in these."

"I'm not so sure. But I'd be willing to run a little science experiment. Being a teacher and all, that kind of thing is important to me."

Lily nodded. "Of course. It's important to expand your knowledge. So, what are you waiting for? Let's commence the experiment."

Parker unzipped the two sleeping bags and zipped them together to make a blanket. She then gently rolled Lily onto her side and became the big spoon behind her. Running her fingers up and down Lily's back and gently kissing the back of her neck, she noticed Lily pressing her butt into her. She rolled Lily towards her and under the sleeping bag blanket, under the canvas tent, under the stars, they made love in total silence, connecting only through touch. Somehow, the silence of it all made it feel more intense, and they felt even more connected than ever before.

Chapter Thirty-Three

LILY

Holding each other, Parker fell fast asleep, but lying in Parker's arms, Lily couldn't drift off. That moment had been the most intimate moment she'd experienced since Megan. That moment she'd reached into Parker's soul, and Parker had reached into hers. In that moment, and for the first time, they were one. It was beautiful and amazing, but it had shaken Lily in a way she hadn't anticipated. Sex with Parker had always been fun, and naughty, sexy, and sometimes a little dirty, but it hadn't felt like making love. Until now.

She had worried that this moment—the moment when she realised she was definitely in love—would be difficult. She had worried she would feel like she'd betrayed Megan. She had worried she'd be scared. She had worried she'd feel that she was replacing Bodhi's mother.

She felt none of these things. She felt happy. She felt excited for the future. She felt pleased to have had her life with Megan and pleased to have a future with Parker. But that was what she struggled with the most— if Megan had not died, she wouldn't have a future with Parker. Once she started to ponder it like that, she couldn't rationalise her feelings. It was all too much to think about.

*

LILY WOKE TO the sounds of Bodhi and Tyson close by. It turned out they were sitting outside the tent but talking loudly. Far too loudly, given it wasn't even seven am. She unzipped a series of tent doors before pouncing on the boys. "Shh," she said. "You're so loud, and it's so early."

"Sorry, Mum," Bodhi said, grinning bashfully. "We didn't think you'd ever wake up."

"It's not even seven am," she whispered. "People are going to be asleep. And not just the people we're with, but…" She gestured around the campground and added, "All of these people."

"Okay, but can we have breakfast?"

Silently, she nodded and handed them a box of cereal and a box of long-life milk. "Bowls are over there, and so are spoons," she whispered. "Now, I'm going back to bed til about eight o'clock. Just play cards or something quiet when you finish brekky, okay?" The boys nodded, and Lily climbed back into the tent and onto her air mattress.

Parker rolled towards her and breathed in. "Everything okay?"

"Yes, just kid stuff. They were being loud. Go back to sleep, baby."

*

HOURS LATER, THE men took Bodhi and Tyson fishing on the rocks. Parker and Lily joined them, but rather than fishing, they went for a walk through the beachside bush together. They reached a cliff face with a stunning beach view, and sat, in awe, looking at it, while holding each other and talking. It was a beautiful moment, and Lily looked Parker in the eyes and smiled. "Thank you for bringing me here."

Parker shrugged. "I didn't know we'd find it either."

"Not here," Lily said. "Although it's beautiful. Here, camping. It's lovely, and I'm loving having a family holiday with Bodhi. With his new, extended family." She smiled, embarrassed. "Don't worry, I'm not locking you in to a lifetime of parenting if you don't want it, but you're still our family. At least, as long as you choose to be, and it works."

"I can't see me choosing otherwise," Parker said, smiling, but looking a little bashful.

Lily reached out for her hands. "I love you, Louise Parker."

Parker laughed at Lily's use of her full name, but then turned serious as she looked into Lily's eyes and responded with, "And I love you, Liliana Delaney-Jones."

"Wow," Lily said, grinning. "So now my mind runs in a thousand directions. What's next? And not just for us, but—" She shook her head. "—for all of us. For Nathan and Scott too. For Bodhi."

"Stop," Parker said kindly and kissed Lily on the lips. "Don't worry about the future. Just live in the here and now."

Lily nodded. "And the past. I think about the past, too, not just the future."

Parker looked at her quizzically, and Lily wondered if by sharing her thoughts she'd make Parker want to run a mile. She finally decided to open up. "I'm excited about us, and our future together though."

"Me too," Parker said, smiling.

"I can't help feeling that being excited means I'm happy about what happened. And I'm not happy. At all. But I am excited. So excited to have a future with you." She had tears in her eyes, and Parker gave her a gentle hug, and then stroked her hand as she talked. "I've never been in your position, Lily, but I can only imagine what you're feeling is completely natural. I don't know what to say, but I guess you can be sad for what you've lost, and still happy about a new future. An alternative future—something you wouldn't have planned on but one you're happy with anyway. And I know you've said Megan didn't want you to be alone forever."

Lily was amazed. Parker always seemed to know what to say. "She didn't want me to be alone forever," Lily admitted. "But in my head, I always thought I'd date, but never really fall in love. I had that with her, and I didn't think I'd have it with anyone else. But, last night…"

"Just last night?"

She shook her head. "No, not just last night. Every day and every night leading up to last night too." She paused, and then added, "Hell, even our first night, all that time ago. Meeting you in the club that night. It was a one-night thing for me, but only because I was scared. I'd never met someone I was so instantly connected with, and I wanted to run a mile from that." Parker gave her a small smile, and Lily continued talking. "But last night, I don't know if it felt that way for you, but…"

Parker nodded with a tear in her eye. "It felt like that for me, Lily. It was…wow."

For the longest moment, they were silent. They gazed into one another's eyes. Suddenly, Lily made a move to stand. "We should go back to the fishermen."

"We should," Parker agreed and stood with her body facing Lily's. "I'm so pleased we had this chat. Please keep talking to me about Megan. I'm not here to replace her, but I'd love to help you have happiness and love in your life, and I'm sure, from what I know about Megan, she would want that for you."

Lily nodded, smiling, with even more tears in her eyes. "She would. She absolutely would. Thank you."

"And stop thanking me," Parker said and winked. That killer smile gave Lily butterflies and in that moment, she felt like the luckiest woman alive.

*

"MUM, WE CAUGHT a fish," Bodhi said when they returned. "Look, Parker, we caught a fish!"

"Wow," Parker said. "It's a big one too."

"I won't be able to eat it," Lily said, screwing her face up. Everyone laughed. "I just don't think I could."

"Trust me, once I'm finished, it will be a gourmet dinner," Nathan said, grinning.

"He's right," Parker agreed.

"And not just one fish. I just caught another!" Scott exclaimed.

"I have a nibble too…" Tyson added.

Suddenly they had a few fish and, soon enough, were ready to return to the campground.

Chapter Thirty-Four

PARKER

Dinner was great—Nathan made parcels of fish and noodles cooked in sauces and baked in aluminium foil on the barbeque. They also cooked a batch of sausages and bought some salads at the little shop across the road. Nathan and Parker even baked a steamed cake in the camp kitchen, and Lily and Scott supplied bottles of wine, and soft drinks for the children. It was a joyous night of family togetherness.

"I don't want to go home tomorrow," Lily said at the end of the night. They all agreed they felt the same way. Bodhi and Tyson were keen to go camping again in the school holidays some time.

Nathan nodded. "I'll have to talk to your mum and dad about that, but I reckon we could make it happen. In the meantime, I think we ask Scott and Lily to host a barbeque for all the families to meet. I know we've met Jacqui, but…"

Everyone nodded.

"And friends? Maree is desperate to meet you both," Lily said, clearly agreeing to the idea. "And I haven't even thought about the school mums yet." She grimaced.

"Hmm, maybe we hold off on the school mums," Parker said but then felt bad for a moment. After all, they were Lily's friends. "Unless you really want them there."

"No, it's okay. It could be strange for you."

"Less so now that Anthea knows, but…" She took a deep breath, then added, "Maybe it's better to wait until Bodhi isn't my student."

"I'm not changing class, am I?" Bodhi looked confused, and Parker reassured him that she meant the next year. "Oh, good," he said, clearly relieved. Parker was flattered, until he added, "I'd hate to be away from Chris!" Everyone laughed in response.

*

BACK TO REALITY on Monday, Parker was tired but content. She was photocopying some papers in the staff room at lunch time when Kelly bounded up to her. "What's the go with Bodhi Delaney-Joneses?" she asked.

"What do you mean?" Parker frowned. She was genuinely confused about what Kelly meant.

"Anthea has asked me to moderate his report card and work with you on it. That only happens if the parents are a little difficult or could be…or…maybe if it was a family member or something. So what's up? Are the parents awful? Do I need to go in to bat for you?"

Nathan strolled over to them, seeing the two of them talking. "Hey grade three, what's up?"

Kelly smiled in response. "Hey Nath. Apparently, the Delaney-Jones family are giving Parker grief. I'm trying to find out more."

"Giving her grief?" Nathan looked baffled, and Parker was amused.

"The parents." Kelly rolled her eyes, then stage-whispered, "Apparently, they're difficult."

"See, this is how rumours start," Parker said, bemused. "They're not difficult. Anthea didn't say that, did she?"

"No. Anthea was super discreet as she is about these things. So I had to fill in the gaps because she wasn't giving anything away."

"Well, your imagination is shit, Kelly," Nathan said. "Parker is dating one of Bodhi's parents."

"Oh!" She was shocked. "The woman, right?" she clarified, and Parker nodded, surprised she even needed to ask. "And Nathan is dating the dad," she said, her eyebrows raised.

"Wow," Kelly said, looking even more shocked. "Now I feel left out. And single. Is there a third parent?"

"There is a third parent, but she's deceased, I'm afraid," Nathan said, and Parker shot him a warning look. She didn't really think it was up for them to be sharing that information when Lily and Scott didn't really publicize it. "But keep that to yourself," he added, quickly.

Kelly nodded. "Will do. Wow, you guys are dark horses. I can't believe you told Anthea before you told me." She pouted.

Parker raised an eyebrow again. "C'mon, if Anthea found out we'd been sharing before we told her… Well, I'm only new around here, but I'd imagine she wouldn't like it."

"You're right. This is exciting though. I thought I had to come in to fight with you against some precious family, but it's just your romance. Sure, I can moderate Bodhi's work. It'd be a pleasure to." She smiled.

"We're not really announcing around here. At least not until Bodhi is in grade four."

"Understood. I won't tell anyone. Let's keep it a grade three secret," she said, and smiled. "Now I'm trying to remember which ones are Bodhi's parents."

"Oh, here," Nathan pulled out his phone, and started showing her photos of their camping weekend.

*

LATER IN THE week, Parker was walking through the front office, when Anthea caught her eye. "Oh, Parker. Are you in a rush?" She shook her head. "Pop in to my office?"

Parker nervously walked into the office, and Anthea gave her a friendly smile. "I just wanted to check in and see how you're going. New school, new relationship, that kind of thing."

"Really good," she said but wasn't sure exactly what the right answer should be. Did Anthea have an agenda?

"Great. All okay with the Delaney-Jones lady?"

"Yes, Lily. It's all going really well. I really appreciate your support, and I promise, I'm being professional at work. Bodhi seems to understand there's a difference too. He has been respectful at school."

"Great." The principal smiled. "I just wanted to let you know I spoke to Kelly, and she's happy to moderate."

Parker nodded. "Yes, she told me. Thank you."

"Ah, good. I would have told you earlier, but I have had a crazy week. Also, I spoke to my colleague—no dramas with my plan." She paused. "And Nathan and his beau are going well?"

Parker secretly cringed at the term *beau* for Scott but hoped she hadn't shown her reaction. She smiled and nodded instead. "Yes, they seem really happy."

"I've never known much about Nathan's personal life, but I never really thought he had a boyfriend. It's nice for him." She smiled. "Well I'm pleased you're going well." She glanced down. "You know I met my husband through work. He was another teacher, admittedly not a parent." She giggled lightly. "But it was a lovely time…the courting. I never loved going to work more than I did back then. I would dress up and flirt to get his attention. He had the pick of the women. There weren't many male teachers back then." She smiled as she clearly thought back, and Parker tried to picture a young Anthea flirting with her colleague. "And nowadays, well, Nathan certainly wouldn't want the pick of women," she said. "Robert and I finally got together. We worked at the same school for a few years after that. Six, I think. And then we ended up going to different schools after I had our first baby. Years later, he became a principal and then I did." She smiled. "Anyway, have fun with Lily. Courting really is a lovely time, and I want you to know you have my full support."

Parker was so grateful. She grinned and told Anthea her story of meeting Robert sounded lovely. A small part of her was desperate to leave the principal's office—her anxiety still remaining just a little—and another part of her was surprised about how comfortable Anthea had made her feel. "I hope to meet Robert someday," she said and actually meant it.

"Oh, yes, that sounds lovely. I'm sure I'll get him to some school event. And you'll have to bring your new lady sometime too. Of course, I've met her." She smiled. "She seemed nice."

"She's great," Parker said, grinning.

Chapter Thirty-Five

LILY

Scott stayed at Nathan's house on Friday night, while Parker stayed over with Lily. Bodhi fell asleep on the couch during a movie, so Parker carried him in to bed—he had gotten far too heavy for Lily to lift these days, but Parker managed it with ease. Seeing how good she was with Bodhi made Lily happy, and Bodhi seemed to really adore her too.

"He's sound asleep," Parker said, returning from the bedroom, and Lily was relieved.

"Great. Let's snuggle in bed," she said, leading Parker to the bedroom. Parker went to the bathroom and came out, then climbed into bed straight away. Under the covers, they found each other, and Lily began kissing Parker. "I love you," she said for about the millionth time that week. She'd never thought she'd feel such emotions again and was so happy she did.

"I love you too," Parker said, kissing her. Lily moaned, and Parker's hands starting tugging on the elastic of her pyjama pants. Lily helped her to manoeuvre them, and then moved toward the elastic of Parker's pyjama pants. She gently tugged on them and then noticed them pulling on something.

"Is that…?" Lily looked questioning at Parker and then realised Parker wore a strap-on.

"Is that okay?" she asked. "I should have checked, but I wanted to surprise you."

"Yes! Let's do it. It will be fun again." Lily enjoyed it so much the last time, and though she didn't want to only ever do it with toys, she was excited to try again.

After kissing and touching some more, Parker was inside her, and Lily, who had chosen to sit astride Parker, cried out in pleasure, arching her back. Parker started to gently thrust her hips, but soon Lily took over, grinding down on Parker. She was feeling sexy—Parker made her feel that way—and a little silly. She lowered herself gently so that her breasts dangled in Parker's face. Parker's eyebrows raised in excitement, surprise and pleasure—Lily would always remember that face!—and Parker reaching up to touch her, and kiss her. After a bit of playfulness, they got a rhythm going, and soon they were moaning in unison, feeling connected and in love, before falling asleep happily in each other's arms.

*

THE NEXT MORNING, Lily and Parker began discussing the family celebration. "Reckon your family would come to Canberra for it, or is it a little premature? I'd love to meet them."

"Really? I hadn't thought about it, but Mum and Dad are always up for a road trip, and I guess it depends on Briony and Nick, what they're up to. I can always ask. Should we wait and discuss plans with the boys?"

Lily paused for a moment, then said, "Let's make it a big thing. Your family, mine, Nathan's, and Scott's."

"What about Megan's family?" Parker asked gently. Lily thought it over.

"Maybe I should talk to them. It could be quite confronting for them. But I definitely should tell them about you. I'd hate for them to see us out and about and be caught by surprise. I can't believe I hadn't thought of that before now."

"Yes, probably a smart idea," Parker agreed.

*

THANKFULLY, THE GUYS agreed with the plan, and text messages and phone calls were made, planning an afternoon barbeque the following weekend. Parker's family could stay at Parker's house, and all the other families were local. That left one last phone call. To Megan's parents.

"Hello, Betty," Lily said nervously. Ringing Betty and Tom was not unusual—after all, they played a very active role in Bodhi's life and still visited her and Scott regularly—but somehow this felt different.

"Hi, Lily. How are you? How are things?"

After general chatter, Lily finally told her. "Betty, Scott and I are having a little celebration next Saturday evening, and we'd love you to come if you're keen, but before you say anything…" She rushed to continue, hoping Betty wouldn't answer before she had a chance to tell her—that could be awkward if she then changed her answer. "Before you say anything, I want you to know, well you already know how much I love Megan. How devoted to her I am. But recently I met someone…"

She heard Betty suck her breath in, and for that moment, she felt like the worst person in the world. Then Betty spoke, sounding so caring and warm, "Oh, darling. That's lovely news. I've been waiting for this moment. I'm surprised because it has been so long now, but I'm happy. I know it doesn't take away from what you and Megan had."

Lily grinned, but tears were forming in her eyes. Not for the first time since Megan's passing, she thanked her lucky stars for Betty and Tom. "Thank you," she said in response. It was all she could say.

"Anna told me Scott's met someone recently too. Unless she got it mixed up, and she meant you?"

"No, she got it right. Scott and I are dating two friends actually. His boyfriend's name is Nathan. He'll be there on Saturday. Anna and Frank are coming too," she said, referring to Scott's parents. Suddenly it became very important to her to have Megan's parents there.

"And what's your friend's name, darling?"

"Parker. She's great, Betty. Very different from Megan, on the outside anyway, but I'm sure you'll love her when you get to know her."

"Let me talk to Tom, but I think we're free. I'd love to meet Parker and Nathan. I'll get back to you."

Within the hour, Betty and Tom had confirmed they would be attending the party.

Chapter Thirty-Six

PARKER

Lily and Scott had been fussing all week. Nathan hadn't been. The little get together that Nathan had proposed was suddenly a catch-up for thirty people. And yet Nathan seemed more relaxed than ever—and that was saying something. While Lily and Scott had planned everything with near-military precision, Nathan was acting like nothing was happening.

"So who do we have coming?" Scott asked on Friday night. "Let's do a final run through."

Lily nodded and grabbed her notepad. "Nathan's mum, Margaret, stepfather Christian, sister Julie, her husband Matthew, and ten-year-old Tyson, who we all know. Scott's parents, the lovely Anna and Frank. Megan's parents, Betty and Tom. I didn't invite her siblings; it was all a bit much. Another time. Parker's parents, Judy and Alan, her sister Briony, and her brother Nick, his wife Jenny, and their kids, Carly, Steph, and Jacob, sixteen, thirteen, and nine. Then my parents, Robin and Peter, my sister Jacqui, John, her husband, and their three kids. Rebecca, Penny, and Isabelle, sixteen, fourteen, and eleven." She sighed loudly. "Plus the five of us and my friend Maree who probably won't stay the whole time. If she even turns up at all."

"Wow, that's a lot of people," Nathan said, as if it had only just occurred to him.

"It sure is," Lily said, worry creeping across her face. "Thirty exactly."

"We'll be okay," Scott said, "but we do have a lot of cooking to do tomorrow. The plan is that we'll have most of the food cooked on the barbeque. Salads are already done. And some bits and pieces to be picked up at the store. Already ordered."

Lily nodded. "I know, but it does feel overwhelming."

"It'll be okay," Parker said, in an attempt to reassure her. "The goal here is that everyone meets us all. Gets along."

"And we cement our relationship statuses with them all. I don't think we're a traditional family. We're a bit of a package deal, aren't we?" Lily said.

"I suppose we are, by virtue of the friendships, the co-parenting, everything," Parker agreed.

"One big happy family," Scott said, grinning.

*

JACQUI, JOHN, AND the girls were the first to arrive, and Jacqui went straight to the kitchen to help her sister and Parker, who were busily finalising some salads and dip platters. Lily looked overwhelmed, and Jacqui sent her to go out and get drinks.

Once she'd gone, Jacqui turned to Parker with a look of concern. "Lil okay?" she asked.

Parker nodded. "I think a little nervous. I'm not sure if it's just about the numbers, or if it's Megan's parents or mine that are panicking her."

"Probably a combination of all three. I hope it wasn't a crazy idea to have all the family on the same night."

"Gets it over and done with," Parker said. The doorbell rang, so she answered it to Nathan's family, who she knew really well—Christian and Margaret, Julie and Matthew, with Tyson. Tyson ran to the lounge room immediately to find Bodhi, and they started playing the games console, along with Jacqui's kids. Jacqui went out to the driveway to greet her parents and bring them in to the house. Gathering Lily, they walked over to Parker. "These are our parents, Robin and Peter. Mum and Dad, this is Parker."

Parker went to shake their hands, nervously, but Robin gave her a kiss and, watching on, Peter followed.

"Hello, love," Robin said, "I've heard a lot about you, more so from Jacqui than Lily, I must say, but it's lovely to finally meet you."

Parker smiled and made small talk about the weather and the chaos of the house as the chatter began to get increasingly louder.

Scott's parents and Megan's parents were next to arrive, and they travelled together, which Scott had expected. While Nathan talked to Scott's parents, Anna and Frank, Lily greeted Betty and Tom, Megan's parents.

"I'd like you to meet Parker," she said and brought them over to Parker in the kitchen. "Parker, I'd like you to meet Betty and Tom, Megan's parents."

Parker hadn't known what to expect, whether they'd size her up and down, compare her to Megan, or be a little stand-offish, but they couldn't have been warmer than they were. Betty instantly gave Parker a hug and said it was lovely to meet her. They shared a laugh about how Bodhi barely looked up from his games console when two sets of his grandparents arrived. "They're all here tonight—he has three sets of grandparents." Betty shook her head, grinning. "And now with you and Nathan, well, perhaps he'll have five sets of grandparents one day." Parker hadn't thought of it like that, but she was delighted at how welcoming Betty sounded. "Now," Betty said, glancing around the bustling house, "Where are your parents?"

Parker shrugged. "They're often late, but they haven't arrived yet. They had to travel in from Sydney along with my brother and his family and my sister."

"Oh, right. Well I'm sure they'll be here soon." She smiled, and Tom smiled just as warmly.

"Gee, it's nice of them to travel from Sydney. Where are they staying?" he asked.

"They're staying at my house, only about ten minutes away from here."

"Oh, okay. Nice of you to have the company," Betty said.

"Well, I think I'll stay here tonight, but we're having breakfast together," Parker said, and then instantly regretted it. She felt awful for suggesting that she shared a bed with Lily, even though Betty didn't look like she was born yesterday. Thankfully, they were interrupted by Lily appearing with her parents and sister.

"I just met your parents," Parker said, smiling. "And Nick and Jenny are on the way."

Chapter Thirty-Seven

LILY

Once everyone had eaten dinner, Tom, Megan's father, stood and the chatter went quiet. "What a lovely gathering. My thanks to the organisers for inviting us, and for all the work they've clearly put into tonight. When a couple establishes a relationship, there's usually a family meeting, and sometimes two families meet. This is a complicated web of relationships. It's not my party to do a speech at…"

Frank, Scott's father, interrupted, "And yet he's going to anyway."

Tom continued, as if Frank hadn't spoken. "It's not my party to do a speech at, but I do want to express my happiness that our girl, Lily, has found someone who makes her happy enough that, for the first time, she's wanted us all to meet. To Lily!" Everyone raised their glasses and toasted Lily. Tears instantly appeared in her eyes, and motivated by Tom's words,

Lily got up to talk.

"I'm not usually a public speaker," she confessed. "And thirty people is public enough! But I want to thank you all for coming. The people around these tables are meaningful to us all. I don't know what else to say, except thank you to you all. For everything." The smiles around the table motivated her to continue. "I didn't want to date. Megan had my heart. What I've realised in meeting Parker is that meeting someone else doesn't erase everything that we had. It's a new future, but I know Megan would be happy. I'm delighted to get to know Nathan and Parker's families a little tonight, and I look forward to a happy future all together. One big crazy family. So let's raise our glasses and toast, 'To everyone!'"

"To everyone!" they all cried in unison.

"But there is one special person I wanted to acknowledge," Lily said. As people looked toward Parker and toward Bodhi, she figured they all assumed it was one of them, but it wasn't. "To Scott. I couldn't do this parenting thing without you, and Megan and I were so lucky to have you in our lives, and Bodhi and I have been so lucky to keep you in our lives. And now…you're part of my life with Parker. I couldn't be any more grateful for everything we have. To my best friend, Scott!"

"To Scott!" everyone cheered and grinned. Scott raced around to Lily and gave her a kiss and a cuddle, and then spoke up, "I want you all eating and drinking, and chatting, so I won't do a speech, but thanks for coming, and I look forward to talking." Scott was never a man of many words.

The evening ended late. Bodhi had a ball with his cousins and new extended family members. As everyone was retreating to the bedrooms, they all agreed it had been an amazing night. "Megan's family are great," Parker said. "And your parents seemed lovely too." She directed that last comment to Lily.

"They're all great. We all lucked out in the family department, didn't we?" Scott said.

"I know," Lily said, nodding. "Pretty great, really."

Chapter Thirty-Eight

PARKER
Four months later

"Grade three, wow. This is the end of the school year! I can't believe what a great year we've had," Parker said over the chatter. "I hope you all have a wonderful Christmas, and a wonderful summer holiday. Come back next year, as big grade four kids! I can't wait to see you next year."

As the bell rang, the children grabbed their bags and raced out of the classroom. Parker stood with her hands on her hips, smiling as she surveyed the scene and said farewell to some parents who popped their heads into the room.

"Annnd, that's a wrap," Nathan said, appearing out of nowhere and into her classroom.

"That it is."

"And now for the next steps."

Kelly suddenly appeared. "Hey, how's your packing going?"

Parker and Nathan both grimaced a little. "Remind me to never move house again," Parker said, laughing. "I think I'm making headway on boxes, and suddenly I notice an entire cupboard I haven't tackled."

"But you're excited?" Kelly asked.

Parker nodded. "I am. I can't believe I'll be living with this boofhead again though," she said, gesturing toward Nathan, who smiled. "That's one thing we haven't done in many years. We used to live together when we first became teachers."

Lily, Parker, Nathan, and Scott had decided to live together, in Lily and Scott's house, but they had all agreed to wait until Bodhi had finished grade three. As of today, Parker and Nathan were going to start moving their boxes across. Kelly grinned. "Well, I'm excited for you all. Perhaps mostly for Bodhi. I think he'll love having lots of parents to care for him."

Nathan nodded. "I've never moved in with a guy," he confessed. "I've only ever had flings with my housemates."

"And not this housemate," Parker said, deadpan, pointing to herself.

"So, I'm going away for a few nights with Dave," Kelly said, excitedly bouncing on the spot. "I know, it's only been a couple of weeks, but I have a good feeling about this guy."

"Gawd," Nathan said, "slow down! You're starting to sound like a lesbian. Soon, you'll be moving in together on your fifth date."

"Hey! You can talk," Parker said, pretending to be wounded. "I've never seen you run as fast as I saw you run into Scott's arms."

"True." He grinned and then turned to Kelly, suddenly serious. "Actually, I'm happy for you, mate. I think it's great if Dave happens to be the guy for you. Where are you off to?"

"Batemans Bay," she said, smiling.

As they kept chatting, Parker picked up her bag and steered them out of her classroom. "Let's go for a drink. But we really only have time for one, two at the most. Then we have to take a carload of boxes home."

Acknowledgements

With every novel I write, I like to acknowledge those who supported me in getting it to fruition—whether that be practical support, or just support through the phase of my life as I was writing and editing it.

In practical support, huge thanks for my editor at NineStar Press, BJ Toth. Always appreciate your guidance in enhancing my work. Also thanks to Raevyn McCann, Managing Director, for all her support and encouragement. Thanks also to the copy editing and proofreading team.

A huge thank you to my family—my children, my parents, my sister Melanie, my author sister, Larissa Johns (check out her wonderful books!), my brother-in-law, my nieces and nephews—for all your encouragement.

Huge thanks to Nic for everything. And to my friends, thank you for constant support and fun distraction. Huge thanks especially to Ruth, Naomi, Amanda, Helena, Suzanne, Anni, and my writing group for everything during the writing and editing of this book.

And finally, to Emma Rossi, my writer 'bestie' and the person I dedicated this book to. During a difficult time, Emma provided me with limitless support, and I really appreciate our friendship.

Finally, a huge thank you to you, my readers. I always appreciate the encouragement and any feedback you share with me, or with reader reviews. I really loved writing Parker's and Lily's fun and passionate story, and hope you enjoy it too. Life can provide unexpected twists and turns that may feel challenging in the moment, but the unexpected can provide happy surprises too.

About the Author

Gemma Johns is the author of five other novels, *The Marriage Sabbatical, Similar Features, Shaken Worlds, Date at Eight,* and *Baby Steps.* She is a professor, fiction writer, and mother. Gemma is never without a notepad and pen, and whenever she gets a spare moment, she is often lost in her head, thinking about the characters she's writing about. This is especially the case when she's hanging the clothes on the clothesline, for some reason. Whenever she can find some down time, Gemma can be found reading, writing, cooking, walking, travelling, or catching up with family and friends. She's a huge fan of podcasts and audiobooks for listening on the go.

Email

gemmajohnsauthor@gmail.com

Facebook

www.facebook.com/profile.php?id=100063466415504

Instagram

www.instagram.com/gemmajohnsauthor

Other NineStar books by this author

Baby Steps

www.ninestarpress.com

www.facebook.com/ninestarpress

www.facebook.com/groups/NineStarNiche

www.twitter.com/ninestarpress

www.instagram.com/ninestarpress

bsky.app/profile/ninestarpress.bsky.social

www.threads.net/@ninestarpress